GORDON MACMILLAN

Blind DATES

hera

First published in the United Kingdom in 2022 by

Hera Books
Unit 9 (Canelo), 5th Floor
Cargo Works, 1-2 Hatfields
London, SE1 9PG
United Kingdom

A CIP catalogue record for this book is available from the British Library.

Print ISBN 978 1 80436 023 1
Ebook ISBN 978 1 80436 914 2

Look for more great books at www.herabooks.com

Printed and bound in Great Britain by Clays Ltd, Elcograf S.p.A.

1

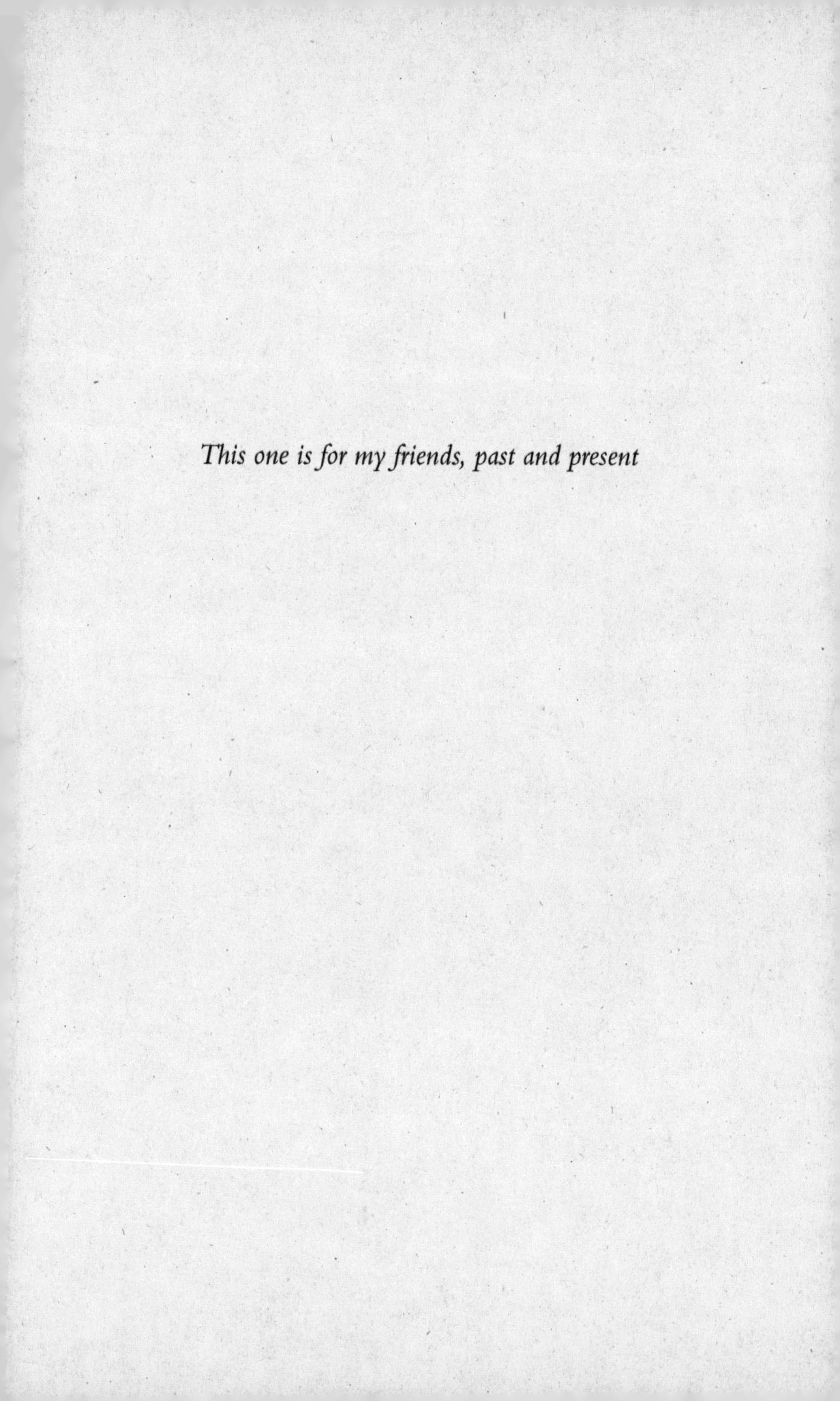

This one is for my friends, past and present

Prologue

Have you ever had one of those moments in life of absolute clarity when you know what you have to do?

Have you heard the voices inside your head telling you what you need to do and why? Sometimes, so loud and insistent that they are impossible to ignore. Like a Greek chorus foretelling tragedy, warning us that we will miss our chance and time if we do not act, and neither will come again.

This is a story about two such moments. The first one is about jobs and careers and how we work away at them year after year. We become so caught up that we never stop to question what it is we are doing with our lives. Sometimes it's hard to stop, hard to give ourselves time to look around and come up for air.

Then suddenly, the whole world actually *did* stop, and we *did* have the time. A global pause that delivered unexpected moments of reset and reflection. I took a chance, and I changed my destination after I got thrown off the career train and then never went back.

The other moment is about a girl, how I lost her and how I tried to get her back. That's what this story is about. It's a mixtape as well, one that is full of love songs, so whenever you're ready, hit play.

Chapter One

'First Day of My Life'

February 2020, I'm staring at the computer screen, reading back over the news story I have written with a sense of dread. I'm not sure why I am having trouble with this one. It's a murder and I'm the crime reporter, and it's going to be the lead story on the *Evening News* website. It's what I do; I was drawn to crime reporting from the start, and I've written about crime for all my career. For most of that time it's been an adrenaline-fuelled buzz that I wouldn't swap.

Tonight, however, it's different and I can't quite put my finger on why. The story itself is no different—another tragedy that is only making the front page because of the grim statistic it represents on this freezing Wednesday evening. It's the only the end of February and there have already been ten murders in the capital, which is gripped by a growing sense of foreboding over what will happen with the spreading global pandemic.

I read the first couple of paragraphs again. My concentration is being tugged at as the news editor, Mackintosh, drums his fingers increasingly loudly as if building to a magnificent drum solo. He wants the story now.

'Tommy, Tommy,' Mackintosh says.

No one calls me Tommy. Not even my mother, who will on occasion call me Thomas when she wants me to stop talking and to listen to what she's saying. Otherwise, I'm Tom, and that's what everyone calls me, apart from news editors and mothers. Mackintosh, however, likes nicknames, calling another reporter 'Bomber' for his ability to break exclusives ahead of rivals. He will then shout out 'boom' when the story is published, and to be truthful, people do laugh at this.

'Tommy, Tommy,' Mackintosh repeats.

I grimace. Try to concentrate. It makes me think we are in the trenches. No mud and slime for us; we're up to our necks in bad news, wading our way through it daily. When, I wonder, will there be any good news? More and more, I have reached the conclusion that I don't think there will be. The bullets keep flying and people continue to fall in the wind.

'One minute,' I say.

'You said that five minutes ago,' Mackintosh says. 'I thought you had somewhere to be.'

It's true; I do. I want to get out of here tonight. My friends Marcus and Victoria are having a #Leaving-London party in a pub in Soho. They have sold their flat and have bought a big house in a picturesque village up north. It is in Yorkshire, in a place called Todmorden, which is quirky and somewhat hip. The kind of place people fleeing London move to—or at least talk of moving to. It is complete with tall Victorian houses and post-industrial mills, and no doubt the setting of windswept TV dramas where there has been a murder. It is, in short, beautiful, and remote, set-in moors and rolling Pennine hills. The pictures look gorgeous on Instagram but then, doesn't everything?

When Marcus first told me they were leaving London I couldn't understand it. They were leaving behind all the joys of the city. The restaurants, bars, cinemas, theatres, galleries, comedy, and live music venues. All the places I occasionally go to. They were swapping it for somewhere with a fraction of that. Marcus said it was about quality of life and work-life balance. That and other slogans favoured by HR departments in buzzword-strewn emails. As an architect, it's easy for him to work anywhere. Victoria, a solicitor, has taken a job in nearby Leeds.

I reread my intro paragraph and realise I am fussing over a story that is finished. There are no more words to write and nothing more to add that will change the angle or the outcome of this piece. I am desperately trying to make it sound better, dragging it somehow in a new direction when there is no way to do that. Somebody died, people are broken and sad, and people are statistics that we count and forget with far too much ease. Their stories become subsumed by screaming headlines that reduce tragedy to a numbers game.

That's when it hits me, finally dawns. It isn't *the* story; it is *all* the stories. I think they are starting to get to me, as if the weight of them is pressing down upon me, and I wonder how much longer I can keep writing them. But if I don't do this, if I am not a reporter, what else could I do? I'd always wanted to be a journalist; only now I can imagine a life doing something else. I have no idea what that something else might be.

I brush this thought aside. I realise I am unsettled by the departure of Marcus, which has been looming for months and now is happening. We were at university together. There were three of us who shared a house in Bristol. It was me, Marcus, and Adam, and now we are down to two.

I close the story and shout across to Mackintosh that I am done. He claps his hands together, and I sit back in my chair. I pick up my phone and check my messages as I wait for Mac's approval to go. Most of my messages are about the party tonight. Various friends have already arrived or are on their way, having gone straight from the office to Red Lion behind Carnaby Street.

I watch Mac as he picks his way through my story, alert for any flourishes of typing. His fingers go to work, and they are like hammers smashing away at the keyboard. There is silence. He sits back, reads; nodding to himself.

'Good stuff, now go, and have a beer for me,' Mackintosh says.

I don't wait for a repeat invitation. I am out of my seat and across the newsroom of the *Evening News*, and in the lift.

Out on the street, it is dark, and an icy winter wind blows through Kensington. People have their heads down as they walk stiffly along the High Street. The road is packed with red buses, choked with traffic, and taxis and cars jostle for space.

I walk the couple of minutes it takes to reach the tube, and head through the ornate shopping arcade that leads to the station entrance. I run down the steps in time to catch a Circle Line train, which is standing room only, and filled with people coughing and sneezing their way through London, while others pull faces at the constant sternutation.

There's no doubt that this is the worst part of my day; commuting to and from North London where I live in a tiny flat nestled between Highbury and Finsbury Park. That is another thing Marcus expressed great joy about. He wouldn't have to do this anymore. He waxed lyrical about being able to work from home, and the joy of not starting each day on the tube nestled under someone's armpit. Really, I don't care: I would hate to leave London. That said, I have slowly come to recognise some of the benefits of going.

After a quick change to the Central Line, I get off the tube at Oxford Circus and weave my way through the slow-moving crowds spilling over from Oxford Street and cross into Soho. I always get a small sense of joy when I do this. It is as if I am crossing the border and leaving behind the busy shoppers bustling with bursting bags, and heading into a happy space of bars, and restaurants, which I have criss-crossed many times over the years. Walking into Soho always sparks memories of good times and late nights, moments spent hanging outside drinking on the street, or sitting tucked away in a quiet corner.

As my mind flits through a random highlights reel, I cross the road in front of Liberty and turn into the fashion strip that is Carnaby Street, where the scene and the crowd changes. I turn down the first side street, heading past the cafés and bars of Kingly Street to the Red Lion pub where Marcus and Victoria have booked the first floor for their farewell bash.

A few idle on the street, braving the cold, cigarettes, and drinks in hand, their icy breath as thick as smoke, as I nip inside the pub. A red rope is hung across the stairs with a '*Closed for Private Party*' sign dangling. I unclip this and speed to the top floor bar.

Upstairs, it is all dark wood and an old red patterned carpet, giving the ample space a gloomy look. It's a bar I've visited a few times over the years, almost exclusively for leaving drinks. It's always here or in the Crown and

Two Chairman on Dean Street or Soho House. Tonight, however, is different.

I stand at the top of the stairs and scan the room. The small bar is to my left, busy with a crowd gathered, and beyond that is a horseshoe-shaped seating area. To the right, people sit in groups on the padded benches that line the wall of the main area and around the cluster of small tables.

Now I am here, I know it is happening, and that it is real. Marcus is leaving London. I still find it hard to accept. I know it is something people do but I guess I never thought he would. I know his life is changing; he is married, and thinking of starting a family. Victoria doesn't want to do that in London. She wants to be close to her parents, and I get that. Selfishly, I just don't like it.

I can see Marcus—six-feet-three with thick wavy brown hair, dressed in jeans and a white shirt with the sleeves rolled up—standing with a group of five or six people amidst the tables and chairs. I know most of them, people from the architecture practice where he works.

One of Marcus's colleagues taps his shoulder and nods my way. Marcus turns and smiles and throws his arms out. I step towards him, and we hug.

'Mate,' he says. 'This is it!'

My lips are pursed. I give a resigned nod in agreement: this is it. There won't be many more nights like this, is what I think, and the memory of when we first shared a room in halls of residence is fresh in my mind. Only it was fifteen years ago, and now it feels like we are fully grown.

'I can't believe we're here,' I say.

'I know. Come on, let me get you a drink,' Marcus says.

We weave our way through the bar, nodding hello to a couple of people, as Marcus gets us two pints of lager. We clink our glasses together, cheers. As we sip, we are on the edge of Marcus's time in London. This is their last night and tomorrow they drive north.

'So, it's tomorrow then?' I say.

'We're all packed; the bed is about the only thing that hasn't been taken down. We're off at nine. Hand over the keys, and then that's it,' Marcus says.

'Goodbye to London and all that,' I say.

'And all that,' Marcus repeats, glancing around the room. 'I'm going to miss it all.'

When he says this, I know he isn't only talking about the city, but everything else as well. Us, his friends, and life here. The people and the places, and evenings like this when everyone drifts across the city and comes together in a bar or a pub. Where it is easy to do so.

'Me too,' I say, and we tap our glasses together again, and take another drink.

Victoria appears by my side and places a hand on my shoulder. She has wavy strawberry-blonde hair, which is tied loosely back, and is wearing a black dress to her knees, with knee-high black boots. I smile, air kiss her check.

'Glad you're here, Tom. I'm sure Marcus was getting anxious that his actual friends weren't going to turn up,' Victoria says.

Marcus rolls his eyes, and I shake my head, smiling. That sounds like Marcus. I wonder when Adam will arrive. He is the third leg of our university stool.

'I don't know what you're going to do, Tom. You spend so much time together,' Victoria says.

Her words echo my own thoughts. I'll do what everyone does, I suppose and adapt. It won't be the same, but it often seems that new people fill the spaces made by those who move on.

'I'm sure I'll cope,' I say.

'Oh, I'm sure you will, and you know he will be expecting you to visit, if you can bring yourself to leave London,' Victoria says.

'There are some amazing walks to do, with good pubs along the way,' Marcus says.

'So, bracing,' laughs Victoria.

They sound only half convinced. I offer a big smile and say that the pictures look amazing (which they do) and do my best to be happy for him. Besides, over the last couple of years we have gone on regular weekend walks around the UK with a few other friends, visiting Ben Nevis, Snowdon and along the route of Hadrian's Wall, so this will be no different, I tell myself.

'Looking forward to it,' I say.

'I'm sure you are, but if there was ever a time to find someone then it is now. It's been a long time since you dated anyone, and you know I've been dying to set you up with Carolyn,' Victoria says.

On a point of order, it hasn't been that long. Six months, give or take. Is that long? Is that *too* long? I'm not sure, and I'm not concerned by it. I just don't want to meet anyone. I met Victoria's friend Carolyn at their wedding five years ago. She's a local TV reporter in London, blonde and cute, and on the basis that we are both reporters, Victoria is convinced we would be a good couple.

'Let's wait and see,' I say.

Victoria places a finger to lips, and then offers her hands out. 'What is it you're waiting for, Tom?' she asks.

It's a good question, and I don't know the answer. My mind leaps to an image of Elspeth Johnson, who I met when on the Reuters graduate training scheme after university. Elspeth—or Beth, as everyone calls her—is intelligent, sharp, and pretty, with a soft Scottish accent, and we have been friends ever since.

If I had split my friendships into friends and best friend categories, I would put Beth down as a best friend without a second thought. We're on the same wavelength, and while we don't agree on everything, we never argue. I love spending time with her. I'm sure that's why our friendship lasted. I miss the sound of her voice and how, after a few glasses of wine, it gets even more Scottish. At that point, she sounds like her mother, who runs a knitwear shop in the border town of Hawick, and who Beth is the spitting image of. Her mother is a small and elegant-looking woman, and always, whatever the weather, dressed in flowery dresses and pearl-buttoned cardigans.

Beth and I never dated although I have thought about it on numerous occasions. I have just never been brave enough to make the leap from friendship to the dating zone. What if she said no? Or—a conundrum of an equal size—what if she said *yes*? This thought sparks cold sweats. It would from the start be all in with us. We already know each other so well. It would be a case of making it work or bust, and that has always scared me. I've missed my chance now anyway—if she comes tonight, she'll be with Michael, her boyfriend of nine months. The timing for us has never been right, at least that is other thing I tell myself.

I find myself articulating this final thought.

'Is Beth bringing Michael tonight?' I ask.

'Talking of things you're waiting for, it sounds like you haven't heard,' Victoria teases.

Marcus grins, already knowing what Victoria is going to say. I feel my stomach muscles tighten. My thoughts jump to the conclusion that Beth and Michael—who is a dashing doctor, tall with dark curly hair, and a bit too good-looking—are about to get married or move in together.

'Don't tell me he proposed?' I say.

Marcus laughs at this and shakes his head. Victoria finds this less amusing, and she flicks her husband a disapproving look to which he pulls his head back, askance.

'They broke up,' Victoria says.

'Sorry to hear that,' I say.

Marcus laughs, and Victoria shakes her head, shooting me a sceptical look. Victoria is right. Those words fell from my lips without conviction, and they do not match my expressions when I hear this news about Beth, I brighten. Victoria narrows her gaze, watching my reaction. I know I shouldn't, only I can't help it. It isn't schadenfreude. It is that this snippet sparks thoughts about the two of us being together. They flicker in my mind, like a match lit in the dark, before I snuff it out, as I always do. I am a coward and will never do anything about it. I hate myself for this, but I am a prisoner of my fear, and I am fully aware of this.

'It's such a shame, as Michael was perfect for Beth. He was just so…' Victoria pauses, wiggling her fingers as she searches for the right word.

'Good-looking?' I offer, trying my best to rise to the moment, and to be generous.

'Yes, he was. Oh my god, I would even go so far as to say handsome. Like a modern-day Darcy. He was caring, and thoughtful too. You'd almost want to put him in a bottle and sprinkle some of his goodness onto others. It turns out, though, that he was also a bit boring which is, I suppose, the distance between the fictional ideal and the humdrum reality. So disappointing,' Victoria says. She shrugs, saddened by her own conclusion. The words 'humdrum reality' hang in the air, somehow flattening the moment; our situation; our lives at large.

'They came for dinner about a month ago,' Marcus starts.

'He talked and talked. He was making us all quite sleepy. Beth yawned at one point,' Victoria says, shaking her head again.

'And you laughed,' Marcus sniggers.

'Marcus! It turns out, Tom, there's still hope for you. Although even as I say that I know you won't do anything about it.'

'She's got you there, mate,' Marcus says.

I shrug. I know they are right, and let it go, as in the nick of time Adam materialises besides us.

'Ah, the third musketeer! Now your circle is complete,' Victoria says.

At five-foot-nine I am the shortest of the three of us. Adam is six feet, with dark, swept-back hair. An architect, a journalist, and a psychotherapist. All quite different but, until now, as close geographically—within a couple of miles of each other in North London—as we are as friends.

Chapter Two

'Something Changed'

As we continue to stand in our little circle, I make a small announcement to the group.

'Oh, by the way,' I start. 'I invited Larissa tonight.'

Victoria pulls a face, Adam nods thoughtfully and Marcus shakes his head. This is a not unexpected response to my announcement, given that Victoria doesn't like Larissa and neither Adam nor Marcus understand why I hang out with her, since she is my ex-girlfriend and she dumped me not once, but twice. I know it sounds odd that I still see her. The thing is that, while we were a terrible couple, mismatched and with poor communication, I always liked talking to her.

Maybe because she's a serious girl ('dour', Victoria says) and her appearance is similarly ascetic; tall with long straight dark hair, almost black like night. She works as head of research for an advertising agency and loves classical music (Brahms and Chopin); and nineteenth-century literature. If you pushed her on the latter, she would say the Brontës and Russian novels were her preference. Like those bleak windswept Yorkshire moors and Russian winters, Larissa Snowe likes her stories to be austere. I embraced her passions with a good deal of reluctance.

I think that is the way most of us embrace Russian literature despite claims otherwise, which is why *War and Peace* and *Anna Karenina* top those lists of books we claim to have read but never have.

'Why did you do that?' asks Victoria.

'I'll second that question,' says Marcus.

'I'll third it,' adds Adam.

I offer my hands out.

'I met up with her recently for lunch and I mentioned it. She only works around the corner, and she knows you all. I thought it would be nice,' I say.

'She's awkward, and hard to speak to. The silences are not comfortable. You just know Larissa was one of those school swots with no friends, which is, FYI, also her adult demeanour,' Victoria says.

This is unfair—scathing, even. Besides, I am sure that what Victoria really means is that Larissa is posh, and went to Cambridge, which is ridiculous. Victoria is also expensively privately educated, went to Oxford and I am sure studied constantly, which I point out.

'I bet that was you, as well,' I say.

Marcus laughs at this, highlighting a certain truth. Victoria sends daggers in his direction.

'It is true, I worked hard,' opines Victoria, eyes glancing to the ceiling. 'In my case, though, it was because I was gifted academically. But I did other things too—excelling in sport and socially. It just all came naturally to me.'

We all roll our eyes at this, to which Victoria smiles, basking in her own celestial light, which needs no illumination from Adam, Marcus, or me. Victoria ran for the county and is a talented athlete whose invitation to do a 5K Parkrun you should never accept, as she will leave you for dust.

'What she means,' says Marcus, 'is that you and Larissa were poorly matched.'

'No,' says Victoria. 'That isn't what I mean. What I mean is that you were terrible together. So self-conscious, it was difficult to watch; I wanted to cover my face and look through my fingers. Like a square peg and a round hole. There was no symmetry. That is the only way I can describe it.'

'Tell me how you really feel,' I say.

Victoria gives me a small hug, which I accept graciously. I know she is not being malicious.

'She was too old for you, as well,' Victoria says.

I'm surprised to hear Victoria say this. Whatever happened to the sisterhood? Besides, Larissa was thirty-seven when we met last year, and I was thirty-three. Not a big age difference.

'Four years is nothing,' I say.

Victoria smacks her lips together, looks up, and back at me.

'Normally, I would agree, but she wanted children, and you, Tom,' Victoria pauses, pointing a forefinger in my direction. 'Well, I don't know what you want. I do know that she was straight about wanting kids right from when you first met, and you came over in a cold sweat and started your non-committal babbling act in response.'

'That's simply not true,' I protest.

'Marcus told me,' Victoria says.

'Marcus,' I growl under my breath.

'Victoria,' says Marcus. 'That was in confidence.'

Victoria laughs at this; she finds it hilarious.

'We're married, darling! Nothing is in confidence or off the record. Besides, Tom, I just want you to date someone who you might be suited to,' Victoria says. 'Like... anyone really.'

I think for a moment, Victoria is going to say 'Beth', only she doesn't, and I am not sure why. She wouldn't be the first of my friends to suggest it, or to encourage me to act. It has never worked; I always pushed back against these encouragements, never bold enough, always too afraid.

After talking about Larissa, our posse disperses, and we circulate. I chat to a few people I haven't seen for a while. We talk about Marcus and Victoria and what it would be like to leave London. Most say they cannot imagine going, although we all acknowledge how hard it is to live here.

While I am chatting, I get a message from Larissa. She is now, after all, not coming. She doesn't feel up to it. I have a slight pang of guilt, and I wonder if this is down to me.

When we met two weeks ago, it was on a Sunday in North London. We had been out in Crouch End for lunch, and after eating we'd taken a walk, browsing the second-hand bookstore and a little clothes boutique that Larissa wanted to look in. Then I saw a tiny sliver of a shop selling incense and crystals, candles, and quartz. It advertised psychic readings, which promised to 'bring clarity to your life, and give you control of your destiny'. I love that mystical part of life, and even if it doesn't really mean anything, I always want to try it. I tell myself I am keeping an open mind, and I like the idea that our lives might somehow be guided rather than simply subject to a random series of events. If nothing else, it gives us something to talk about.

'Let's go in,' I said.

Larissa looked warily at the shop. Its door stood at forty-five degrees from the street and faced an equally small old-fashioned tobacconist. It was the kind of place that only exists in the cracks of doorways, and stubbornly hang on against the march of time.

'These places give me the creeps,' she said. 'You know it's all fake, don't you?'

'Probably. I had it done once before at a work party. It's weird, but she said I was going to meet someone,' I said.

Larissa laughed at this. 'Anyone could say that, but okay, just for fun.'

It wasn't fun, though. Larissa took it seriously, and the consequences were dire. We went in and met a copper-haired woman named Lucy-Anne, who was dressed in a long floaty dress in shades of amber and orange, red and gold that looked like fire. So far, so cliché. But instead of a dark, musty place hung with tapestries, which I'd expected, the room where she did her readings was bright and white and rather professional. Lucy-Anne beamed reassurance, as if positive psychic energy flowed from her very being.

Larissa went first, and the psychic said we could ask any questions we liked. Larissa jumped straight in with a serious question about something I knew mattered deeply to her—when I had been expecting something light.

'This is what I want to know,' Larissa said. 'Will I have children?'

I am not sure why, but I bristled when Larissa asked this question even though we were no longer dating. I knew the thought of children pressed heavily on her thoughts. Victoria was right; Larissa had told me when we first met, and I had reacted as she described. I was also surprised that she asked considering she saw this as little more than baubles, mirrors, and fakery.

I fully expected Lucy-Anne to gush at this point, and after a suitable pause, to tell Larissa she saw two or three children in her future. This wasn't what happened. Despite Lucy-Anne's earlier smiles, it was as though Larissa's question had caught her out. She took a moment to answer and stumbled, which put me on edge. It was almost like she didn't want to respond to Larissa's question.

'Would you like to ask another question first?' Lucy-Anne asked.

'No, that is the question I want to ask,' Larissa said.

'Maybe we should go,' I suggested.

Larissa shot me an annoyed look.

'You wanted to come in,' she said.

I nodded. I thought it would be fun, now not so much. We were committed. There was to be no turning back.

'It isn't always definite,' Lucy-Anne said, sugar-coating her answer. 'I don't see any children standing around you in the near future.'

'What about further into the future?' Larissa asked.

Lucy-Anne did not answer immediately, and then dodged the question. What I didn't understand was why she didn't lie. It could only be that she believed in her own powers to look into others' lives and see their futures unfold.

'It is difficult to tell sometimes, today is one of those occasions,' Lucy-Anne said.

Larissa looked stony-faced at this and then, without a word, got up and left. Lucy-Anne called after her, and I offered a quick apology and rushed after Larissa, who was standing outside.

'I told you that was a bad idea,' Larissa said and began to walk at speed down the street.

Larissa wasn't the same after that visit to the psychic. It was my suggestion that we go in, so I can't help blaming myself for what happened next, and I am sure it was the reason she decided not to come along to the leaving drinks.

Chapter Three

'Wonderwall'

As the evening wears on, the bar begins to fill, and the conversation levels rise. I mingle, drifting around the room between groups. I always enjoy nights like this, full of unexpected conversation and the chance to see people whose paths we cross only at such gatherings.

It reminds me of the house parties we went to in our twenties. Unexpected evenings when friends lived with three or four others located in disparate parts of the city, and a night out could involve a trek across London to a variety of locations from grand Clerkenwell townhouses to flats in Plaistow tower blocks.

Now we gather in bars like this for birthdays and goodbyes, and catch up with each other, sharing recent highlight reels of life's misadventures.

I am coming to the end of one such update with a woman who is a friend of Adam's called Rebecca. She once briefly dated Adam and Marcus, which had led to disagreement between the two. From this we learnt never to date people our friends have dated as it can create serious and unnecessary disharmony. Happily, this was water long since under the bridge, and we were all friends again.

I am turning towards the bar as Rebecca begins speaking to someone else, when I see Beth come up the stairs.

I am struck by how stylish she looks, dressed in a long plaid coat, jeans, boots, and cream sweater, complementing her willowy figure and blonde hair.

When she sees me, Beth gives a small wave. I imagine she has come straight from home rather than the offices of *The Correspondent* where she is one of the paper's political reporters.

I walk towards her, as she moves from the top of the stairs, and we stop near the bar. It's been ages, I tell her, and it has. It has been a few months now since we last saw each other, which is both unusual and not. Whenever one of us is dating we see less of each other until inevitably coming out of the other side like hibernating creatures reconnecting with the world and certain friends.

'It has, my fault,' Beth says. 'We should do our traditional thing and see a movie or just sit in the pub.'

'That's a plan I can support,' I say, before pausing. 'Sorry to hear about Michael.'

Beth eyes me for a moment, smiles, and I wonder if I said the wrong thing, or she detected a lack of sincerity in my words.

'Yes, well, all good things…' and she gives a measured nod. 'It wasn't right, although I am sure you have already heard the highlights from Allison or Victoria.'

I smile and offer no comment. I order us drinks at the bar, and we shuffle along a little, so that we are standing tucked away. Beth's mention of Allison reminds me that I haven't seen her and her husband Paul for ages either. I wonder how they're doing. Paul is an old friend of Beth's who married Allison, who is a friend of mine, and my twin sister Sarah, from school. She is more Sarah's friend, really, but she spent so much time at our house growing up that she is almost part of the family.

I wonder how Allison and Paul are doing? We haven't seen much of them over the last few months since they had their first baby. They are the first of our friends to have one and were the first to get married. So many firsts.

'So, leaving London? Yes, or no?' I ask, changing the subject.

'Oh, is this the rapid-fire round?' Beth asks.

'It is,' I say.

'Then, I'd have to say leave, at some point, and talking of leaving, I would love to visit Marcus and Victoria once they've settled in. I've always wanted to visit that part of Yorkshire. You know it's where Sylvia Plath is buried?'

I shake my head. How, I wonder, did Plath come to end up there on some freezing northern hill? Beth, however, would know this. She is a huge fan of the writer, who she sees as some kindred spirit, a candle of her conscience.

'I did not. We should go,' I say.

This is entirely like me; taken by enthusiasm for Beth and everything about her, and then being petrified twenty seconds later that she suggests an actual plan to do this. Beth looks at me, and there is an uncertain smile on her face that I cannot quite decode.

'I would even consider such a move, but the problem with leaving London for us though, as journalists, is there are so few opportunities outside of London. We'd have to change careers, and I have no idea what I'd do,' Beth says.

'I've been thinking about that,' I say.

'Oh? Tell me.' Beth is intrigued. 'What conclusions have you drawn, and do you have a back-up career in mind? I really don't. Writing is the only thing I love and can do. I'm useless at anything else.'

'My only conclusion,' I say, 'is that I could imagine doing something else, and wouldn't mind, I just don't know what it is. You should write that book.'

Beth has spoken about writing a novel. It is something a lot of journalists, including me, talk about, and most never act upon. I am in the latter category.

'Oh, I have, and I'm finished,' Beth says.

I'm taken aback when she says this. I thought it was idle talk when it was clearly nothing of the sort. Beth has been busy and keeping quiet about it.

'When did you find the time? And how have you managed not to mention it?' I say.

'I got up at five a.m. three days a week, set myself a goal. I didn't want to say anything as, if I never finished, I'd just be another one of those hacks who talks at boring length about their great unfinished novel,' Beth says.

Before I get a chance to ask her more about her writing, Victoria appears, and hugs Beth and they begin to chat. I peel off after another a minute or two and come across Adam and then Marcus. The three of us find ourselves sitting down somewhere together as we always do.

Before any of us know it, it is closing time, and Marcus and Victoria's leaving London party is over. There is talk of going onto other bars, although it is a Wednesday and there is a general reluctance from everyone to embrace this plan. Besides, Victoria sensibly nixes the idea. Marcus is not going anywhere. He and Victoria are instead saying their goodbyes, touring the room, as friends leave. They are heading back home for their last night in London.

Soon, only the five of us—the departing couple, Adam, Beth, and myself—remain. Marcus is asking us all when we will be visiting, which is something he has talked about often since the move north was announced.

'Spring is a good time to visit,' Marcus says. 'Why don't you all come then?'

Victoria smiles, indulgent and approving. 'That would be lovely,' she says.

'Sounds good,' I say. 'I'm for it. Hop on a train.'

'It's two hours,' Marcus says. 'No one believes it; they think the north is like another country and it takes five hours to get there, but really it takes no time.'

'Count me in as well,' says Beth.

'Me too,' says Adam.

'You know we are going to visit; besides, I don't know what I am going to do with my free time now,' I say.

We walk together through Soho, heading towards Oxford Circus station and home. At the tube, we embrace, pause for a few moments more, and our goodbyes are complete.

At Finsbury Park, Beth and I say goodnight to Adam who catches an Uber to Crouch End, and we cross the busy Seven Sister's Road and walk towards Highbury.

I live close to the old Arsenal football stadium, in the garden flat of a Victorian house, and Beth lives a few streets away. We are talking about Marcus and Victoria, saying again how it will be strange for them not to be around in the way they always have been, and what this change to our lives will be like. Beth says she is envious and mentions her forthcoming visit to a house her family owns on the Isle of Skye. She plans to take a week off, enjoy the quiet away from London. I love the sound of it and joke that I would love to come.

'You should! Why don't you?' Beth says.

It is the second time tonight we have spoken of going away together. First, a pilgrimage to visit Marcus and to where Sylvia Plath is buried, and now this. My reaction is the same: pure fear.

'One day, I'd love to,' I say, pushing the idea away, although such a break for me feels long overdue. I think about the office, and work, of that darkness. Specifically, I think about the story I wrote tonight. I'm not sure, only I cannot escape the feeling that the clock is running down on that life.

I have always been poor at taking holidays, which is what happens, I think, when you are single and not ready to give yourself over to group or activity-based trips. So, as so often, in this situation I am being presented with a chance of something that might be good for me, and a choice to make, and as usual, I am running away from it, like a sprinter down the track.

'I've been thinking about this for a while, so I am just going to come out and say it,' Beth says.

I turn to her, a prickling of hair rising on the back of my neck, like a spidery sixth sense, alerting me to something. There is a strong gust of wind, the bare branches of the street trees creaking as they twist, and cold air burns the exposed skin of my face.

Beth is about to share something of note. Is she, I wonder, about to do something radical with her job? Maybe a career break and six months living on Skye to write another book? Although, given how quickly she has written one, I'm not sure she needs a career break. Or just to be free of commuting, and the grind for a while.

'Oh,' I say. 'That sounds intriguing.'

Beth smiles at me, gives a small, nervous laugh. 'I'm not sure that's the word,' she says.

'What's the word, then?' I ask.

'If there was a word,' Beth starts, 'it would be "overdue",' and she makes inverted commas with her fingers as she says this.

'Like a lost library book?' I suggest and start to ramble. 'I have a copy of *The Lion, the Witch and the Wardrobe* from my local library when I was a teenager. I loved that book. I wonder if I could still take it back. It has been twenty years, and fines would be significant, but I think I owe it to future generations,' I say.

'That would be long overdue, and this would be something similar.' Beth pauses and looks at me, gazing deep as if contemplating something. She holds my gaze, so much so that I started to giggle a bit. 'Tom?'

'Beth.'

'Don't you sometimes think…?'

My first thought is, think what? Beth has lost me. It could be the alcohol.

'What?' I say, throwing my hands out.

'Don't you sometimes think…?' Beth repeats. She opens her hands out towards me, and I look at her, still confused. As far as I can work out, Beth has repeated her last sentence. It sounds like a fragment of a sentence lifted from a complete conversation. I have no idea what that conversation was.

And then Beth asks again, as though she cannot quite bring herself to say it and is struggling to get the words out.

'Don't you?'

Beth draws her lips tightly together and looks down to her shoes, toeing and heeling them together, her boots giving a click, like Dorothy trying to find her way home.

'Beth, whatever it is, come out and say it. Hit me with it,' I say.

Beth nods at me, her expression somehow resigned to what is about to happen, which only adds to my puzzlement.

'Okay, as you asked,' and she breaks again for a moment. 'I have dated people, and it always comes back to this. It always comes back to the two of us standing somewhere like this, and to me, it makes sense. You and I make sense, and when you spoke about the two of us visiting Marcus and Victoria, of visiting Sylvia Plath, it made me think that you feel the same about this. It is a conversation that I have put off, so that's what I'm saying. Now I'm saying it. This is how I feel.'

Boom. I feel like I have been washed away by a powerful wave. My mind is desperately trying to swim in swelling seas, and I am struggling to keep my head above water, as I gave myself enough time to think and organise my thoughts. Beth is right, and I think back to that Plath moment, which is one of several marking our friendship; I did have that thought before retreating from it, post haste.

Now I am struggling, and I do not immediately respond, which is a terrible mistake. All I can say is that as a man, I am prone to making poor decisions and shocking mistakes when I find myself occupying the territory that most would describe as 'the perfect romantic moment'. Beth is doing the grown-up thing, and I am failing.

This is the moment I have thought about many times. The one where I tell Beth how I feel in full knowledge that there will be no turning back; the one where I know

I am ready for a serious relationship that will last and last. It is the one I have always been too afraid to have, and the one that I always run from, as I could not commit. But... I'm still convinced that I should be with someone else—although deep down, I know I will never find anyone I'm better suited to and get on with more than Beth. Those are the cold, plain, and very confusing facts, and as I stand there looking at Beth, I feel as if I'm both running away *and* reacting like a rabbit caught in the dazzling headlights of an oncoming car, out on a dark country road.

I start to nod as thoughts inside my head are screaming at me to tell Beth that I feel the same. However, even as they scream, I shut them out, and I shut them down, and instead I play for time, and try to find a way out of the situation.

'Okay,' I say. Which is the wrong thing to say. It sounds like someone has presented me with a problem, and I am trying to find a solution or a way out, which in sense, I was. Then, as I have the habit of doing, I say the second wrong thing:

'Cool.' As if I am trying to give myself more time.

I should say it. That is my moment: I should say I feel the same way. Only I can't bring myself to do it, and I squirm—then do something incomprehensible: I start to talk about something else. I act like my weak response to Beth's words has concluded the conversation and that now we are moving on.

'I was thinking,' I start, 'of watching that Netflix documentary *American Murder*, later. It's meant to be very good.'

Beth looks at me, her expression one of incomprehension, as though she can't quite believe what I am saying.

Then she calls me on it. She isn't taking my bullshit answer to her telling me how she feels lying down which, to be honest, is fair enough.

'Seriously, that's your response? I tell you I want to be with you, and you change the subject and start jabbering about Netflix?'

I nod at her. What can I say? I can hardly agree with her and admit that she's right, can I? Yet I know that at this moment we're at the cliff's edge, and my mute response has plunged us down onto the jagged rocks and into the dark sea of the night below. Our impending fate was oblivion.

'I'll see you, Tom,' Beth says.

'Yeah,' I say, my voice cracking as I add, 'soon', the word sticking in my throat as if I don't believe it either.

Beth turns and walks in the opposite direction, making for home. I watch her go and cannot bring myself to do anything to stop her. I could call out, and I could run after her, and I do none of those things. Instead, I watch her go; I watch her leave in silence.

I understood right there and then that her words meant the exact opposite. She wouldn't see me. Her use of my name in that final sentence carried with it an inescapable note of finality.

Despite that, I try to tell myself that it's okay, that I will find a way to fix the situation. Only I don't, for two reasons. First, I don't know how I could do that, and second, a week later the country came to a halt. The prime minister announced a lockdown, and the country became a place of ghosts, of fearful, scurrying people, like lonely figures from a Lowry painting.

As we all hid away, I allowed our friendship to wither, and a chance at anything else die a death as well. Even after things started to get better, I did nothing about it. I focused on other things, as I worked to change my life.

Chapter Four

'You & Me Song'

The man at the counter is making a complicated coffee order. I should clarify: if you're me and only order black coffee, with the only variation being the size of the cup, then every order that requires more than coffee and hot water is complex.

'Could I have a triple-shot, venti latte with soy milk, no foam and a decaf, soy latte, but with an extra shot?' he says.

In a previous life, queuing behind this person, I would have been seething, and asking myself, *how do you even come up with a coffee order as convoluted as that?* It sounds more like a recipe than a hot drink, which will in turn take the barista an age to make. However, times have changed. I am not angry; instead, I am smiling, and I'm about to make polite conversation with Ralph—which happens to be his name—and I know he has a pug he adores, which his boyfriend is looking after outside the café, as he has told me this. I also know that the first coffee he is ordering is for his partner, and the second for him. That's the way Ralph does it.

That's the other thing; I am not in the queue for coffee. I am the person making the coffee. I'm no longer furiously bashing away on a keyboard writing about a soul sucking court case or somebody who got killed, I am serving coffee, and I am much happier for it. More than a year ago, while the country was still stumbling from lockdown to lockdown, I lost my job as the *Evening News* made swingeing redundancies, and opened a café with my twin sister, Sarah, who I could not have done this without. She has not only provided money, but together we wrote a business plan and found someone to help run it.

I didn't know one end of a balance sheet from the other. Luckily, my sister, who works in the city as an investment banker, does, and she insisted that for the business to work, I needed to go on a crash course, and so I did. Her idea is that one day in the next few years before she is forty, she will quit her job, and open another café or three if we can make a success of this one.

The idea is one—and excuse the pun—that has been brewing for years. There are lots of good cafes out there, only I always thought that what was missing locally was the perfect combination of a café bookshop.

I idly told my sister this one day as we spoke on one of our regular calls during the grinding months of the first lockdown. I was jobless, rarely leaving the house and on a downward spiral. I had started looking for a new job in journalism, but the truth was a combination of there being few jobs around, and my heart no longer being in it. My problem was, I had no idea what I would do instead. I had always been a journalist, and thought it was part of who I was, but no longer felt that way.

The 'downward spiral' bit was according to my sister, who is as blunt as a hammer when it comes to providing feedback. To be fair, this was, in part at least, the result of soul-crushing and tragic news of a personal nature. I am not sure I have quite recovered from this, which came on top of all the pain and suffering the pandemic brought to so many. That combined with my redundancy, about which I was fifty per cent sad and fifty per cent relieved, and the loss of Beth as a friend. The two of us had not spoken since the night of Marcus and Victoria's leaving drinks.

So, with all of that going on, I vaguely mentioned the bookshop/café idea.

'I love that,' Sarah said.

I was so surprised to hear her say this that it took me a while to respond, and I thought about the things we have in common. We love books, we're both big readers, and my memories of us in the town library as kids, sitting on the big, soft, long-slung seats, reading after school while waiting for Mum to finish work are lodged in my mind.

'You do?' I said.

'Absolutely,' Sarah said. 'But don't sit around talking about it and never leaving the house—do it. You hated your job in the end, you don't seem to be getting another, and there is no café close to you. I bet we could find somewhere to open one.'

The thing was, I knew nothing about running a café or anything else. Yet in the face of my sister's enthusiasm for the idea, I began to think seriously about it. How hard could it be? (The answer turned out to be harder than you think, but not nuclear physics.) I started messaging my sister, asking her how she thought we could do this. First, she said, we needed to take a walk around the area, and that's what we did.

On the parade of shops at the bottom of my road was a former carpet shop, which had closed months ago. It was available and we took out a lease.

We agreed on a name, calling it the Shakespeare Café, which we both liked. The idea made me think of Bohemian Paris, of Fitzgerald and Hemingway, of New York's literary salons, and San Francisco's beatnik days and coffee houses. That was the inspiration. Of course, the North London experience is somewhat different.

Sarah brought in Julie who had managed a coffee shop in the City, which had closed for lockdown and never reopened. The two had become friends, chatting as Sarah bought her morning coffee on her way into the office.

Julie, who is French Moroccan, slight, with long soft curls of dark hair and big brown eyes and freckles, is forthright, and graceful under pressure. When the two of us first met, seated on old office chairs in front of a rickety old desk in the half-painted café, we hit it off straight away. She is a woman who puts others at ease and is easy to be around. The cast-off furniture, was, at the time, all we had, left behind by the Williams family who had run the former carpet shop for forty-three years. People don't want carpets anymore, Mr Khan, who runs the newsagent a few doors down, told me.

'You have some impressive experience,' I said.

Julie smiled and told me she knew what needed to be done, and that this was the kind of café she had always wanted to run.

'I can tell you I know exactly what you need to do to make this café a great success,' Julie said, her voice like honey, her accent smoothed by years in England.

We talked for almost two hours before ending the interview, which was a foregone conclusion following instructions from Sarah ('She's perfect: hire her').

We talked about books and coffee, and about how she came to England as a student with a plan to stay a year and was still here more than thirteen years later.

'I fell in love and got married, and we are still in love now,' Julie said, and as she spoke, she gave a slight smile, which was warm and reassuring. Her words were ones that I could not imagine an English person saying, so innately French was the way she expressed her position in life.

Julie followed this up with a lift of her left shoulder and a raise of her eyebrows. It was a slight shrug, as if by way of explanation, and to say that there was nothing that could be done about it, she did not understand this either, but *c'est la vie*. Her gesticulation conveyed so much. I came to understand her gesture more later, when I met her husband, Jasper. Tall, bearded, and solid, he is a prematurely grey forty-something film studies lecturer, who towers over her, and is rather fond of a tweed jacket. To look at them you would never put them together. Julie says he is the ultimate romantic, and his knowledge of romantic films and the joy he takes watching them is what drew her to him. This only goes to show that sometimes people don't know much about putting people together. Sometimes they get it all wrong, which says more about people than it does about happy couples.

Together, with Sarah, we got the café up and running and I made it my life. We designed the interior with light, wooden floors, and grey walls. The tables are dark wood, the chairs vintage and mismatched, and bookcases line the walls. The critical thing is that the café is split into three and sells second-hand books and a selection of new novels.

First, at the front you have the books, and the grown-up café section. This is populated by people sitting for long hours with Apple laptops who don't buy enough coffee. Julie has no qualms about materialising beside their tables and suggesting they might like another coffee. Her disarming smile and French manner always do the trick.

Then at the back we have a section of the café dedicated to parents. There you'll find a seating area and a soft play section for parents, babies, and toddlers. It is essential to the success of the café to make sure that mums—and it almost always is mums—are constantly coming through the doors with buggies, bags, and small children, and a desire for caffeine.

Since we opened the café, I've been bouncing back and forth like a human tennis ball between my flat near Finsbury Park and the café, which is a ten-minute walk away. I have been okay with that.

The café always feels less like work and more like hanging out. I like making coffee and taking orders and cleaning. And telling customers that yes, that is the WIFI code on the blackboard, directly under where it says, 'WIFI code'.

At the end of the day, I take a walk to the park a few times a week. It's one of those rituals that, like everyone else, I started doing during those first apprehensive, tense, dark days when the country had its first lockdown. The first one, the one that feels like it happened an age ago, when the 2020s were young and ready to roar, and before they were gloomily interrupted.

I never thought I would be one of those people who goes to the park and takes a walk. I am, though, and taking regular walks saved me in a way that I never thought possible. It is exercise for the soul, not the body. At first, I would listen to music, then podcasts about absolutely anything.

Then I got to a stage, like many people, where I felt as if I had completed everything, listened to every podcast and had enough of my music. After that, I walked with my thoughts. I'm sure that this was one of those small acts of self-care that helped me keep my life from spinning away from me.

Being free of news helped as well. I had come to hate the news, the constant doom scrolling, and hot takes, and that's hard when it is your job. So, when it wasn't my job anymore, I felt as if a weight had been lifted. I didn't need to look at the news; I didn't feel I needed to keep up. I was free of the news. I don't know why, only to me now, at a slight distance, that is what news feels like, something you must try to keep up with, when you can't. There is too much news, too much bad news, and it is like a terrible game you can never win.

Mostly, however, I go to the park to meet up with Larissa. She's always there as well.

That wasn't the only thing that happened. There were other things. One of them close to the beginning of the first lockdown was and still is unspeakable. It knocked me off my feet, like I had been punched hard in the stomach, and it took the air right out of me.

The other thing was that as the world closed in on itself with the pandemic, I became anti-social. I cut myself off from other people, and I didn't know I was doing it. I thought I was working hard, focused on starting something new and getting the café up and running. Only that wasn't quite it. I wasn't talking to people, not even taking part in group video calls, or making any other effort to contact my friends to chat. First, I stopped going out because we had to, and then I preferred not to.

My friends were concerned about me and a few weeks ago, at the start of June, almost sixteen months after the pandemic hit, they staged an intervention. My friends, led by Adam, became convinced that at the age of thirty-four years and more than half a dozen months, my time was running out to find someone, and that staying in and not seeing enough people wasn't helping. They said I needed to kickstart my life and start dating again as soon as possible.

Do people need rebooting? Did I need rebooting like some troubled laptop with software problems? The thought never occurred to me. I thought I was happy. It was a different kind of happy to before—quieter, but in general I felt happy all the same, if more contemplative. At least I thought I did.

I had come to enjoy many aspects of my life after the pandemic. The introverted facets of my personality had risen to the surface. I could still chat and smile around people, only with a lot less socialising and transactional conversations.

That's why Adam led his intervention. He wanted to get me dating again, meeting people, and moving on with my life.

Adam got Allison and my sister involved. They unkindly described my existence as 'hermit-like' and 'weird'. The last one, to be fair, was my sister, who pointed out that she did not help me start a café with our joint money so that I could turn into some anti-social weirdo who shuffles to and from work and does little else.

This is where Adam came in. He had a plan to get me out of my 'flat funk' and outside into the world. It culminated with the intervention, where my friends came en masse like some uninvited committee of local neighbours overflowing with community spirit. They were going to get me dating again.

Today, as I enter the park and walk around the edge of the boating lake with its rusting metal fence, I notice fresh flowers tied to the railing. I wonder who put them there. I had been in the park a couple of days ago, and the flowers were dying. They've been replaced today. It's been more than a year now, and someone or several people continue to leave flowers to mark what happened here.

Today, it is a pretty bouquet of oranges, yellows, and pinks. The orange flowers are striking, although I am not sure what they are called. There isn't any note with the flowers, and nothing to indicate who might have left them or their particular interest or reason for this continued act of remembrance.

I know spots like this, where something tragic has happened, can be morbid, and some people don't like it because it creates something of a shrine. That said, I understand why people do it. It is warming to see people do such things, to take the time and expense to remember people we have lost.

Standing by the railing, I am joined by a jaunty, slight-looking woman in her mid-sixties. I recognise her and am sure I have seen her energetically doing speed walking circuits around the park. Dressed in a loose-fitting purple tracksuit, she looks as though she, too, is out on her regular evening walk and has paused like me, drawn, I imagine, as we both were, by the fresh flowers.

'Absolutely tragic, isn't it?' the woman says.

'Yes,' I say.

'I couldn't believe it when I first read it,' she says. 'A woman drowning herself here in the lake. Another victim of the pandemic.'

Was she that? It is something that none of us will know. Some got sick and died; others found it too hard to carry on. I shake my head, give a reflex shiver. The story always chills me, makes me uneasy, as things to do with water always do. People say that drowning is not a terrible way to die. I find it hard to believe. I would be flailing and splashing madly, gasping for breath, and thinking every second that there is nothing that is not terrible about it.

After a pause, a few moments of refection, the woman says: 'They called her *the lady in the lake*.'

I wince at this. That is what some headline writers came up with. Even after I lost my job and moved ahead with the café plan with my sister, there were quite a few stories in the end about the woman who drowned in the lake. It isn't often that someone drowns themselves in your local boating lake, after all. The news made the local and national press, and I remember seeing a couple of TV news crews here.

'I remember,' I say. It is an evocative headline, sending most of us reaching for images rooted in Arthurian legend. However, there have been no reports of any figures rising from the shallow waters of Finsbury Park's boating lake to greet surprised families or teenagers rowing around the island with news of England's new dawn. Not when darkness continues to stalk the land.

'I always see you in the park,' the woman says.

I feel like I have been seen when she says this and am uncomfortable. It is the elephant in the room psychologically speaking for me. For some reason, despite often seeing the same people, I convince myself that they don't see me, and that while I notice others, people aren't noticing me. I am somehow, I imagine, unseen, incognito, a shadow who passes unnoticed.

I think it is something about how we see ourselves as people who live in large cities. We prefer to lose ourselves to the vastness of London rather than connect. However, since everything that happened, since we ended up becoming more local in our lockdown lives, we have been forced to notice each other more— some, like me, more grudgingly than others.

I have an absolute fear that she will introduce herself, tell me her name, and share other biographical details. Since the pandemic I have found myself fearful of getting close to people—I can chat with customers in the café but tend to share little more than basic pleasantries if I can help it. There are one or two who push for more. That said, it is enough for most.

I offer a slight smile. 'I've seen you too, although I think you set a better pace than I do,' I say.

The woman nods, pleased at this. She looks at her Apple watch, checking, I suppose, her distance covered so far on today's outing.

'I do try, and on that note, I had better press on, I have two and a half kilometres to walk yet,' she says.

'Enjoy,' I say.

'You too, enjoy your...' She pauses as if searching for the right word, and shrugs. 'Well, enjoy the rest of your day,' she says.

The woman gives a wave and walks off past the café towards the tennis courts. For a moment, I watch her before she turns down the hill and begins to loop around the edge of the park, where the railway line runs and the skatepark can be found.

I turn to look at the lake, casting a final glance at the flowers—maybe they are orange poppies? A fitting note of remembrance. I set off again; ahead of me, I can see Larissa, dressed in black trousers and a white T-shirt, which she is always wearing, sitting where we always meet in the park, on the bench which looks across the mid-point of the lake. She smiles when she sees me, and I grin back.

'I see you were making some new friends,' she says.

'Oh, you know me, I try as hard as I can to make no new friends, but the social repellent I use is only of limited help,' I say.

'It amazes me how anti-social you've become, and yet you chose to open a café.'

'I know, it makes no sense. I do enjoy it, though.'

'I know you do, and I'm happy for you, I think you made the right choice.'

'Thank you.'

'What were you and your new friend talking about over there?'

I'm flustered for a moment, as I don't want to mention the flowers. I know Larissa doesn't like to talk about it.

'The weather, of course,' I say with a bright smile. 'The same thing British people always talk about.'

'Not something that concerns me that much,' Larissa replies. 'What I do want to hear about is what is happening with this intervention? When are you going to start going on these dates?'

Chapter Five

'Heart-Shaped Box'

Early last Wednesday evening, Adam, Sarah, and Allison descended on my flat and staged an intervention. When the bell rang, I had initially planned to do what I always do in the evenings when the doorbell rings; I was going to ignore it. I do this in the likelihood that the person ringing the door isn't someone I know, and instead is trying to sell me something.

However, on this occasion, whoever is out there will not give up. They press the bell three times. *They must really want my money*, is the thought that strikes me, and I cross my arms, strengthening my resolve not to answer the door.

At this point, my mobile phone rings. I glance at the screen and see that it is Adam. It has been weeks since I have seen Adam despite his frequent suggestions we go to the pub. I answer the phone, wondering as I do, what is going on. My bell is buzzing, and my phone is ringing. It is a really busy night.

'I'm standing outside your flat, ringing the bell. I know you're in, your light is on. Are you going to answer?' Adam asks.

My first instinct is to say *no*, as I was engaged in an important project, which I had only started a couple of weeks ago. Things were progressing well.

I'd decided to watch all seven seasons of *Gilmore Girls*, which is not a TV endeavour to take on lightly, even in these weird days. People kept talking about it throughout lockdown. I didn't think it was for me at first. Only now I realise it is for everyone. It is a slow start, and once you are over that, you discover the most perfect vanilla TV. It's glorious and comes complete with whip-snap dialogue, a truckload of cultural references, and with one hundred and fifty-three episodes. It is the kind of suitably substantial TV challenge that I've enjoyed taking on over the last year or so. Julie recommended it by saying it was very popular in France. Besides, during lockdown, I had watched so many boxsets and had already completed *Luther*, *Schitt's Creek*, *House*, *30 Rock*, and *Line of Duty*.

'You are a man in much need of comfort TV,' Julie said.

Despite being in London for many years, Julie has not lost that certain directness that the French can possess. This comes with a deadpan sense of humour and a terrific capacity for organisation. Besides, Julie is not wrong.

When I open the door, I am greeted by the three of them standing there on a clear warm June evening, looking not unlike a group of random out-of-season festive singers.

'It's a little early for carolling, isn't it?' I quip.

It was half past eight, and I thought we were all agreed that people turning up on your doorstep uninvited was a thing of the past now that we have a myriad of ways to connect. It is now much easier not to turn up than it is to… well, turn up.

'Oh, you're very droll,' Sarah says, rolling her eyes at me. 'I bet you say that to everyone who knocks at your door. And for the record, I am only here as Allison dragged me along.'

Without waiting for an invitation or offering explanation, they troop in like weary, respite-ready ramblers.

I watch them walk past me, thinking as they do what reason I could have given to refuse them entry. Other than that, I was happy watching TV on my own while sprawled on the couch, as I am most evenings, I had absolutely none. Although that is not a bad reason.

I realise I could have tried lying and said there was a woman in the flat with me, only I could already see them staring at me blankly, peering into my soul and through my lies.

As they enter, Allison gives a slight shrug, as if to say this wasn't her idea either, and Sarah gives me a small sisterly hug. Adam, on the other hand, gives me a censorious look that tells me this must be his doing. Of course, it is. It's always the person with the PhD who comes up with these ideas.

The three of them cram into the small sitting room of my flat. Allison and Sarah sit on the small, two-seater couch, nestled neatly together, while Adam plonks himself on the oversized couch.

'While it is nice of you all to drop by unannounced, is someone going to tell me what you're all doing here?' I ask.

Adam throws his arms out and his head back. I have clearly missed something obvious, and the reason for their visit should be blindingly apparent to me, when it isn't.

'Isn't it obvious? This is an intervention,' Adam declares.

I look at Adam, nonplussed. He must be joking, right? This is why I start to laugh, only no one else is laughing. Allison and Sarah look at me with long, serious faces. Adam shakes his head and continues to wear a grave expression. This isn't, in fact, a joke. I am the subject of a real-life intervention. I feel like I'm on TV.

For a minute, I think they might have two burly oversized silent men outside ready to manhandle me into a waiting van and drive me off to an unspecified location. When I arrive, I hazard, I will be shown a room and given one phone call. Of course, I'll phone my mother only to be told in a solemn voice that it is for my own good. Too late, I will realise I have wasted my call. Damn. Although, given that I speak to so few people, I am not sure who else I would call. I could try Marcus, although he is too far away now to be of any help.

No burly men appear; instead, the next worst thing happens.

'We're here to help,' Adam says.

Why are there three of them? Since when did interventions need a quorum? Can one person intervene, or is it, strictly speaking, only an intervention if the whole cast of characters is in attendance? Perhaps there is a rule from the sitcom writers' handbook that has since slipped into popular culture stating that if you are going to hold an intervention, you must ensure that at least three characters are in attendance.

I suspect the real reason is that Adam likes an audience to work with. I'm surprised to see Allison here, of all people. She has had a tough year, splitting up with her husband Paul during that long first year of the pandemic.

Allison and Paul were the first friends to get married, the first to get a house and have a baby. They've been the grown-up model for marriage for us all, the blueprint of how to do it, when we find the right people to do it with. When I think of them, I think of how things can work out right if you get serious with the right person.

They seemed like the perfect couple: they looked good together, he cooked wonderful food—making much mess and using many pans—and they had the best Instagram account. This turned out to be all presentation and no substance, your basic social media problem.

Their boxes were all checked; I thought in a year they would have another baby and their model family would be complete, and then the pandemic came, and lockdowns and unpleasant truths emerged from the gloom.

Sometimes I wonder why I even use social media. As a former journalist I find the doom-scrolling through bad news depressing. Julie does our social media for the café. She doesn't trust me to do it. She told me my posts needed to be more upbeat.

When Allison told me that she and Paul were splitting up, I asked her what had gone wrong when they had been such a great couple.

'We were a great couple and then we stopped being so great. I think that's true of a lot of couples; it's like your "greatness" has a time stamp, and ours expired. Having Dylan changed everything. Paul's idea of helping with childcare was going to work and changing the odd nappy. He didn't want to do any of it, so we argued all the time. I told him he couldn't play golf, play football, go out with his mates, and expect me to do everything. He responded by saying he didn't want to spend all his time babysitting. That was the end. I yelled at him that time, and you know me, I don't yell. I told him you can't *babysit* your own child. I said he needed to do more, and he said he couldn't, so he left. He's at his dad's house in Dulwich. Like father, like son. Two overgrown teenagers together.'

After I served beer and wine, we sit looking not unlike a reluctant book group, which has been forced to read something that only the person who recommended it enjoyed. Today's choice of book has been chosen by Adam and the title is: *The life of Tom Martin.*

Adam wastes no time in jumping in and setting out the problem as he sees it.

'You, my friend, are facing a time bomb,' Adam says.

'What he means is—' Allison starts.

'He means,' Sarah interrupts, 'that you're getting old, and lonely, and well, it is sad and depressing to watch, and… oh, so many other kinds of things, and—'

'Sarah? Remember what we spoke about?' Adam says. 'Let's all try to remember why we are here. Try to use positive phrases to allow better communication, such as "I feel".'

Sarah smiles indulgently at Adam and gives him an appreciative nod. He is pleased by this, thinking that he has got through to her. Does he not know her and her wily ways by now?

'*I feel,*' Sarah starts again, 'that you are getting sad and lonely, and as my twin brother, you need to pull your socks up and sort yourself out.'

'Sarah,' Adam and Allison say together.

Sarah smiles at me, and I am the only one who finds her performance amusing, and I think she knows I do. Sarah is channelling my dad. He might be dead but his spirit lives in her. A former soldier, his attitude to anything in our childhood from falling and cutting a knee to being punched in the playground was to sort yourself out and 'crack on'.

'Sorry. I will try,' Sarah says.

I wonder what they have spoken about. It sounds as if there has been some kind of pre-intervention meeting. I imagine them sitting at Allison's nearby house. Adam would have insisted on taking notes. He probably called them 'minutes', although he likely delegated this task to someone else, as he was 'chairing' the meeting, and then proceeded to do most of, if not all, the talking.

The hairs on my neck prickle like a storm is in the air, and I'm uncomfortable. I wish they would leave. How long before I can reasonably ask them to go? Is thirty minutes enough, is forty-five enough? Or do I have to stretch to the whole hour?

Besides, I am thirty-four, and since when was that old? I am sure that thirty-four is the new something-or-other and that you are not old in this century until you hit your forties.

'For the record, I'm thirty-four,' I say.

'Yes,' Adam says, 'and very soon you will be thirty-five and beginning your demographic slide.'

What on earth was a demographic slide? As theme park rides go, it needs work. It is a terrible name. It sounds like something that should have the word 'of doom' at the end. Perhaps, the Demographic slide of Doom, accompanied by a logo featuring a man in a grey suit and words of warning: 'You will not enjoy this experience.'

After a pause, as if to let his words sink in, Adam continues: 'Your chances of meeting someone and making a life for yourself are about to decrease exponentially.'

He pauses again for, I imagine, dramatic effect, and looks at me. Is this one of the tricks and tips he picked up from his media training? He presses on.

'Have you tried going on a dating app as a thirty-five-year-old man? The research says your chances of meeting someone diminish by forty-seven per cent.'

After saying this, Adam folds his hands together, crosses his legs, and makes a temple with his fingers. He looks pleased with himself as if the words spoken are meant to impress me and drive home the realisation that I am in terrible trouble. He has got to be joking.

'You forget I was a journalist. I know how meaningless these statistics are. They probably asked one hundred and fifty people before coming up with this headline-generating news story designed to fill websites and keep people mindlessly browsing. Research can say almost anything you want it to say, and if it didn't, everyone in research would be out of a job,' I say.

Adam shakes his head as if to tell me that I do not fully appreciate the gravity of my situation. I would happily say that he is correct in this assumption, as I do not.

'By the time you hit thirty-seven, your chances decline by sixty-seven per cent. And that isn't far off—if you think about it in terms of months, it is only twenty-four months away.' He snaps his fingers, and everyone seems impressed by this (to be fair, his fingers do make a strikingly loud click). 'To put it another way, give it a necessary pop-culture spin people more easily understand, that is just two seasons of your favourite TV show. It'll pass in the blink of an eye. Think about that,' Adam says.

I'm surprised that Adam hasn't insisted on connecting his laptop to the TV to show his compelling PowerPoint presentation chart. I am sure he considered this.

'It's true; women don't want to date older men,' Allison says.

Older men? Aren't older men like sixty-five or older? The kind of person who your mother would describe as 'an older gentleman'. Someone keen on bowls and strolls. They are not talking about people like me who don't like going out anymore. Besides, why is Allison saying this? She is meant to be one of my oldest friends. I almost find myself protesting and pointing out that she is no longer married nor dating anyone. Unless something has changed. Is she back out there?

'Thank you for your support,' I say.

'We want to see you happy, that's all,' Allison says.

However, I feel about it, Allison has a point. There is a stigma attached to men who are eternally single. Women—and I have no evidence to back this up, so in that sense, it is almost exactly like most research—see it as a sign of failure and ask themselves why these men haven't managed to commit by the age of thirty-seven, possibly concluding that there is something wrong with them; and then wondering, if something *is* wrong with them, is it a) fixable? b) worth the trouble?

Is that the way I'm heading? I have a little way to go but not too far. Two seasons of a TV show do pass in a flash, and decent story arcs can take much longer to develop. When you think about how long it takes at the beginning to work your way into a relationship, the stages you go through before you reach a place when you have an inkling that this is probably 'It', then you start to realise that maybe you don't have much time when you hit your mid-thirties.

This makes me think that it isn't only women who have a ticking clock. I have found myself thinking that it might be nice one day, at some unspecified point in the future, to have children. Thinking this, I find myself taken by surprise by my own mind. I am not sure where such thoughts came from. Or when they first started to appear, as lately I have not been myself. Or at least the best version of myself. It is like they slowly and stealthily sneaked up on me. They made their way through the long grass of my life, and now they have presented themselves. Maybe it is my subconscious, simply doing the maths and figuring out that I don't have as much time as I previously thought. My unconscious seems to be saying, *get a move on*.

The clock belonging to women has added biological pressure if they want to have children. For men, it is different. There isn't such a reproductive element, although maybe there is something in our DNA and nature that drives us. If you're a man, and you take reasonable care of yourself, your sperm will (despite steeply declining levels of male fertility) probably hold out for a while before your guns are exhausted and all you are firing is blanks. Of course, that's not the only thing to consider: there is the joke that Charlie Chaplin still had children in his seventies, although by that stage was almost too old to pick them up.

Besides, Chaplin would almost certainly have been mistaken for the grandparent when standing next to some mum or dad in their twenties or early thirties at the school gate. And I really don't want to be that person. So, my clock is ticking as well. Is early-onset male broodiness a thing? I don't know. It could be. Maybe it is for men like me, and I mean men of a certain age and demographic grouping, who are predisposed to dicking around and failing to make choices.

'Allison is right,' Sarah says.

'You are getting married,' I say to shut my sister up.

This was the source of some contention. My mother likes to call me up and talk to me about Sarah's impending wedding and has on occasion asked me how I feel about my sister getting married. My mother, I think, applies this question like a pressure point, hoping that it might generate some reaction and spur me into action by following Sarah's example. My answer is always the same: I am okay with Sarah getting married if she is. Only, I really can't stand her boring banking boyfriend, Jack. He is so full of himself, with his tall, good looks, and slicked-back hair; he is just so smug. He looks down on most people around him, like certain Tory MPs.

Sometimes, I don't think Sarah likes him much either. I have seen her roll her eyes at him. I have no idea what that means. Jack appears impervious to Sarah's eye-rolling behaviour. He thinks it is all an enormous joke. He laughs at it and acts like it is part of their relationship dynamic, and it might well be. However, I suspect most of the time, the joke is not what he thinks, and he should not be laughing quite so much.

That said, they have been together for almost five years, and Jack did pop the question. He did all the right things, with a textbook proposal, which I am sure he got from Google, having typed in the search term 'what is the best way to propose to a girl'. He then duly followed the AI-generated advice to the letter. Jack took Sarah on holiday to Greece, they island-hopped before stepping off the ferry in Santorini where he got down on one knee on a beach and whipped out a chilled bottle of Dom Perignon from his backpack, along with a ring. Sarah did say yes. However, women do seem inclined to say yes to those handsome, rugby-playing types. So, on that front, Jack does appear to be winning at life.

'The issue is,' Adam says, trying to get things back on track, 'that it's been a long time since...' He pauses and there is a brief silence, during which everyone takes a sip of their drinks and does a spot of shoegazing. '...the last girl you dated.'

'He means,' Sarah says, 'Larissa Snowe.'

'I know who he means,' I say.

'That girl was cold as ice, no pun intended,' Sarah says.

Allison gives Sarah a look of admonishment.

'I apologise. That was in bad taste,' Sarah says.

It's fine I tell her, and I know she did not mean anything by it.

'Well, it was a relationship that preceded the pandemic; it was almost two years ago now,' Adam says.

When you put it like that, in real human years, it does sound like a long time. In my defence, the pandemic and lockdowns did throw a lot of people off course, and I have not quite corrected yet. It is more than that, though. I avoided dating altogether and, I suppose, gave up on it. Even when the world unlocked, I didn't start dating again. I put dating in a box, and then I put the box in a draw and moved on with the rest of my life. Dating was something that I had been putting off, and the idea of going out and meeting new people and starting over made me queasy. Working was easier, and it was a new kind of work, and one that provided the perfect distraction from other parts of my life. I started to tell myself I didn't need anyone; I didn't need to go dating.

There is a good reason for that. Let's face it, dating is hard. I would go so far to say, dating is *horrible*. It is not unlike a gruelling, spirit crushing, long march through the night that feels like there is no end in sight. Yes, it is great being with someone, or being with the right someone, only you have to go through a lot of pain and make a good deal of mistakes along the way to get there. That could just be me, and maybe I am bad at dating, and doing it all wrong. I won't lie, that thought has occurred to me many times.

'Yes, I know it has been a while and thank you for pointing that out,' I say.

Sometimes I think about that and wonder how it is possible to get dumped twice by the same girl. The answer is if, like me, you do not know when to quit and never should have been dating in the first place, then it's easy. People enjoy reminding me of this fact in the same way that people like to quote compelling statistics when making their case.

'Well, it is true,' Sarah says.

'I never knew what you saw in her. She was…' and Allison offers out her hands like someone trying to conjure something from thin air. In Allison's case, this would be why anyone would go doolally over one particular girl as I did. '…just so troubled, if very well read.'

This is classic Allison because she is not a mean person and always tries to end on a positive, and it is true; Larissa is well read. However, I know what she is saying. Larissa wasn't the classically attractive woman that I have chased in the past. Not like Rachel, Sara or Lucy who were all identikit small brunettes. Larissa Snowe was tall, a good two inches more so than me, gawky and had corrective braces on her teeth when I met her. None of that mattered as I liked her, and I think I was somehow in awe of her. There was also a sense of darkness around her, an almost otherworldly detachment, and her mood could become gloomy. The darkness was almost a reflection of the bleak novels she liked to read, which I was drawn to. I think at the start, the same was true for her. Briefly, she saw a kindred spirit. She once told me that it was okay for me, as I was good-looking. 'So are you,' I shot back, which was a response met by silence.

In the end, when I think of Larissa and of wanting someone like that, I am drawn to what Emily Dickinson wrote: 'The Heart wants what it wants—or else it does not care.' We have no control over our hearts, and sometimes they make poor choices for us.

'Let's not get side-tracked or dwell on past failures,' Adam says. 'It's important to stay focused.'

That is a classic Adam putdown, dropping in 'past failures' as a throwaway comment. Is getting dumped twice a failure? I imagine if you checked it against the chart, then yes. At the same time, I am glad I met Larissa and we spent that time together, even if we were mismatched, as we became friends. However, I let it go, and allow Adam to continue with his focus.

'Lockdown is long over, and apart from the café, you never leave your flat. You don't see anyone, you don't socialise anymore, and—'

'You're becoming reclusive which, combined with your conversation about buying a cat, is worrying,' Sarah interrupts.

'People say cats are good company,' I say, and I do so with a straight face.

Everyone laughs at this—I mean, really laughs. If it had been another year, I would have laughed as well. Before the pandemic, I had not considered owning a cat a positive attribute in a person. I don't know what to tell you, other than that I have changed my mind. In the same way that I once thought *Die Hard* was a Christmas movie, when it isn't. In retrospect, I might have been a cat person all along—a secret cat person hiding in plain sight after all these years. I like the idea that someone else will be softly padding around the flat, even if said creature has no interest in me much of the time.

'No one says that,' Sarah says. 'Cats are for single people who have given up on life. Get a dog, take it for a walk, meet a girl in the park. Or a boy. If that is your thing.'

'You know that's not his thing,' Adam says, doing his best to keep this show on the road. 'But a dog is not a bad idea.'

'I don't want a dog,' I say.

'Okay,' says Sarah, who, for someone who was dragged along, has a lot to say. 'But why do you have these cassette tapes? And a cassette player? What is all this crap you've acquired? It's like you're living in a nineties museum.'

Sarah is talking about the tape deck and old stereo equipment I have assembled in the corner by the TV, which previously belonged to my dad. It amazes me how much equipment it used to take to play music before everything was replaced with a phone and a few Bluetooth speakers.

All this 'crap', as Sarah puts it, is what I have been using it to make old-school mixtapes on cassettes. Actual mixtapes on tapes, which became my lockdown hobby. I have sat for hours on the floor wading through boxes of dusty old CDs and making mixtapes of my favourite songs. I have not made them for anyone else. I made them for myself. I know it sounds weird, only I fell in love with the process of creating them; the careful song selection, and the small joy it gave me to lie on the couch and listen to the tape once complete. I have found it very satisfying.

It was Beth's fault. Sort of. At the start of the first lockdown, I thought I would have a spring clean to cheer myself up and while sifting through old boxes I stumbled across two mixtape cassettes tucked away in a box. I had forgotten all about them. Staring at the tapes, I found myself reading the track list and smiling to myself. I made them years ago for Beth, and never gave them to her.

I started them not long after we met. So almost ten years or so ago. Beth had people over to her flat, where we ate and drank and then sat up for hours talking and playing music. As the evening wore on, and people left, Beth and I started to pick songs we liked to play for each other. It was one of those nights that you look back upon that was full of possibility. At that moment, Beth was always on my mind, and it was an evening when something could have happened. At the time, I always thought that nothing did occur. However, thinking about it later, I realise it did.

'I love some of your music suggestions,' Beth said.

'Let me make you a mixtape,' I enthused.

As soon as I said this, I felt awkward, like a dopey teenager. There was a pause, and Beth smiled, I think, delighted by the suggestion, and thus I was committed.

'I'd love that! No one has ever made me a mixtape before. You need to give it a title, reflecting the theme and the person you are making it for,' Beth said.

'Are those the rules of mixtapes?' I asked.

'As far as I know, those are the rules.'

That evening, the music we had played featured quite a few love songs of different varieties, so I wasted no time, and I worked on the tape, which turned into two, most of the following weekend. I was swept up in the moment and the challenge, enthused by what I thought it all meant. I painstakingly wrote out the band names and song titles by hand. I gave the mixtape a title, following Beth's mixtape rules. I called it: 'Love Songs for Girls'.

I then proceeded to tie myself in knots about the title. I worried about what it said, and that it said too much. However, in the end, I went with it. It was what so many of those songs we had listened to were about. It was also a reference to one of Sylvia Plath's poems, called 'Mad Girl's Love Song', which I knew Beth would appreciate. She loves Sylvia Plath.

After I finished, and the rush of excitement of making the tapes faded, I was embarrassed by what I had done, and too self-conscious to give them to Beth. Instead, I stuck the cassette in a drawer. When Beth casually asked me about it a few weeks later, I brushed it off. Been so busy, I lied, and I would 'definitely do it' at some point.

Neither of us ever mentioned it again. If it hadn't been for lockdown, I would never have found the tapes and started to make more mixtapes while I was stuck at home. They would have remained tucked away with other memories and fragments of my former life until one day being lost or discarded. Now I wonder if I have only been making them for myself.

'I've been making mixtapes,' I say.

'For a girl?' Allison asks with a grin.

'You've met someone?' Sarah asks with disbelief.

'No, I make them for myself.'

The faces looking at me are those of the lesser known three monkeys: 1. Deflated Monkey, 2. Incredulous Monkey and 3. Puzzled Monkey.

'Why would you do that?' Sarah asks and turning to look at Adam. 'This is much worse than we thought.'

'Oh, come on Sarah, hobbies are a good thing,' Allison says.

Sarah rolls her eyes; incredulous monkey is not buying that.

Adam raises his eyebrows. 'Let's get back on track.'

There is a pause, and Adam gives me a long look. He takes a deep breath and rests his chin on his hands, his fingers locked together.

'What we are most concerned about is that…' and he pauses again as if he is struggling with his words and how to voice them. 'You are lonely, and I think you just emphasised that yourself.'

When he says this, everyone is quiet. You could hear a pin drop. The room is silent, and I feel exposed, and like I could break in two. Only the murmur of distant traffic can be heard. Adam has stunned everyone with his words.

I don't know why but there is a stigma to an admission that someone might be lonely. I think somehow, it is seen as someone failing at life when it is nothing of the sort, particularly in these strange times of pandemic and lockdown when many of us are no longer the people we used to be. Some have been harder hit than others and struggled. Others, like me, tell ourselves we are happy enough, allowing their introverted selves to bumble along without the need for so many people in our lives. Some people are more content without other people all the time—I know most find this hard to believe but it is true, all the same.

'I am not lonely,' I say. 'Honestly.'

I realise I should not have said that, as no one believes you when you use the word 'honestly'. You might as well come out and preface whatever you are communicating with the words 'this is a lie, but I will push it anyway and please do your best to believe it'.

Adam looks at me kindly, and I wonder if this is a professional look he has developed and spent time practising with a mirror to perfect.

'It is okay to admit it,' Adam says.

'I have plenty of friends. I can count more than six, not even including the people in this room,' I say.

'But you don't see any of them,' Adam says.

'I know...' I thrust my finger forward. 'And I will try harder.'

It is at this point that Sarah changes the subject, as sisters do.

'Are you even washing or changing your underwear?' she asks. 'I've seen what single men are like. It isn't just single men. It is men if you leave them to their own devices. They need constant direction. Your sheets, as well. I hope you are changing them.'

'Yes, I am showering, and changing my underwear and sheets. I find it helps when running a business,' I say.

'Just checking,' Sarah says. 'And yes, I know you run a business, and I am proud of what you've done.'

'Thank you, and I in turn appreciate all the help. I could not have done it without you,' I say.

I am offered a satisfied sisterly Sarah smile. I know it well from our childhood squabbles, and I know we are reconciled.

'She has your best interests at heart,' Allison adds.

What is with those two tonight? It is as if they are synched. I know they have always been close. Allison and Sarah were in the same class at school, and I time travel for a moment back to when Allison would help Sarah with her advanced maths homework because, as well as everything else, Allison was always best at maths.

'The point is,' says Adam. 'We have come up with a plan. It's almost guaranteed, and it's based on a programme I've been developing for my clients.'

For a moment, I think Adam is joking. He can't mean he's here to sell me a twelve-step programme that he has cooked up like I am his personal science experiment.

'You have to be kidding me,' I say.

'We're not,' Sarah says.

'You need to get out there again,' Allison says.

'It's time,' says Adam.

I feel like I am being kept in suspense. While the idea of having an intervention and a plan foisted upon me is the last thing that I want in my life, I am at the same time intrigued to know what it is they have come up with.

In his work as a therapist, Adam's practice touches on elements of spirituality. He runs a course in self-realisation, which, to be honest, although he has explained it to me, I am not sure I understand. It involves something to do with liberating the knowledge within yourself to fulfil your inner potential. He hangs crystals in his office as part of this practice, which to me always seems like mystical, pseudo-scientific hokum and nonsense. I am not sure he believes in the crystals himself, or whether they are more for window-dressing and general ambience than anything else.

What I do know is that I am not, no matter what anyone says, going on any kind of spiritual journey. Besides, this last year has felt like a personal spiritual journey, only one based in a reality where I have changed my life. Sometimes, that feels like the hardest thing in the world to do, and I am sure many of us do not think we have the power or the bravery to do it when I fiercely believe that most of us do.

Switching my career from journalism to opening a café might sound like the easy option but to me it has felt like a revolutionary act. Making flat whites for the population of North London probably wasn't what Marx had in mind when he encouraged people to throw off their chains, but revolutions come in different forms, and this one started within. Heavy chains were what my so-called career, the thing I'd chased so hard for so long, had come to represent; heavy, thick chains that dragged down my soul. Now I feel free, even if I am on my own, and I cannot imagine going back.

'I'm not going on a spiritual journey,' I say.

They laugh at this, apart from Sarah, who rolls her eyes. Despite her MBA mentality, she does a lot of yoga and meditation and owns a lot of candles. People are laughing so hard about the spiritual journey that they are spluttering into their drinks.

'Don't worry, no one would ever suggest you go on a spiritual journey,' he says.

'You're too cynical and closed-minded, sometimes I can't believe we shared the same womb,' Sarah says.

'Maybe you sucked up all the good karma,' I quip.

'At least your sense of humour hasn't deserted you,' Sarah snaps back.

'You two,' Allison says.

'Okay, so, what are you suggesting exactly?' I ask.

'Dating,' Adam says, and then he lets this word sit there and I stare at him waiting for more. 'You are going to go on ten dates or dating experiences, and you do it in quick succession. That's the key part to the success of this process,' Adam says. 'It is part of a programme I am developing for my practice, and it is the basis for my book. It's called "Ten Dates to Happiness". Let me explain.'

Chapter Six

'Love Fool'

The book and programme Adam is writing and developing sounds exactly like the kind of title that makes it into the *New York Times* bestseller list. The title alone will have people queuing around the block and climbing the charts.

Essentially, it is an intensive step-based programme, at the end of which, I will, according to Adam, be in a happy relationship.

At this point, Adam stands and starts to pace around the small sitting room of my flat as if it is a stage, and he is delivering his TED Talk. He appears to be setting himself up as a relationship guru. The kind of person who appears on morning TV, sitting on brightly coloured sofas wearing pastel-coloured shirts and chinos, and looking super relaxed and smiling, as a presenter flashes his book to the camera.

'This experience will change your life,' Adam says. 'We are going to take over your dating life and organise ten dates for you. For each date we will provide you with a short bio and some background on why we have chosen them for you. The idea is that it takes some of the stress out of dating.'

Adam stops his pacing and turns to face me, pointing his two forefingers in my direction like they are dowsing rods and mystical energy is directing his movements.

'The key to this,' Adam says, 'is that you need to give yourself over to it fully and be open to whatever and whoever you meet. You need to free your mind and invest in each moment. You need to ensure you are present.

'Push your scepticism aside and trust the people who know you best. This is what you need. Try to think of it as an emotional healing process that will allow you to connect with people again. Meeting new people can be freeing,' Adam says.

This, to me, sounds exactly like what the writer of self-help books would say and like a speech he has given before, or maybe he has written it down. That said, I'm relieved when I hear the plan and glad Adam is not trying to encourage me to engage on a spiritual journey of self-discovery.

'Let me get this straight; you want me to go on ten dates?'

'Yes, although we are not just talking about dates. It is a programme, an exploration of experience that must be seen and engaged with completely. It's a holistic approach to dating. People too often think of dates as separate events that they go through one after the other. They don't connect them, which is why they end up going on so many and why dating becomes such a negative and empty experience, as people continue to make the same mistakes.'

Adam turns and looks at me, his forefingers in a steeple, pressing against his lips. He seems to be asking me if I understand any of this.

'Okay,' I venture.

Adam nods at this, satisfied, and continues.

'What I am talking about, the essence of my idea, is dating as an expedition of the self. A series of interlinked experiences—a journey that culminates in a destination. What we don't want you to do is find yourself in a series of bars, waiting nervously for calamitous social encounters to take place, a.k.a. modern dating. That said you might meet the love of your life on date one. Or it might be date ten. All you need to do is fully invest yourself in each date,' Adam says.

'We're going to help you,' Sarah says.

'Please just let us try,' Allison says.

Allison gives Sarah a shoulder squeeze when she says this, and it is like they are in it together.

That is the situation. My friends and my sister have appointed themselves as my dating advisory panel. Big Brother is taking over and now regulating my dating life. Red tape, rules and form-filling is sure to follow, with a subsequent inquiry to discover what went wrong. Don't ask me why but I know something will go wrong.

On the plus side, these are the people who know me best and so there is that.

'Let's face it, you need the help,' Sarah says. 'You are terrible at dating, absolutely the worst, and I know this might sound harsh—'

'That has never stopped you before,' I say, interrupting.

Sarah scowls at me. '...I was going to say, you are smart, and quite good-looking. I know this because girls used to say it to me at school. Of course, I did try to put them off you—it would be weird if my friends dated my brother—and if I haven't said sorry for that before...'

'You haven't,' I say.

Sarah smiles beatifically at me. 'Then I apologise now. What I am trying to say is that you have a lot going for you.'

I nod my thanks at this. I do appreciate her saying it, and it means a lot coming from her. It brings a smile to my face. However, I do object to the assertion that I am terrible at dating. I am not *terrible*, although maybe not as accomplished as some. There have been some successes along the way. Admittedly, they have been minor and mixed in with poor results, like a middling sports team always threatened with relegation to a lower league. I think that happens to everyone, though, at least that's my explanation and I am sticking with it.

After I have refilled everyone's drinks and thought about what Adam is proposing I feel a mix of trepidation and excitement in a way that I have not felt for a long time. There have been highs in these long pandemic months, like opening the café, but few interpersonal ones. Maybe this is what I need, dating with the painful aspects removed. As I arrive at this realisation, I feel immensely grateful for the fact that I have friends and family who care enough to help me.

'So, tell us what you think?' Adam asks. 'Will you do it?'

'I must admit, I did hate the idea when you first said it, but I need to do something. One question though, why is it ten dates? Why not five or seven?'

'We're taking advantage of the special meaning and power of the number ten,' Adam says. 'For instance, ten is the Pythagorean symbol of perfection or completeness, and in numerology, it resonates with the vibrations and energies of optimism and success, among other things. It also has a place in Modern Portfolio theory,' Adam says.

'Modern what?' I ask.

'It's how risk-averse investors—in this scenario that would be you, the reluctant dater—can create portfolios to maximise their success. Those portfolios can be financial or, in your case, romantic, on a given level of market risk. To put it simply, you need to do X amount to win,' Adam says.

I want to argue with this and not give my life over to some mystic or market economic-led experiment, only I am tired, and so instead, I give in. I mean, how bad can ten dates be?

'The key thing is that this works. At the end of this process, you will see real progress, if not ultimate happiness. And it's progress that we are here for, as tonight isn't so much an intervention, as it is prevention, stopping you getting stuck. From prevention, we progress,' Adam says.

'From prevention, we progress' sounds like a slogan from George Orwell's *1984*. I turn over the phrase and imagine myself chanting it at my cult meeting. I'm not in a cult, but if I were, I am sure we would have a catchy mantra like that, which at a given point in one of our meetings we would all monotonously intone before handing over money to a minion of our leader who has joined us for ten minutes via video chat from California to offer an inspirational thought or two. I imagine it is also a title chapter of Adam's book that falls towards the midway point. He will use it in his talks, as he turns to the audience, and booms this phrase out—the audience then duly repeats the words and then the crowd goes wild.

'If you say so,' I say.

'And the good thing is, unlike normal dating on apps which, let's face it, can be useless, we are selecting your dates so there will be no duds,' Adam says.

No duds? I almost laugh at this. Have these people been on any dates? In dating, there are no guarantees, that's almost its number one rule. It is a battlefield: trenches are dug, and full-frontal assault tactics are the only ones being employed. The chances of making it to the other side are slim, and Pat Benatar is one hundred per cent right on this matter, of this much I am sure: love *is* a battlefield.

'It's a good plan,' Allison says, to which Sarah nods her agreement.

'Some of these dates are going to surprise you—and in a nice way,' Sarah says.

I wonder what Beth thinks of this. It is not the first time I have thought of her since that night I last saw her, when she told me how she felt, and I ran for the hills like an idiot. I have thought of her so much, only I have not seen or spoken to her since. I know I am fishing when I ask the question, but I want to hear the answer all the same.

'Where's Beth, by the way?' I asked. 'I would have thought she would have been all on board with this.'

After I say this, there is an awkward silence. Allison looks to the ceiling as if trying to locate a spider's web tucked in some corner of the room. Even Adam looks uncomfortable and gazes around.

There was a time when we would have spoken every week or so and been messaging back and forth all the time, but that was before. I can't quite let the subject of Beth go, and I press it a little more to see if my friends will reveal anything more telling. Is she dating, what's happening in her life? I look to Sarah, who is the only one that will give it to me straight, sibling to sibling.

'Still, I thought she might have come, you know, just to watch, if not to participate,' I say.

'You know why Beth is not here,' Sarah says.

This is short and sharp; it is the honesty that I asked for. After Sarah has said this, I feel hot. The collar of my T-shirt feels scratchy on my neck.

Everyone else has been speaking to Beth apart from me. What I have been doing, as far as Beth is concerned, is hiding. I stuck my head in the sand and have left it there. I think that sums it up. I've been doing it since the night of Marcus and Victoria's leaving drinks as we stood in the cold, and Beth told me how she felt, and I bottled it. At the time, I told myself I wasn't prepared. I wasn't ready, and I was not brave enough to make the leap. I also told myself that it might blow over and that we would be able to move on as friends. I was lying to myself, as deep down, I knew it wouldn't.

The annoying thing—no, the *confounding* thing—is that Beth took a gamble and voiced thoughts that I'd previously had myself and never done anything about, and so here we are. I thought about it a lot through our twenties. Only it was never the right time. These thoughts were full of self-doubt and second-guessing. What if I said something, and she said no? That would be the end of our friendship for sure, and I didn't want that; and yet it happened anyway, only not in the way I expected.

Worse, I fretted about what I would do if she said yes. That was almost worse. I worried that if that happened, then that would be it. This wouldn't be a one-night stand, or for the short term, it would be for the long haul, and I wasn't sure I was ready for that either. If I had said yes, I would have been all in, and I could not bring myself to roll the dice.

Chapter Seven

'Islands in the Stream'

Sarah snaps me back into the room, pulling out of my reverie as my thoughts tangle around Beth.

'What did you expect, Tom? You blew it,' Sarah says.

It sounds harsh when it's put like that. This must be what they mean when they say the truth hurts. The thing is, I don't know what to say to Beth in response to what she said, even after all this time. I don't know what to say in response to 'You and I make sense'. I tried for ages not to think about it and found that I could not escape. Thoughts about Beth are there always there, bobbing at the edge of my mind like a sailboat on the horizon.

'I might be guilty of that,' I say.

A train goes by, and the clatter of its wheels on the track fills the room.

'Life has moved on,' Allison says.

When she says this, it hits me how life has been flowing around me for a long time now, and until this point, I haven't minded. It makes me think of Dolly Parton, and I almost break into song which would be weird and besides, I don't think anyone wants to hear my rendition of 'Islands in the Stream'. However, it does make me think this track belongs on a mixtape, and I start to wonder what else would work with it?

'I should go and see Beth,' I say, and I have no idea why I say this because with Beth I am frozen in time. I am stuck in that one moment, and with one question hanging over my head and it is a question that I am still too afraid to answer or to do anything about. I cannot message or call her as I have no answer, and I have nothing to take us forward. What would I say if I turned up on her doorstep? In my head all I hear is the sound of silence, and now I am thinking of Simon & Garfunkel and Disturbed.

'Much good it will do you,' Sarah says.

'Sarah might be right,' Adam says. 'Best to focus on the future and move on. You're going to enjoy this.'

'You never know, this could be it,' Allison says.

The cynic in me says no chance, but the romantic says maybe. Besides, if not now, then when? If I don't act soon, I will die old and lonely. It is only ten dates, and maybe I will meet someone who, at the very least, I might like and who might like me. Isn't that, after all, what everyone wants?

The dating conversation winds up, the intervention is at an end, and everyone is leaving. Adam leads the way, guiding his ramblers out of the door. It is like I am only one stop on an ongoing tour and Adam is some on-call dating doctor who has more interventions to conclude before the night is out.

Allison is the last to exit the flat, and as she is leaving, she turns to me. She has that look that says she has something on her mind. I get the impression that she doesn't want anyone else to hear.

'Dinner next week at mine, after your first date? Sort of like a post-dating debrief? Besides, it has been so long since you came around. It would be lovely to see you,' Allison says.

I'm sure Allison's post-dating debrief is code for some kind of pep talk that may or may not also be Adam's idea. He is a bit like the wizard hiding behind the curtains in all this. That said, it has been a long time since I went to Allison and Paul's… only it is now only Allison's. There is no Paul. I used to love going before. Going to their house was like a trip showcasing the next level of life—an actual house, rather than a flat; domestic harmony with the perfect partner, now complete with a small child. Besides, Paul was an excellent cook and never shy when it came to opening the wine.

'I'm there,' I say.

After everyone has gone, and I am alone again in the flat, the only thing I can think about is Beth. I am, I tell myself with a sense of purpose, going to do something about it. I pick up my phone and decide to call her right there and then. I go to my address book. I have to search for her number, as it has been so long since I called or messaged. My thumb hovers over the dial button.

Only I don't dial her number. I do not have any more of a response now than I did more than a year ago. So, what is the point?

What I'll do, I tell myself, is go around to her house and visit her. Maybe tomorrow, or sometime this week. I don't know what I will say… Maybe I will start with hello and go from there.

Chapter Eight

'Lover, You Should've Come Over'

In the morning, I get up at seven as I always do, and get myself ready for work. I do the same thing each day. My routine invariably does not change, and I do everything in the same order and way. I blitz some berries, make some porridge, and drink a glass of water.

By the time I leave the house at seven thirty, the day has not quite warmed up. However, the morning light on the trees that line the streets makes the leaves shine as they shift in the breeze. It looks like it is shaping up to be another bright and warm June day.

Despite my initial misgivings, my optimism about going on these dates has grown. Adam might say that this was an early sign of progress. If he and the others had not descended upon me, I would not be going on any dates. Instead, I would carry on with my life, going back and forth to the café, visiting the park, making mixtapes, and binge-watching TV.

I think, truth be told, I do need to shake up my life. I wasn't about to do it myself. If it hadn't had been for Adam and everyone else gate-crashing with their intervention, I would have probably continued, as I was stuck deep in the hole that I had dug myself into. I would have kept on digging merrily away like an unhappy dwarf.

I hate to say it, but Adam is right. If I'm honest, while I don't like the idea of dating in general, based on previous experience, I am excited about doing something different. Am I going to go on ten dates? It sounds a daunting prospect—although, to serial daters, it's a typical week or two.

I turn the corner and make my way along the parade of shops, which completes my walk to the café. I always find myself looking up at the black shop front sign, with the café's logo and image of Shakespeare's head in gold on black. It is one of my favourite parts of the day.

When I came up with the name for the café, I wanted it to be as much about books as about the coffee, and I have always loved the Paris bookshop, Shakespeare and Company, which made hiring Julie a happy coincidence. With her, Julie brought a little of the magic of the City of Light to North London.

Through the window, I can see the lights are already on and I stare at the bookshelves, tables and chairs, all empty and neatly in place, like a stage missing only its players.

Julie invariably beats me to the café. I always think of myself as a morning person. When I told this to Julie, she said she was a morning person, too. However after we compared notes, it became apparent that our interpretations of what this entails differ wildly. I mean rolling out of bed at seven, while Julie gets up at five-thirty and does an hour of yoga and meditation. After she has done this, she still makes it here before me. That was the day I learnt that there are different kinds of morning people.

I love this part. Getting into the café when it is clean and empty and ready for the day. This always begins with the two of us having a coffee and talking over anything we need to cover.

The surprising joy of running a café, which I had given little thought to, is making the coffee. Good coffee is part of the essence of the café, and I'd thought making it would be a simple function: press a few levers and steam some milk—how hard could it be? The answer is, more complex than you imagine. There is a science to it, and you end up getting rather ostentatious about the process. It is hot and hard work, but I like it. There is a beginning and end, and a sense of satisfaction that I enjoy.

Julie suggested I take a short course to learn the basics, so I didn't have milk exploding everywhere every time I tried to make a flat white or cappuccino. I then took another, more advanced class. I'm not as good as Julie or Fabio, our full-time barista, but I can make a good cup of coffee.

On the wall in the café, we have a quote from Gertrude Stein, which I think is the best thing anyone ever wrote about coffee:

> *'Coffee is a lot more than just a drink; it's something happening. Not as in hip, but like an event, a place to be, but not like a location, but like somewhere within yourself. It gives you time, but not actual hours or minutes, but a chance to be, like be yourself, and have a second cup.'*

I'm pretty sure people read that and think to themselves, *I will have a second cup*. It is almost like it was written by an advertising copywriter trying to sell more bags of coffee who attributed it to a famous literary figure. It is pretty perfect.

I wish Julie a good morning in French, which we have been doing for a while, as I try to learn a little. It is the bonus of hiring a French person.

'*Bonjour, il semble qu'il fera beau aujourd'hui,*' I say.

I feel positively liberated by doing it, by learning. It feels like progress. Julie worked at the café for a while before she suggested we have 'French mornings'.

When she first said this, I thought it was some odd French tradition. It wasn't that at all.

'What are French mornings? Are you thinking we employ grumpy waiters that take ages to bring you a coffee and croissant? I'm not sure people will embrace that,' I said.

I thought I was hilarious. I thought I was killing it with my child-free dad jokes. I wasn't. Julie looked at me, formed an 'oh' with her mouth, and placed her hand on her heart.

'I feel pain for French waiters everywhere and all they have to put up with from English customers, whose first question is always, "do you speak English?". To which the answer is, almost without exception, yes. Even if this answer is delivered with a sigh of disappointment which, in case you were wondering, translates to: *why would you come to our country without being able to order food for yourself in the local language?*' Julie says.

I reflected for a moment when she said this. This was true and a terrible indictment of the English abroad.

'Okay,' I said. 'Point taken. What do you have in mind?'

'We speak French for the first five minutes each morning,' Julie said.

'But I don't speak French,' I said.

'*Exactement!*'

Julie gives me a bright smile and tells me to take a seat while she finishes making the coffee before we begin our French.

Julie brings over our coffee, and I don't know what it is, only she is able to pick up on something about me. Maybe a change in my disposition, I don't know, and she waves her finger at me.

'You seem different today. More smiley. Did something happen to you overnight?' she asks.

I take a sip of coffee and dither for a second or two about telling her. Working so closely together, we have shared the secrets of our lives, mostly as we busy ourselves getting ready to open for the day. I share with Julie in the same way I share with Larissa in the park.

For instance, I know that Julie and her husband Jasper have been going through a long and torturous IVF process. They have tried twice and are about to start a third round.

Julie is many things. She is funny and direct, brilliant at running the café, and hopeful. When she said they were to start IVF again after two miscarriages, she said: 'Third time lucky, no?'

Today, my news feels trivial, like I am light relief, which I suppose is not a bad thing to be. Although if you're not in the comedy business, you probably don't want to make a career out of it. That said, I imagine someone already has. Hearing about dating disasters is something we all seem to enjoy, and why, I think, people love columns like the *Guardian's* 'First Date' so much.

I start to explain how I had visitors last night and what I am about to undertake.

'Ten dates? That's a lot of dates, but you know what? I think you are ready,' Julie says.

I swell with confidence when she says this and feel even more sanguine about the prospect of the dates.

I realise that right now, Julie probably knows me almost better than anyone does. We spend so much time together.

Julie is the only person who has said that I am ready to start dating. This wasn't something any of my friends mentioned, not even Allison.

When I started withdrawing from life, my sole focus was the café, and it was my only means of interacting with other people. Julie could see what was happening to me and I feel now that it might all have come off the rails if it hadn't been for her. She told me it was okay not to be okay, and that she was there to listen if I needed to talk. She didn't make a big thing of it and didn't say anything else, and neither did I, other than to say thank you.

'You know what? I think I might be. I mean, I hate the idea of dating, which is why I stopped, or at least never started again. I think I was waiting for something else, and I think I found that here, in the café,' I say.

'We all need something,' Julie says. 'The trick is finding the right thing, and this might be it for you. I'm very pleased to hear this.'

After the café closes at five and we have cleaned, I head out for my walk. Today I am running late as I'm going to stop by Beth's house, which is only a few streets away. I still have no idea what I am going to say, and the only thing I know for sure is that it has been too long. I am just going to wing it in the hope that as I get closer to her house I might—by pure luck—think of what I need to say.

Despite her proximity she has not visited the café, but I do know that *The Correspondent* allows her to work at home for a day or two a week.

I walk to the end of the parade of shops and turn left down the tree-lined Victorian street and then take a right onto Beth's road. I walk halfway down, past neat rows of Victorian terraced houses, and stop outside Beth's house.

Painted a tasteful darkish grey, it has a navy-blue front door, which I stand staring at for a moment or two. I realise as I stand there that I might have triggered her Ring doorbell. Oh crap. If that's the case, Beth could be looking at me now on her phone hanging here like some stalker.

I stand for a little longer and there is no luck with me. I realise that, even after all this time, I still do not know what to say. I feel a twist in my stomach when I think of her words, and I know deep down that I want to reciprocate them, but I can't. I am as afraid now as I was then of committing myself and I hate myself for it.

I suppose I could say hello. I could start there, offer Beth an apology and hope for the best. If nothing else, I would like her back as a friend—if she will have me.

I could tell her that I've missed talking and spending time with her.

I could ask how's she doing and tell her I have missed hearing about her life and sharing mine with her.

However, I worry that, standing here now, I am still not saying enough or anything of consequence. Despite being here, I can't help but feel that there is never going to be any going back, it will never be how it once was. Not after feelings have been shared. I know I should share my feelings with her, but I am infected by that deep fear, which has seeped into every bone of my body. What if I commit and I change my mind? Or worse, what if Beth does? When this thought strikes me, I am possessed by the same paralysing fear that gripped me the night of Marcus and Victoria's leaving party.

I hear footsteps walking down the street towards me. Approaching is a tall blonde woman walking her small dog. I can see suspicion in her eyes as she probably asks herself what I am doing lurking on the street outside someone's house. Maybe she knows Beth. The closer the woman comes, the more uncomfortable I am. I realise I do look like a stalker or worse, and instead of knocking on Beth's front door and pressing the Ring bell, I turn and leave.

I tell myself that I will come back another day. On that occasion, I will endeavour to make it up the garden path rather than loiter on the street looking in, like someone of dubious intent.

I walk to the park and when I am a few feet away from her, Larissa looks up at me and tells me that I am late. I glance at my watch and realise that I am, in fact, much later than expected. My diversion and failed visit to Beth's house took up more time than anticipated.

'I am; apologies,' I say. 'I didn't know we were on such a strict schedule.'

'I like to organise my day.'

I give her a sideways look and she smiles, acknowledging how ridiculous her comment was.

'It's a joke. I was far too serious… before,' she says.

I nod at this. It's true, the aforementioned love of Russian literature being a keen indicator of this trait.

'I always liked that about you,' I say.

'No, you didn't, you had no interest in most of the things I liked, but you did try, and I always appreciated that. Tell me you finished *The Brothers Karamazov*?' Larissa asks.

This makes me smile for two reasons. I wasn't sure she ever noticed that I made an effort to like the things she liked, and any time Larissa says anything nice to me, I feel one hundred times lighter.

'Thank you,' I say. 'And no, of course I never finished that book. I did start it.'

'If you read a little, it is better than nothing. Besides, the thing you liked about me is that deep down, you knew I wasn't right for you. It was a classic case of you wanting what you shouldn't or can't have. I knew that too, of course, which is why I dumped you,' Larissa says.

'Thanks, as always, for bringing that up.'

'You're welcome. Besides, I did it with the best of intentions.'

'I know you did.'

I believe that and it is the reason we remained friends afterwards, which is a record for me as I have never been friends with any other ex-girlfriend—it never works.

'I can't quite put my finger on it, but you seem very cheerful today, and I must say, I like that. I sense you have some news to share with me,' Larissa says.

What is it with the women in my life? First Julie and now Larissa. They can read me like a book. How does it end, I wonder?

'Funny you should mention that,' I say.

'How funny exactly?' she asks.

'Fairly funny in a sitcom kind of way. Adam led an intervention last night. They came to my flat. They think I need to start dating again. Adam has a plan. What do you think?'

'Before I answer that question, do you tell your friends about me?'

She has never asked me this before, and I'm curious why she is asking now. I am sure she already knows the answer.

'Of course I don't.'

'Is it because I dumped you twice?'

'No, it is the other reason. They would think I'm unbalanced,' I say.

Larissa thinks this is amusing and smiles. I always liked that smile when we were going out. It was a secret smile that she hid away, and its warmth held everything. It was sunshine and light, and I never saw it often, which is a shame.

'I think your friends are right,' she says. 'You need to move on with your life. You know it too, which is why you are sounding more chipper today. As nice as it is to meet you in the park, I think I am holding you back, which has been fine in this strange in-between time, but that is coming to an end.'

After Larissa says this, we are quiet. It is what happens when someone voices what has not been said, but is known to be true. I want to tell her that I like coming here, and over the last year or so, have enjoyed taking a walk and chatting to Larissa in the park.

'Maybe you're right,' I say.

Larissa beams. 'You know I am. So, tell me about Adam's plan.'

'They're arranging for me to go on ten dates, the theory being that at least one of these dates will work out,' I say.

'That is exciting. I wish someone had done that for me, and I cannot wait to hear how these go. I expect it will be highly entertaining,' Larissa says.

I give Larissa a wry look. 'Entertaining for you?'

'No, I mean for both of us. Don't we all love dating stories?'

'We do,' I say.

'The only thing I would say to you is, do it for the right reasons. I do hope you haven't said yes in the not-so-secret hope you might end up sleeping with some of these women,' Larissa says and pauses. She raises her forefinger to silence me, as she knows I am about to interject here and protest my innocence. 'Save the protests for the government. You know there is at least some truth in it, and you know, you might get to because they're bored, or they just want to have sex or—unfathomably—they might like you. But don't do it unless you believe it is something real.'

I protest again, and this time Larissa gives the nod, like an umpire at Wimbledon silently communicating with the players, signalling that she will allow this.

'Unfathomably? That's a little unforgiving, isn't it?'

'You're right, it is. I apologise. Besides, I know you are about to say I once told you that you are good-looking. That is still true, but I also told you who you *should* be going out with, and it probably won't be one of Adam's magic ten dates,' Larissa says.

Larissa is talking about Beth. She knows all about what happened.

'I want to lodge a second protest,' I say. 'That was before anything happened and she said anything.'

'All the more reason why Beth is the right girl for you. You already know she likes you. There are only so many people who come along in one lifetime, and while there might be more people after that, they are all wrong. I'm telling you this as your friend,' she says.

I don't tell Larissa where I went before coming to the park and how silently I stood outside Beth's house with nothing more to say to her now than I did that night after Marcus and Victoria's leaving party.

'You know I appreciate your advice. I always do,' I say.

Larissa nods at this. It is a note of acceptance, as she knows that I will not, and cannot, act on that advice. No, my plan is now Adam's plan, and after all this time living only half a life, I am ready for something new.

I feel like a light has been shone on the path ahead of me, and sometimes it takes friends and family, the people who know you best, to light the way. Whatever happens next, I am ready for it. And who knows? I might even meet the one. At the very least it might be, as Larissa says, entertaining.

Chapter Nine

'Into My Arms'

Bright summer sunshine fills the empty pub and makes the varnish on the wooden floor sparkle like gold as I sit waiting for my date to arrive. She's late, and I'm nervous to the point of being shaky. I lift my beer and spill some on my jeans. It is not a good look.

I am always anxious on dates. Even more so today, given it has been so long, and the fact that this is a genuine blind date with no messaging beforehand, no flirty chat, and no establishing we like the same movies or bands. All I have had are a few biographical details and a picture. Therefore, I suggested an afternoon date. I thought there would be less pressure and that it would be more relaxed for both of us after the strangeness and insular lives we have been living over the last eighteen months. However, the pub is empty, and I'm reconsidering the plan. It is none of the above. Where are the casual afternoon drinkers, and those engaged in illicit daytime affairs, quietly enjoying a drink? They have gone and not returned. Either that or these people were a product of my imagination.

The angst is a feeling that started during the pandemic and never went away. I don't go out much or have significant conversations with people I don't know. I worry that I have no chat and that the conversation will run dry.

Worse still, Adam only emailed the dating profile and picture to me an hour ago and I have been poring over it on my phone as I sit here in the pub. This is what he has sent me about Alice, my first date.

Dating Profile:

Name: Alice Carter

Age: 32 Height: 5'3 Build: Slim/medium

Hair: Blonde Eyes: Blue

Occupation: fashion journalist

General: I've known Alice for years. She is an absolute gem. Smart, funny, very bright (went to Durham), and is one of those people who could have done anything.

I'm surprised I've never put you two together before, which is why she has made this list of women I think you would work well with.

I should mention, she can be a little prickly on occasion. In a cute way, though. This, you will find, is an outer shell, and if you can demonstrate you're her equal then you will find the real Alice a delight.

I have high hopes for this date and look forward to a debrief. I will also be hugely surprised if your date with Alice does not progress, not only to the next level but most likely, several levels.

In short, Alice is a total catch, and I'm surprised she is still on the market. Good luck and give me a call afterwards.

My first thought on reading this on my phone was, fashion? I don't know anything about fashion. I am the least fashionable person you have ever met. I live in 501s, buy T-shirts in five-packs, and own a wide assortment of flannel shirts.

Okay, my lack of fashion knowledge was my second thought, to be honest. My first thought was, oh, she's attractive. I do worry that I will be a disappointment when my absolute lack of fashion knowledge or interest is laid bare. I consider this second only to my lack of knowledge about *Love Island*, about which I also have next to nothing to say.

The only other person in the bar is the woman behind the bar. She is a twenty-something, dressed in black with short, peroxide-blonde hair, and black eye make-up. She looks like the singer in a punk band.

Alice, who suggested the pub, as she lives around the corner, is thirty minutes late and counting. I've finished my beer and am considering another when a text arrives.

> I'm running late, will be there in fifteen minutes, sorry!

I sit there trying to be cool, to relax, and tell myself this is date one, and post-pandemic people are not quite back in the swing of dating. They might have forgotten that turning up on time is important. As this thought rattles around my head, I also think, who turns up forty-five minutes late for a date when they live around the corner?

I scan Alice's profile again on my phone. I feel better. I don't think it matters how many dates you go on. The nerves don't go away. I also realise that my nerves are directly affected by how excited and hopeful I am about a particular date. On paper, this one looks strong, and Alice sounds interesting. Her profile picture is striking. Alice has great cheekbones and a long blonde bob, and is one of those people who knows how to smile in a picture in a way that draws you in.

I am still turning this thought over in my mind when the door to the pub creaks open. I find myself holding my breath in anticipation. A woman walks in wearing killer heels, and somehow managing to walk with an elegance that defies physics. Her blonde hair, much longer than in the picture Adam sent, is around her shoulders and shines as it catches the sun. She does look stunning, and it is only then that I take in the fact that she is wearing a tutu skirt with a crop top, which exposes her belly. I'm aware of my mouth falling open, and for a moment, I am in genuine shock. I am lost for words looking at this tutu. I have so many questions. My brain is firing neurons like they are spitting from a machine gun, and all my wires are crossed. The word 'tutu' repeats in my mind like the chorus to a song, so much so that my brain converts it into a sentence.

'Pleased to tutu,' I babble, struck down as I am by verbal incontinence. What is happening to me? I try to get back on track before this date sinks beneath the waves with all hands lost. 'I am so sorry. I mean. pleased to meet you.'

This is a long pause, as we look at each other, and I would not be surprised if at this moment tumbleweed blew through this empty bar and signature music from a Sergio Leone film started to play—those haunting two-note melodies which sound like the howl of a distant coyote.

As the moment stretches, at this precise point in time I want nothing more than to run for the door. Dating is as horrible as I remember, and all it has taken is a matter of seconds for this to turn into a car crash. I'm reasonably fast. I think I could make it before Alice is able to say a word. However, I don't want to be the run-for-the-door guy. That's a hashtag waiting to happen. Knowing my luck, Alice would snap a picture of me looking over my shoulder as I exited the pub looking leery and weird, and would tweet it:

> I just had the worse date of my life. Guy took one look at me and ran. So, humiliating. His name is Tom. Stay away from him. #WorstDateEver

I'd be destroyed on Twitter and would become a meme faster than you can type 280 characters and shout Twitter storm. No doubt someone I have no memory of would pipe up and identity me. 'Oh, *that* Tom,' they would quip. 'He's a douchebag, I dated him as well.' The punk behind the bar would turn out to have an unfathomably large following on social media because her band is the next big thing, and would amplify the message on Instagram. There would be nothing to halt it going viral. From there, it would jump again and be included on a BuzzFeed listicle of 'The 20 Worst Dates Ever'.

Before any of this can happen, I force myself to act and course-correct. I thrust my arm out in a chopping motion like I'm Bruce Lee, and breaking wooden blocks is my jam. In my mind, I am doing this to emphasise my correction. However, the reality is that it only serves to highlight my horrible mistake.

Alice stands there and stares at me, and then she laughs. I mean, *rocks* with laughter, and drops herself down into the seat beside me without ceremony.

'That was genuinely funny, thank you. It has been so long since I laughed like that,' Alice says.

I notice she has striking dark blue eyes that appear violet in the dim light of the bar.

I am not sure what to say to this, and the only thing I think of is to apologise and try to do the thing that I have previously been told I do not do enough. I offer Alice a compliment and try to reboot this date before I say anything more idiotic.

'I am so sorry; that is a great outfit,' I say.

Alice smiles. 'Thank you, I know it is slightly out there, but I promised myself I would wear this on a date after all this shit was over, and here I am. Lucky you.'

I smile. I get it. Alice wanted to wear this exact outfit. Fantasised about it, and now the day is here, nothing is going to stop her.

'Good for you. I didn't think about dating at all in lockdown and wouldn't be dating now if it hadn't been for Adam,' I say.

'So, I heard. It's fun though, and different, and when Adam mentioned it, I thought, why not?'

I realise I am forgetting my manners—I ask Alice if I can get her a drink.

'Thank you, a gin and tonic. Can you make sure it's a light tonic?'

'Of course,' I say.

At the bar, punk barmaid smiles, and mouths the word *date*, with a smile.

'How did you guess?' I ask.

'The nerves. Take a breath,' she says.

'Got it, thank you,' I say.

I return with a beer and the G&T to the table where Alice is sitting looking at her phone.

'Here you go,' I say.

'Thank you. My turn to apologise. I'm so sorry I'm late, I really wanted to wear this outfit and then I had second thoughts, so I changed a few times. And then I decided to go for it,' Alice says.

'No problem,' I say.

'Thank you. I bet all this makes you want to run for the door, right?'

'Only out of embarrassment, and nothing to do with you or your dress,' I say.

'I know how out there it might be, but I had to do it. I watched all six seasons of *SATC* in lockdown, and became obsessed with Sarah Jessica Parker, and the tutu she wears in the opening credits. Besides, I'm convinced the tutu is making a comeback,' Alice says.

The mention of *Sex and the City* starts us talking about the shows we watched during the long months of lockdown. From there the conversation is easy and we hop around. Alice wants to hear about the café and how I quit my job as a reporter.

'I've fantasised about living in a cottage somewhere remote. I just don't know what I would do once I got there, and I always come back to my current career. My job is so much of who I am,' Alice says.

'I thought that as well. I just had enough bad news, and the last year made me realise I wasn't my job, and I could do something else,' I say.

'I'd miss the parties, the social life, the lunches and meeting cool people. You gave it all up for a café?' Alice can't quite believe it.

'It definitely isn't for everyone, but I like it,' I say.

We sip our drinks and the sunshine falls into the bar, and we are quiet. We have hit that point in a date when the initial burst of conversation has run its course. I do what I always do in this situation and fall back on classic dating conversation.

'So, how's dating going for you?' I ask.

'It's been an absolute nightmare,' Alice says.

'That bad already?'

'Yeah, I know this is your first date in a long time, I have been on a few, and it is as bad as ever. Maybe it is the men I go for; they have always been a commitment-shy, only now they are also skittish as hell. It's just sex, like they are on a mission. Last year did weird things to people. I thought it might improve people's approach and make them realise what they want, only it hasn't, mostly at least,' Alice says, and takes a sip of her drink.

Without thinking through what I am saying, I try to announce that my intentions are good.

'I'm not here for sex,' I say.

This makes Alice splutter into her drink and burst into more laughter. This declaration of mine came out all wrong and has not quite been taken how I intended. God, I am terrible at dating.

'Sorry, I know what you are trying to say. Maybe put it on a T-shirt and wear it to your next date. I shouldn't have laughed like that. It's sweet of you to say,' Alice says.

This makes Alice guffaw some more and I find myself smiling as well although it does tell me that this date is not going to progress much further than this bar. The mention of my 'next date' makes it sound like Alice has mentally moved on.

'It's okay, at least you're not offended,' I say.

'I'm really not, and I always take it as a good sign if my date makes me laugh even if he didn't mean to, so I will say nice things to Adam. I should at this point tell you about my last date. While it was awful, I think I liked him,' she says.

This sounds intriguing and I remember that dating is good for swapping war stories. I'm not sure why I love to hear them. Maybe it has something to do with the sheer dreadfulness of most of them – but also the hope because, just like Alice's date, sometimes you go on one and even though it *is* terrible you still think there might be something there. A small salvageable spark, and that sounds like what has happened to Alice. However, before Alice can expand on this point, her phone rings, and she looks at the screen and back at me. She shakes her head in dismay.

'Sorry, it's the guy I was talking about, Albert. I have to take it,' Alice says.

Alice stands up from the table and takes a couple of steps away and answers the call.

'Hello Albert,' she says.

Then Albert must say something funny, as Alice laughs. I am no expert, but to me it sounds like they get on. I am then struck by the thought that Albert and Alice sound like they should be a couple. If ever there were two names bound together, it is these two. They sound like a royal couple. If they were to get married, there would have to put an announcement in *The Times*.

Alice is now telling Albert that while that she might be interested in doing that, it isn't a good time.

'I can't see you now. I'm busy. Maybe later,' Alice says, looking up at me and smiling.

I smile back and try to be relaxed. I am no expert, but it does appear that Alice is already dating someone else. I know I should be offended that Alice is agreeing to meet up with another man not long into our date, only I am not. On any other date, this would be a major red flag. Today, I am taking it as a clear sign that as a reintroduction to dating, this hasn't been too bad. Alice is attractive and funny, only I am not sure we are heading in the same direction. I think Alice is heading in the same direction as Albert.

Alice hangs up, and settles back down opposite me, and gives me a smile. It is apologetic, the kind of look you offer someone when you are about to share some bad or disappointing news. I have seen this look before on dates, and I have worn it with awkwardness on my own face.

'Sorry, that took longer than I thought,' Alice says.

What I want to know is the status of Albert-and-Alice whose names in my mind will now be forever linked.

'I have to ask, what is going on with Albert?'

'We've been out a few times,' Alice says.

I nod at this, trying to work out what this information means. What's the distance between dating and going 'out a few times'? I have no idea. In the age of dating apps, however, I am inclined to believe there is no distance at all. A few dates is a relationship. Marriages have been built on less. A 'few times' means you have already navigated through the crucial First Three Dates (FTD) and been your best self, not doing anything stupid enough to put your date off. To my knowledge, the FTDs breakdown in the following way:

> The Nervous First checking-each-other-out date.
>
> The Tricky Second get-to-know-you date.
>
> The Difficult Third date where the conversation might run dry and is the point

> where many potential relationships founder
> or florish.

'Oh right, I see,' I say. 'So, do you think you'll be seeing Albert again?'

To this question, Alice gives an enthusiastic nod.

'Yeah, tomorrow, for lunch,' Alice says and takes a long drink of her G&T.

'It does sound like you are dating,' I say.

'Yeah, I know. The thing is, when I met him, I didn't like him. Our first date was terrible and our second not much better. He's very awkward. I do think his communication skills suffered in lockdown, but there is something there. He runs a gallery, and he's a bit taller and has floppy hair, and is one of those guys always wearing crumpled suits but, you know, with T-shirts?' Alice says.

He sounds ridiculous and cool, I think, and I can picture the two of them together—especially with Alice in her tutu. My own dress sense—jeans and T-shirts with one too many plaid shirts—is not on the same level.

'And after you first met him?'

'I liked him a bit more, and he has pursued me a bit. There were flowers, and dinner, and he has been nice. You know, like, whoa, who is ever this nice? And I don't know… it was a lot,' Alice says.

I am no expert, and I want to emphasise that, given that it has been a long time since I had any dating success, but it does sound like Alice is displaying a basic fear of commitment. I only say this because I think that's what I had with Beth, and it has grown over the last eighteen months. To be honest, I think it is true for many of us. We have all changed; like mice in some grand social experiment, we are dealing with the repercussions of forced isolation and being ejected from work that many of us had shaped our lives around. There is no playbook for how we bounce back from this, and I am not sure we do, at least not straight away. Whether we like to admit it or not, everyone's mental health has been impacted, only some more than others. I put myself in the second category there. Not that I would admit this to Adam or anyone else. Now we are all thrown back together. Things are not going to plan. We are changed, and people are different. Reintegration is going to take time, and sometimes it takes other people to see that for you. In my case Adam, my sister and Allison.

It sounds like Alice has been taken by surprise as you can be after years of bad dates when you meet someone who is good and decent, and it is a shock. Your instinct is to push them away.

Alice and Albert might not go the distance, but they will go somewhere, and if I have learnt anything, it is that it is better to be with someone who you have a chance with, and which might be scary, than anyone else. It's weird, as this is advice I can hand out to others, but cannot follow myself.

I know I shouldn't be saying this, as I am supposed to be on a date with Alice, only it does sound like she has already met someone.

'That does sound like a lot, but it seems as though you like Albert and he likes you?' I venture.

Alice considers this, looks to the ceiling, and I can almost see the battle that is being played out in her head projected there, her thoughts like dancing shadows.

'I think you might be right,' Alice says. 'Sorry, I think I have wasted your time—and lots of it as I was so late as well.'

I smile at this and shake my head. I don't mind at all. While I feel a tinge of disappointment, this is just the start for me.

'It's okay, it really is,'

'Thank you for being so nice,' Alice says. 'I think you're right.'

From there we relax and chat about other things. I ask her about her job as a fashion journalist for a glossy magazine, and we compare notes about working in journalism. I find I can make her laugh by telling her about some of the regular characters who pass through the doors of the Shakespeare Café.

We buy a couple more drinks, talk, smile and laugh, and the conversation flows, and the afternoon slips away as we sit in the sun-lit bar. Then we are standing outside, saying our goodbyes, and I feel much better for having come out and sat down with someone new and had the chance to talk in a way that I have not done for a long time.

'Come here, I want to hug you,' Alice says.

I smile at this and acquiesce. I was never much of a hugger before covid, but I probably need it, and we embrace.

'I enjoyed today,' Alice says. 'Whiling away a sunny afternoon in a pub is on my list of favourite ways to spend time.'

'Me too, and I had a nice time,' I say.

'If it had been any other time, I would definitely go out with you again,' Alice says. 'God, that sounds awful! Forgive me. It's just the timing.'

It makes me think that, as with so much in life, so many of our relationships come down to timing, and this is one of those occasions where you meet someone a day, a week or a month too late, and maybe if your paths had crossed earlier, it might have worked out. If I take nothing else away from today, I take that.

I smile at Alice, I tell her it's okay, and it is. We walk off down Essex Road together, and we are winding up our chat. When we reach the junction, we say our goodbyes.

'I do hope we bump into each other again,' Alice says.

'Yeah, so do I, and good luck with Albert,' I say.

'Thanks, and say hello to Adam.'

Alice walks off. I make for Highbury Fields, which is one of my favourite places in North London. The ample green open space bordered by its rows of Georgian and Victorian houses is one of those untouched areas of the city where time has stood still. I always feel a little better after walking along the edge of the green and past the tennis courts, which are full at this time of year.

As I walk, I call Adam. When I talk to him, I am sometimes not sure who I am speaking to. Is it Adam the friend? Or is it Adam the psychotherapist, who deals with depression and mental health issues? In my case, I think it is a combination of the two.

Even though my life is on an even keel I don't think my friends believe it even as the café starts to look more aand more like a success. It is almost like no one can make such a drastic change to their life and be okay. More so, perhaps, because of what happened with Larissa. It did hit me hard. I mean, it would hit anyone hard, and while I am not over it, and I may never fully get over it, I am, I think, doing okay.

I am glad I lost my job, and I am more thankful for it every day, because if that had not happened, I don't think I would have changed my life. For that, I have the pandemic to thank. The right conditions might never have emerged again in my lifetime. Or, as others see it, the wrong conditions. I think of all the people who died, and how lives were upturned. A perfect storm where we entered a new normal in which many others lost their jobs as well, causing utter heartbreak for some, and for others like me, a welcome pause in life's unrelenting momentum, which carries most of us forward throughout our lives without a chance for pause or reflection.

Adam answers on the second ring and asks me how the date went.

'You know when you said you were surprised she was still single? Well, the breaking news is, she isn't. She met someone. She is lovely, though and if we'd met at another time, who knows?' I say.

'Hmm,' Adam says. 'I'm sorry, I had a good feeling about you two. How do you feel in yourself?'

I always wince at this question. I would go as far to say that I hate it. My dad used to ask me this, and was never satisfied with my answer ('I feel fine'). It is almost that the person asking the question is demanding you dig deep within yourself, and that you root around in the long grass of introspection, for an answer that sounds true. So, when I hear this, the question I answer, is 'how do you feel?', and that's what I do now with Adam even though I know this is not what he is looking for. I say it quickly, and try to move the conversation on.

'I feel good, and more than that, I feel optimistic. I'm looking forward to date two,' I say.

There is a pause as Adam considers my answer, and I wonder whether he is going to push me to delve deeper, to search my feelings. He lets it go.

'I'm so glad to hear that. Despite Alice not working out as I'd hoped, it sounds like you've made a great start, and even if I say so myself, you are going to really enjoy your second date; Allison chose it.'

I press Adam for details, as off the top of my head I have no idea who Allison might have chosen. Adam is giving nothing away. I have to say I am intrigued and find that I am eager for the next date.

Chapter Ten

'Fade into You'

The next morning, I arrive at the café early, and today Julie suggests that in our window of French we cover some useful dating phrases.

'Do you think I am going to need them?' I ask.

I cannot imagine my friends will set me up with a French woman. Then again, anything is possible, and it has happened before. One summer when I was in my twenties, I dated a girl called Chloé who I met at a party. For six weeks, we drank a lot of red wine and smoked cigarettes standing outside bars in Soho and spent weekends in bed, before she told me she was going home to Paris. She asked me to visit her, I said I would, and I never saw her again.

'Even if you don't, you can talk about how you are learning French. Women love a guy who is open to new things, no?'

That's something I did not think about. Learning French is one of the positive things I have done post lockdown as a direct result of changing my life and opening the café.

After we have practiced a few key phrases, Julie presses me for details of my date, and I tell her about the tutu, and how I had inadvertently greeted Alice. Julie rocks with laughter.

'You must have been nervous,' she says, after her laughter has subsided.

'I'm going with nerves. To be honest, the tutu threw me,' I say.

'I admire this girl for being brave enough to wear what she likes, but I think the tutu would throw anyone.'

We busy ourselves with getting the café ready in the knowledge that today will be hectic. One mum approached us a few months ago asking if she could host a mum and baby club coffee morning in the back of the café once a week. It is a winner for us, as they buy lots of coffee and sandwiches, and for the mums who get a space where they can meet as a group.

After work, I leave the café and wind through the back streets of Highbury towards Finsbury Park. I want to see if Larissa is there and to tell her about my date.

I enter the park via the main gates opposite the Happening Bagel Bakery, which has the best smoked salmon and cream cheese bagels for miles around. I walk up the long, sloping wide avenue that runs to the top of the hill as runners move past me in either direction and turn and head towards the boating lake. I pass the adventure play area where children are laughing and running, pulling each other back and forth on the zip wire. Walking anti-clockwise around the boating lake, I finally spot my favourite bench. It sits in a shaded nook of trees and bushes and looks across the centre of the lake and island. Approaching the bench, I can see Larissa is sitting there.

When we dated, we would come here now and again on a Sunday morning, get a coffee, and feed the ducks. Larissa took a lot of pleasure in feeding the ducks. For her, it was about a simple connection to nature, the closest thing to getting away from it all that you could achieve in the city. I rather enjoyed it too.

As well as standing by the railing and tossing handfuls of oats and seeds into the water, Larissa also liked the boats. A few times we rowed around the lake, at one with the ducks and geese. If we were feeling adventurous, we might walk up to Alexandra Palace where there is a bigger boating lake. Larissa was always drawn to places with water, although she never learnt to swim.

'Here he is, our top reporter from the dating zone, what's the news?' Larissa says. 'I can't wait to hear how it went.'

'She turned up wearing a tutu,' I say.

'Oh, that sounds promising. You have to give a girl credit for not giving a fuck and wearing what the hell she likes. I like her already.'

I give Larissa a rundown of the rest of the date and tell her that despite it not working out, I'm feeling positive about the future dates.

'You don't have much luck with women, do you?' Larissa says, giving me a knowing look.

Thinking she is referring to us, I let this pass. It is true. I suppose it all comes down to our choices. We do not always make the right ones.

'I suppose not,' I say.

'Do you remember when we met?'

'I do,' I say. 'Funnily enough, that was the evening you told me you had the worst luck in the world with men.'

'I did, although I am always glad we met,' Larissa says, a sweet, sad smile on her lips.

What is it with first times? Those nights we first meet that we always remember. They linger like stardust in our memories, glittering neurons sparkling in the dark and lighting up our thoughts. Maybe it's that people want to have good stories to tell so that they can look at each other now and again, smile, and enjoy a shared moment of happiness no matter what followed.

How we met is like this. It was a birthday party in the upstairs room of a bar in Notting Hill called Beach Blanket Babylon. Adam was dating a friend of the birthday girl named Annabel.

Adam was off chatting, and I was fending for myself and making a good impression of surveying the party scene from a corner wall. I'd seen Larissa earlier, noticing her as she moved through the party, and I saw her again later when she was on her own and she paused mid-room. The second time I looked her way, and she looked back.

Larissa gave me a half-smile and continued to look. I returned her smile and went one step further—boldly, I thought—tipping my bottle of beer in her direction. I am a big fan of the beer-tip move, classic that it is.

Larissa walked over to where I was standing. Her arms crossed and her feet closed together as she came to a stop. 'So, you're one of those people who turn up at parties and like to try and populate your own bit of the party and set up camp in one little spot.'

'Yes, that is me. I like to try. I was successful at one stage. My corner was buzzing, only it led to a party power struggle. The host wasn't into splinter groups, and my fringe group crumbled.'

'I see and you are always in kitchens at parties?'

'I am. I can be rented by the hour to stand in your kitchen. My attendance can make you look more popular than you are. It is an essential part of modern party planning: don't forget to invite the fake guests.'

Larissa smiled at this, putting a forefinger to her lips as if she were considering a particular thought. 'You're quite funny for a guy who hangs out on his own at parties. What you're saying here is that you are waiting for people to stop and talk to you as you hold court with your bottle of beer.'

'That would be an alternative interpretation, but yes, I will concede, that does sum it up well.'

'It's a good job I stopped by then.'

'It is. Otherwise, I could have been standing here all evening on my own.'

And at this, we laughed in unison for a second or two.

'I should tell you that people are talking about you,' Larissa said.

'Already? That doesn't usually happen until much later.'

'Annabel, who is the host, long ago noticed you standing here. She considered calling security.'

'Security? Okay, wow, I should at this stage point out that I'm not technically on my own,' I said, sweeping my beer bottle hand out in front of me. 'I'm with him,' I said, pointing to Adam, who was deep in conversation with a tall blonde woman.

Larissa looked over her shoulder. 'Oh, that's who Annabel is dating. He's quite tall. What about you, are you planning to mingle?'

'I was working my way up to it. This is a great spot, and you get a good view of what's going on.'

Larissa turned and looked back across her shoulder, pivoting slightly to look across the rest of the room. She turned back around to face me.

'We don't have to mingle. I could quite easily stand here for a while.'

'You could?'

'Sure,' she said.

And so, we did.

After a while, when it was getting late and when, it seemed, we had talked about everything from London to San Francisco, and with that feeling of departure creeping in, I started to ask her a question.

'Look, I wanted to ask you...' and I let the question trail off.

Larissa smiled. 'I'm not seeing anyone, and besides, I have the worst luck in the world when it comes to men. I thought I would tell you that in advance.'

I nodded. 'Oh, me too,' I chimed.

Larissa arched her eyebrows. 'Really? I am not sure I believe you.'

I dipped my head. 'Absolutely, it's true. I spend a lot of time chasing unobtainable women. I frequently hang out on the unrequited scene, and if I am not there, you can find me in the friend zone. Feel free to drop by.'

Larissa laughed at this, throwing her hair back as she did, and she had a laugh like honey; one that, when you heard it, you also felt better.

'Oh, we should definitely date, then,' she said.

That is how we met, how we started, and what led to us now sitting opposite the cold, dark water. I don't know why but the way we met still strikes me as more romantic, meaningful even, than any online date. I'm not sure why.

'I'm not sure people meet like that anymore. Maybe it is just me,' I say.

'Tom, you barely leave the house. You spent lock-down *doubly* locked down, and even before that, you were famous for being difficult to get out of the house,' Larissa says.

'That is true,' I say, nodding, and then, offering my hands up, I add, 'I know, but now that I am out meeting people again, I'm enjoying myself.'

'When is your next date?' Larissa asks.

'In a couple of days, and that is all I know.'

'Well, I look forward to hearing about it. Onwards and upwards, isn't that what they say?'

'I think it is, and on that note, I should go.'

'Well, you know where to find me,' Larissa says.

I always know that, although I don't say anything. I stand up from the bench and walk back through the park and to home.

Chapter Eleven

'Song Bird'

The following week, I take the bus to Allison's in Harringay and get off on the high street. It is a warm evening, and I enjoy my walk down the bustling high street, which is well known for its eclectic mix of Turkish restaurants, twenty-four-hour food stores and bars. I pass one bar called Jam in a Jar, which is buzzing with people. There are tables outside and there is a guy singing inside with an acoustic guitar. His voice is authentic and clear, and I stop as I recognise him.

It is the English guy who comes into the café with his American son, a six- or maybe seven-year-old boy. I've never said more than hello to him, and I am always intrigued as to what his story is.

I stand there on the street listening as his voice floats out onto the street. He's singing:

I ran and ran and ran,
I walked and walked and walked,
I kept on going forward all of the time
In the hope I think would arrive
Just where I'm supposed to be
But I think I missed a turn
Somewhere down the road

Missed where I was supposed to be
I missed you too, and I need you now
You're all I need like I hardly know
So won't you come and find me
I'm looking for you too
So won't you come and find me
I'm looking for you too
I'm running now, and I'm on my way
So forgive me if you think you can
It's late I know but I finally have a plan
And I'm on my way back to you
As I miss you and I need you now
You're all I need like I hardly know
So won't you come and find me
I'm looking for you too
So won't you come and find me
I'm looking for you too

I wonder what the story behind the song is and how personal it is. I am half-tempted to go inside, lean against some wall space, and listen to his songs, only that might be weird. He would recognise me, which would spark a conversation next time he saw me.

I can't remember the last time I did that: just went into a bar on my own. When I look at the bar again, there are so many people inside that it fills me with a slight sense of dread. This overrides my desire to go in, and I carry on down the street towards Allison's.

As I walk, I am thinking about my date with Alice, and partly trying to rehearse it so that it comes over as amusing when I tell the story, and all I can think of is 'pleased to tutu' and what an idiot I am.

I turn down one of the roads of neat Victorian houses which line each side of the street, and continue until I am halfway along. I can see Allison's red Mini Cooper sitting outside her house. I am always somewhat envious of this. I stand outside Allison's red-brick terraced house with its neat terracotta-tiled path and elegant black door.

I'm not at all sure what to expect. Maybe some kind of Allison pep talk before my next date.

This is the first time I have been to Allison's house when it is only her and no Paul, and I wonder what it will be like. If this had been before, when they were still together, Allison would do all the talking and Paul the banging of pots and pans as food is prepared. The cooking was all his domain, and he is one of those people who can produce something delicious even when the ingredients don't look like they add up to all that much. I will miss the food.

Allison opens the door. Her long dark hair is tied back. She's looking summer-cool, wearing a white T-shirt and blue trousers. A wide smile is offered, and she looks quite beautiful as she does this. Some people look grim when they give huge smiles as everything flies out of proportion. That doesn't happen to Allison. Somehow there is a proportionality at play with her face, and the lines flow.

'You're right on time. I just finished story time,' Allison says.

I follow Allison inside, and the first thing I notice is how quiet the house is. There is no sound at all, and when we arrive in the kitchen, it is empty and silent. It is like a different world to the one I last visited. I look around, alerted by a beep from the baby monitor. Dylan, Allison's two-year-old, lets out a soft snuffled murmur.

I stand there for a moment, taking it all in. Allison must notice this, clock what I am doing, and she comments on it.

'I know, it's quiet, isn't it?' she says.

'Sorry. I didn't mean to… I don't know.'

'Really, it's fine. More importantly, I ordered Indian food. Hope that's okay,' Allison says as she takes a fresh bottle of white wine from the fridge and unscrews the cap.

I sit at the kitchen table where two glasses sit ready. Allison pours the wine and sits down.

'Cheers, it's good to see you. It's been a long time since you were here,' Allison says.

Thinking back, it's been more than a year—like a lot of things in my life. I've missed coming here. I always liked the dinners and the nights we had hanging out in this kitchen, eating food, and drinking wine, as we often did pre-pandemic. It is almost as though we have yet to find our rhythm again, to find our old selves. I know that is true of me. I am not my old self, although I am not sure that is all bad either.

'Good to be here, good to be out,' I say.

'I'm glad to hear you say that,' she says.

I ask Allison the question I feel I should ask, the one about Paul, who has been gone for a long time now, and who has shown no signs of returning.

'Have you heard from Paul?'

'Yes, I've heard from him; and to head off your next question, no, he isn't coming back. He wanted to but I've moved on. The truth is, we're done, and I am more than happy with that,' Allison says.

Allison speaks like a woman who is very sure of herself, and with little emotion. Her words fall with finality, like stone-cold tablets onto the table, dust rising around us, the debris of once happy lives, and that is all that is left.

'He's an idiot,' I say.

'Of course he is. A word to the wise should you ever start to procreate, and I'm sure you will. You must pull your weight. Otherwise, you'll end up like Paul,' Allison says.

'He's going to regret it,' I say.

That is something I'm sure about. You read about those fathers who part company with their wives and partners and end up playing a minor role in their children's lives. They become the supporting act. They often end up unhappy and regretful about the situation. This is what happened to my sister and me after our dad left. We seldom saw him, and then we stopped altogether, and then it was too late, and we live with our regrets.

'I'm sure he will. Just not yet. He thinks he's single again. Besides, I'm sure he was cheating—you know what people who work in advertising are like. His only contribution to our child so far has been insisting we call him Dylan because of Dylan Thomas. I have no idea why. He couldn't quote a line of poetry to save his life,' Allison says.

'To be fair, you wanted to call him Atticus.'

'Yes,' and Allison holds up a forefinger. 'That is true, and I loved that name, and I had at least read the book.'

Allison has tears on her face, and she is crying, and I am swept up in her emotions, close to tears for her. I lean forward and hug her. This isn't something that comes naturally. We were not big huggers. Instead, I would usually shift awkwardly in my seat and wonder if I should offer to make some tea. This time, because of the years we have known each other and all the good times we have spent together, I feel the need to do something more. We embrace for a few moments. I ask her if she is okay, and she tells me that despite all appearances, she is.

'Thank you, I know you are not big on hugs, and I appreciate it,' Allison says.

The Ring doorbell goes; our takeaway has arrived to punctuate the moment. I go to the door to collect it. Walking back into the kitchen, I find Allison placing bowls and cutlery on the table.

We tuck into our food—two vegetarian curries—and drink more wine. I ask Allison how she has been coping with being a single mother, which is the last thing I ever expected would happen to her. Allison is good-looking, successful, and a wonderful human who I always feel lucky to know.

When Allison was sixteen, she had a girlfriend, and she was the coolest girl I knew at school. It was only later, after university, that she ever dated boys, and then met Paul.

She asks me how my first date went. I recap my encounter with Alice, and she laughs on cue about my tutu gaffe.

'That is mortifying. It sounds like she had a sense of humour,' Allison says.

'She did, she was cool, and it is okay that nothing came of it. I still got something from it,' I say.

'Do tell, what revelation did your re-introduction to the world of dating deliver?'

'Don't be afraid to take the leap,' I say.

'Oh, that's very good advice, you should definitely follow that,' she says, bursting into laughter. Which I understand: it has become very clear to me that I can hand out advice, I just can't follow it.

'Look, the most important thing is, I am genuinely looking forward to my next date,' I say.

'That's so optimistic of you, Tom.'

'I realised that dating can be horrible, but sometimes it can be okay, even if it doesn't work out and going out there again is what I need. So, I am going to crack on.'

'I'm impressed,' Allison says. 'You sound like your dad. Sorry, I probably shouldn't say that.'

I shake my head. It's fine. Allison is right, though. It is the kind of thing he would have said.

'It's cool, and it's true. Ask me again after date four or five,' I say.

'I will, but before then, I should admit I had ulterior motives for inviting you around tonight.'

'Okay,' I say slowly, and for a moment, I have weird and inappropriate thoughts. Is Allison about to make a surprising declaration? This seems unlikely. I am almost sure that she always saw me a bit like the brother she never had, albeit the kind that followed you around like a dopey teenager. 'Allison…' I start to say.

In almost the same way Sarah does, Allison rolls her eyes when I say this, as if sensing I am about to say something spectacularly dumb.

'No, silly, not that kind of ulterior motive. What I wanted to say is that you don't have to continue to go on these dates; you know that, right?'

Now I am confused. I was under the impression that Allison was involved in putting this whole plan together. She was part of 'team intervention' along with my sister.

'I thought you were all for this, and that you are personally responsible for my next date?'

'That is true,' Allison says. 'I just have reservations. I did think it was a good idea to descend on you, but you know the dates are all Adam's idea. He's worried the rest of us will upset his plan.'

What is Adam's plan, exactly? To get me dating and write a book? I think that sums it up.

'I do, and I don't mind that this is all Adam's doing. The worst that could happen is that I meet no one, and the best is that I meet someone, and it goes somewhere,' I say.

'What about if you meet the wrong person?' Allison asks.

What does the wrong person look like? That's the problem with dating. People don't come with helpful warning signs. You know like: *Be warned: date me, and I will mess up your life like a hurricane inside a doll's house.* Every person I have gone out with in the past, including Larissa—who I always, for reasons I don't quite understand, wanted to be the right person—has been the wrong person. We broke up or never managed to last.

'I'm baffled,' I say. 'How will I know?'

'That's the difficult bit. You might end up going out with one of these women. I mean, worst-case scenario, you could end up living or married to one of them, and they could still be the wrong girl for you,' Allison says.

I thought ending up with one of these women was the whole point of this endeavour? What if Allison is right? How do you ever know for sure? The answer is, you don't. There are no guarantees. You have to take a chance. It is the subject of thousands of pop songs with titles like 'You Belong With Me' (Taylor Swift), 'I'll Be Waiting' (Adele), or 'True Love Will Find You In The End' (Daniel Johnston). The point is, they are all singing about the same thing. Loath as I am to admit it, Phil Collins was also right: 'You Can't Hurry Love'.

I cannot believe I have not made this mixtape yet. I mentally make a note to start this project as soon as possible. This will be an awesome mixtape, although it will not include Phil Collins.

'If I meet one of these women and we end up in a church, that does on paper look like a traditional metric for success. My mother, at least, will be pleased. Who knows, I might even be happy as well,' I say.

Allison offers a smile at this and takes a sip of her wine. She is not convinced.

'What I'm saying is that you could end up like Paul and me,' Allison says.

I'm not sure how to take that or what to do with that information. Until they separated, I had always considered Allison and Paul a success story. The gold standard in relationships. It goes to show you can never tell. Their relationship turned out to be a house of cards, and Paul an absolute dick. The thing is, there didn't appear to have been any signs that this was going to happen. They were the perfect couple for a long time, they got on well, and everyone loved being around them. People gravitated towards them. There was no gradual deterioration. Instead, there was a complete breakdown of communication and support with the arrival of Dylan. It is another reminder that dating, relationships and marriage, are the biggest of life's gambles. When you throw your lot in with someone else, there are no guarantees and, in the end, that has to be okay. The alternative is doing what I've been doing. It's being on your own, and there is only so long you can do that before you start to lose yourself.

'To be honest, this is not the pep talk I was expecting,' I say. 'I was thinking you were going to be a major supporter of this dating enterprise.'

'I know, and I'm so glad you are doing this, doing something. You know what it is, don't you?' Allison asks.

When she says this, I get it. I know what tonight is about now. It is about Beth. I feel an ache in my chest, and a sense of disquiet settle over me. Allison has always liked the idea of Beth and me getting together on the basis that we got on well, and have known each other a long time.

'I know what you're going to say,' I tell Allison.

'There's a reason why you know that. It's because I'm right. Beth was the perfect girl for you, and you know it. Not just that, you were perfect for each other. It breaks my heart that you let it go,' Allison says.

'Because Beth and I are friends?' I offer.

'That's your excuse and you're sticking to it.' Allison pauses, and I think she will say something else, only she doesn't. 'All I am saying is that you should have done something when you had the chance.'

'What's the line? *The past is a foreign country;* they do things differently there.'

I don't tell Allison I went to Beth's house, as there isn't much to tell. I didn't see her, and if she was in, Beth didn't want to see me. I don't want to examine this any more deeply than I already have.

'You know what's going to happen, don't you? Someday soon she's going to meet someone. They'll start dating, and before you know it, they'll be talking about moving in. Five minutes later, in the well-worn tradition of early thirty-somethings, they'll be standing at the altar and very quickly after that, you'll be sitting there thinking to yourself, "I blew it". That's the future, and the only way to avoid it is to speak to Beth before it's too late.'

'I can't do anything about the future,' I say.

Allison nods. 'Okay, well, I have said my bit, and I won't push it other than to say reconsider before it is too late… Adam was right about one thing; time is short.'

I have the feeling Allison is trying to tell me something else. Only I am not sure what. I shake it off. I am confident this is the right thing to do. Besides, I have nine dates left, and maybe, just maybe, one of those will go somewhere.

'I think you might have mentioned that before,' I say.

Allison smiles and sits back in her chair, and shrugs, resigned, signalling we are moving on.

'Okay, well, I hope you get something out of the dates and that your trip into Wonderland isn't repeated. Everyone has done their best to find people who we think you'll get on with. Besides, I can't wait to hear how the rest go,' Allison says.

'We haven't talked about you, yet. I know everything with Paul must be raw, but maybe you need Adam to set you up on ten dates as well,' I say.

Allison laughs hard at this, which I have to tell you I find disconcerting. It is also like she knows something I don't.

'What and end up in his book? No, thanks. Besides, I don't need to,' Allison says.

I do a double-take when Allison says this. Unless I have misunderstood her, she is saying that she has already met someone else. How is that even possible? Why is it that some people can do this—move seamlessly from one relationship to another—yet other people find it all a gargantuan struggle?

'You've already met someone?'

Allison gives a couple of small nods and takes a sip of her wine without elaborating.

'Well, don't leave me hanging,' I say.

'Oh, I'm afraid I am going to do just that. Sorry, I know that is a bit of a tease. It is early days. It is all a bit in the air. We're just waiting for things to settle.'

'Okay, that sounds intriguing. Is it anyone I know?'

Allison makes a weird shape with her mouth and then snaps her mouth shut, like she was going to tell me something and then thought better of it. 'I promise you will hear all about it soon,' she says.

Chapter Twelve

'Girl from Mars'

It is a bright early evening, with clear skies, and full of warmth. Long rays of sunshine fall onto the top deck of the bus I am riding on my way to date number two. As the bus rumbles through North London and down Islington's Upper Street, I read the profile Adam sent over, written by Allison.

Her name is Juliette, and she does something in children's TV, which makes me think of happy smiley people wearing primary colours. This could, of course, be an erroneous impression of what children's TV is like.

> **Dating Profile:**
>
> Name: Juliette Jones (Jules)
>
> Age: 36 Height: 5'7 Build: Medium
>
> Hair: Red hair Eyes: Green
>
> Occupation: Children's TV exec
>
> General: You will have the best time with Jules. She is one of the funniest women I know. Not just outside, inside too. I met her working when we were starting out, and we

had so many brilliant nights together (admittedly, most of these were Prosecco-fuelled).

Jules is a pretty redhead, with a brilliant laugh, and is so incredibly knowledgeable that you can talk to her about almost anything, and she will generally have something interesting to say. Whoever Jules ends up with will be a lucky guy.

Her feminism is also very important to her, and she expects to be equal in everything she does with her partner. I can't think of any downsides when it comes to Jules.

That said, there is maybe one thing to mention; she has terrible taste in men. I think she's had some bad experiences. Don't worry though, as I'm sure that's changed since I last saw her. This was a few years ago. All you really need to know is, she is pretty, single and looking forward to meeting you.

I can't wait to hear how it goes. Allison.

The phrases 'bad experiences' and 'a few years ago' do set off alarm bells. I wonder, though, what happened to Jules in the intervening years since Allison last saw her. My thought processes stop at this point as though tripped by a rut on life's stony path, as I realise that this also describes me. I wonder what Allison told Juliette about me. She must have told her something.

The words 'hermit', possibly 'a little agoraphobic' and 'anti-social' spring to mind. A radical career change from high-flying crime reporter to glorified barista, maybe? People either think this is great and say well done for getting out, or they think I have lost the plot. All some people are interested in is the status of the job you hold and the money you earn. To them, my new life, on paper, appears less valuable than my old one. What they don't see is life as a whole, and the work-life balance people talk about. I don't want to work to live, I want my life to be the other way around.

I imagine Allison concluding with the phrase: 'other than that, he's a real catch'. For some reason, this makes me laugh. I am not sure if this is a good or bad thing.

The picture accompanying the profile Adam emailed is that of a slim woman with long, thick red hair. This got me thinking about how prescriptive we can be when dating and how this can lead us to make bad choices. For instance, I always tell myself that my ideal woman has a blonde bob, sometimes a brunette. I don't know why or where this even comes from because I do find Juliette's picture attractive.

It often feels like I've been programmed at the most basic level to continue chasing this ideal when it ends in total disaster. Generally, because we were not well-matched and could barely stand each other. It also means that I'm more likely to casually reject people who don't fit this mould. This is, of course, not the smartest way to go about finding someone.

We're meeting at a local pool bar in Islington tonight, which I take as a good sign. I love playing pool. I'm not sure why, as my pool skills are mediocre at best, despite having spent long afternoons and evenings smashing balls around tables at different times in my life.

I weave through the waves of people making their way along Islington's Upper Street as they leave work and head for bars and home. I turn down Liverpool Road, past

Marks & Spencer and then onto Chapel market. Stallholders are tidying up, and shoppers are ambling along.

As I approach the bar, my anxiety levels are spiking. I don't linger outside. I push on through the double doors and enter the pool hall bar. Inside, I stand for a moment in the entrance gazing around as my eyes become accustomed to the gloomy, open space, which is split into two. On one side are tables and chairs and on the other, rows of pool tables with purple felt.

There are groups of men playing together and more at the bar. Apart from a couple of women sitting at a table, it is only men I can see. As I scan the pool tables, I see one woman standing on her own, holding a pool cue, ready and waiting.

She looks straight at me and waves. The good news is that Juliette looks like her picture. She is slim, and her red hair is longer, and falls to her shoulders in soft waves. She is wearing a white linen jacket, and a blue and white striped T-shirt with jeans, and she is like a bright beacon in the dimly lit bar.

I wave back and walk through the rows of empty tables towards where Juliette has positioned herself.

'You must be Juliette,' I say.

'Call me Jules—and correct. You look like your picture, which is a welcome change. Isn't that the worst part of dating?'

I smile at this. It is definitely one of the worst parts.

'I know! Why do people think they can get away with putting ten-year-old pictures on their profiles?'

'I would never do that,' Jules says.

'I recognised you straight away: red hair and pretty,' I say. When I say this, Jules offers a fake laugh, and not in a good way.

'Wow. You didn't just say that did you? That I'm "pretty",' she says, making quote marks with her fingers.

I give a small, dry, awkward laugh. I try to analyse how, seconds into this date, I am in trouble. My mayday call is going out over the radio as we speak.

'I did,' I say, and I almost add, I meant it in a good way.

'Without going radical feminist on you, pretty is what you call little girls,' Jules says, twisting her mouth.

I open my mouth, making a big 'oh'. I'm flummoxed. I did not get that memo. Thinking about it, I can see her point. For a moment, I think about telling Jules that 'pretty' was how Allison described her and then reject this approach. I put my small shovel away, fold it carefully into my pocket and stop digging right there and then.

'Now you mention that I can see your point. Fair enough,' I say. 'Beautiful?'

'That's cheesy, isn't it? It's something people say in 1930s movies. Besides, that isn't how I feel about myself,' Jules says.

'I think that's harsh,' I say. 'There's a great F. Scott Fitzgerald quote: "She was beautiful, but not like those girls in the magazines. She was beautiful, for the way she thought. She was beautiful, for the sparkle in her eyes when she talked about something she loved."'

Jules holds her hands up and gives me a nod.

'Okay you win. I am always impressed by anyone who can quote anything, and I do like that, so thank you. You must think I'm horrible, hammering you like this after we just met,' Jules says.

You might think that, only I don't. Jules has a fiery spark, brighter than her tumbling red hair, and a smartness that shines through. I like her, and I don't mind at all how we started.

'Not at all. I think it's perfectly cool to set people straight,' I say.

'I'm pleased to hear you say that. I think we're going to get along,' she says. 'I bought you a beer.'

Jules nods to one of two bottles of beer sitting on a table next to a stone pillar.

'Thanks,' I say, and I pick up the bottle and take a drink.

'Shall we play?' Jules says. 'I should warn you, I'm quite good.'

I smile at this, 'I'll take that bet. I once beat a mate ten games straight.'

'Was he drunk?' she asks.

'Not at first,' I reply.

Jules laughs at this and chalks her cue. 'Well, let's see if you can take one game from me.'

Jules breaks, sending her cue ball hard down the table, hitting the pack like a precision strike. I follow up with a shot and put nothing down. As I step back from the table, I see I have left Jules a couple of options, which she does not waste. She sinks first one ball and then another in quick succession.

This activates my competitive streak, and I take my time over my shot and manage to sink two balls.

'Not bad,' Jules comments, and for the next couple of minutes, this is our conversation as we pot balls and critique the quality of our play before graduating to sharing our pool history.

We talk about pubs we've played in and the people we've played with. We offer biographical snapshots of some of the people who have crossed our lives. All of the games played on those tatty barroom pool tables in different towns and cities, that led us to this moment.

'Best bar you played in?' I ask.

'Oh, that's a good question. It would have to be this local bar in Brooklyn Heights. I spent about five years in New York and lived in Brooklyn. It was the best,' Jules says.

'I'm jealous. I've been a couple of times to New York, not spent much time there, but love the city,' I say.

'Me too, although dating in New York, I have to say, is god awful. I prefer London for a lot of things, and dating is one of them. I had some terrible dates in New York.'

'Dating is hard, or maybe it is just the first bit, getting started.'

'Absolutely, it often feels like progress is an uphill struggle. Unless, that is, you meet someone who you feel right with and… oh, I don't know.' When she says this her words slow, as if she is having trouble with them, and there is something more to say, only she cannot bring herself to say it.

'So has there been someone you came close with?'

Jules scrunches up her mouth, and I can see she is thinking this over, and considering whether she wants to tell me the story. 'There was. We were engaged, and I thought that was it, and then he died,' she says, and I can see the emotions building on her face, and that talking about this is not easy.

I do not push Jules to elaborate, as death is, I know from personal experience, hard to talk about.

'I'm sorry to hear that,' I say.

'Thank you. It was a long time ago now, almost six years, and the thing is, I'm forty-two, and I'm so over dating. I wonder some days why I'm even bothering.'

'You're forty-two?' I don't mean to say this. It pops out of my mouth. Allison told me she was thirty-six. I understand that age is a sensitive thing, and I'm not sure men approach it in quite the same way. It seems to me that there is possibly a more significant pressure on women. That might have something to do with biological clocks, the loud and off-putting ticking sounds, and the pressure women feel related to that. So, I can understand why people might knock a few years off their age.

'Ah yes, I always lie about that. I don't know why. I must have lied to Allison about it at some stage as well, and it stuck in her head.' Jules pauses while she gathered her thoughts. 'Okay, that's also a lie. It's because, even though I am not sure I want to go out with most of those men I see on dating apps, they will not date you once you're close to forty,' she says.

'Okay,' I say, not entirely sure how to proceed before it hits me. 'You look thirty-five by the way.'

'That's sweet of you to say, thank you. The thing is, I didn't date anyone in the last year-and-a-half of on off lockdowns, and I think I was happier not dating. Although the other thing is, I probably missed my window,' Jules says.

'Your window?'

'Yeah… Let me ask you this: do you want to have children?'

I'm ambushed by the question, and unprepared. It is a level of detail and self-examination that I was not expecting or ready for on a first date. More than that, it isn't something I have spent much time thinking about since Larissa. I don't have an answer. I think that in the past when I have been asked this question, I might have answered 'yes' on autopilot. I didn't take it seriously, and I said what I thought women wanted to hear. Older, changed, maybe not all wiser, I'm not sure what to say or what people want to hear.

So, I ask myself the question again. *Do* I want children? As I interrogate myself, the question hovers there, and I find it hard to come up with an answer. I'd like to be truthful, and honest, and so I ask myself the question again: *do I want children?* I realise that I do have an answer, which is as much a surprise to me as it is to anyone else. I don't even know where the answer comes from. Maybe it is an innate desire or a drive, even, which is part biological and part emotional.

The answer to Jules's question is: *yes, I would like to have children*. Not immediately, and maybe not for at least a couple of years, but not too long after that. After all, I'm almost thirty-five, and while I don't have a biological clock as such, I do, as a man, have an equivalent. Maybe it is the male counterpart to what women experience, which comes as both a desire and knowledge that time is running out. Besides, my sperm count no doubt started its inevitable downward trajectory long ago and is now picking up speed like a tobogganist going for gold.

Before this moment, I always dimly thought that women were the drivers in wanting a family and wanting children, which is a ridiculous way to think. I had thought before about men being just as broody. And I think about it again, in this moment, as balls are smacked across tables, flying like planets across the stars and colliding with each other.

I have surprised myself with this answer. This date is proving to be illuminating. I think that must be a sign that I am growing, or maybe getting older. I also take it as a good sign that I now know myself a little better than I thought I did. Maybe going forward through this dating process, that self-awareness and honesty can only help me improve how I am. I think that might be key to moving my life on and making progress. I didn't see that coming. Adam is going to love this. It will provide a perfect case study for his book.

'Yeah, you know what, now you have put me on the spot, and having barely consciously thought about it until now, I think so. At some point,' I say.

'Now you can say that, but I can't say that. The truth is that I could probably still have children if I met someone new, and we decided quickly we wanted to be together, and it happened naturally or, more likely, we paid for IVF. But I don't want children, and I don't want to go through the whole IVF nightmare,' Jules says.

'That's okay though, isn't it?' I ask, and I mean this.

'It is okay,' Jules says, and picks up her bottle of beer and takes a sip.

The two of us stand there for a while longer, not saying anything, and it is okay. It isn't awkward, as we have reached a moment that comes when two people show themselves to each other, bare themselves if you like, and the honesty and openness that comes with such moments is a welcome relief. It is as though we are being ourselves, rather than trying to be other people, which is quite hard to do when dating.

We continue to play. We rack the balls and shoot pool, buy more drinks, and are well-matched in our games. In that fashion, we pass another hour together and we chat about this and that, our jobs, our lives, and it is not uncomfortable. We are at ease with each other, and I like hanging out with Jules.

When we leave, it is nearly dark outside, and the street is empty. We stand in the fading glow of the summer light and say our goodbyes. That easiness we had with each other around the pool table is gone.

I am self-conscious, and our conversation is at a tail-end, both of us unsure how to conclude it or say goodbye. I think we are about to depart as friends. That, to me, feels like progress, and I'm okay with that.

'So,' I say.

'I enjoyed tonight.'

'Yeah, me too. You have the skills.'

Jules smiles, beams at this. 'I do, and I am happy with that. I invested my time at university wisely, acquiring the talents that would carry me through life.'

'Look...' I start.

Jules laughs, 'Are you about to say it was lovely to meet me?'

I hold my hands up, guilty as charged. 'Please don't hold it against me,' I say. 'I was drawing from my stock book of dating goodbyes.'

Jules laughs again. 'I'll let you off. Here's the thing, though: I don't know about you, but one of the first things I think when I meet a guy is, *could I kiss him?* It is a fundamental.'

'Okay,' I say, unsure where Jules is going with this.

'And when I looked at you, I thought I could. You have a boyish charm,' Jules says.

I can feel the heat on my face. I am blushing. 'I'll take that, I think.'

'You should—and remember, one day you won't have it.'

When she says that, I am thinking of that ticking clock again, and how Sarah politely told me I was 'getting old', and as I am mulling this over, without warning, Jules takes a step towards me, and we are standing close. I am no expert, and I might be out of practice, but I think we are about to kiss. I'm confused, and for a moment wonder if it is a good idea, and then dismiss this thought and instead, I go with it. I am going to play it as it lays.

I lean forward, and am close to her. Jules gives me a small smile and angles her head. I can feel the warmth of her breath on my face, and then our lips touch.

We are kissing, sensual, slow, and soft.

I feel it from my head to my toes.

It is a first kiss.

It is a good kiss.

And it is a goodbye kiss.

Jules lifts her head away from mine, and we separate. She gives me a final peck. Still standing close, she places the palm of her hand on my chest and rests it there for a second or two. Looking up at me, she says, 'That was nice. I thought it might be.'

'It was nice.'

'I always wanted to try that, a kiss like that. Mostly though, when I end a date with someone I'm not going to see again, I want to leave.'

'And tonight?'

'Tonight,' Jules says, 'was different.'

She shrugs as if she has more to say on the subject. For a moment, I think she is going to suggest we meet again. Only that isn't what happens.

'I'm going to go now,' she says, and points with her finger to her direction of travel.

'It was good to meet you—and, yes, I do mean that,' I say.

'I know you do and, you never know, maybe I'll see you again.'

With that, she turns and starts walking in the opposite direction towards Penton Street. I watch her go, and she does not turn around and does not look over her shoulder.

I see her disappear around the corner, and she is gone. I turn and head back the way I came, with a smile on my face. Jules's parting words accompanying me as I walk; because she's right, you never do know.

Chapter Thirteen

'I Don't Want to Change You'

A few days later, I'm getting ready to leave the house to go to the local pub where I am meeting Adam for my 'Dating debrief'. Adam sent me a WhatsApp a short while ago, telling me that I should be prepared for some tough questions. He makes it sound like I am about to go on *University Challenge* where I will get three answers right and feel like a quiz master.

The last couple of weeks have seen me doing things I have not done in months. This will be only my third visit to a pub in more than a year. Other than my two dates, I have not been anywhere else that involves a social setting, and I am oddly trepidatious. Work is different, there is a separation and distance.

I have fifteen minutes or so to kill before I leave, and I am lying on the couch with the TV on and volume down while listening to the evening show on BBC Six Music when my mobile rings. I glance at the screen and do a double-take: it's my mother.

My mother normally calls me during the morning, which tells me something is up. This, I am almost sure, is an emergency parental call. Despite this being the case, I know that before we get to the heart of the matter, there will be a certain amount of conversational small talk.

My mother is the master of preamble, and it is always a precursor to what she really wants to tell me.

This evening, it is something she has read in the *Daily Mail*. My mother loves to call and tell me about something she's read. More often than not this relates to dating and relationships.

'Hello,' I say. 'How are you?'

'Very good; I've been hearing about you dating again. After so long it sounds like you might be having some fun.'

That will be Sarah, who has wasted no time in updating my mother on the intervention.

'So far so good,' I say. 'It is better than I expected.'

'Pleased to hear that, I will keep my fingers crossed for you. Coincidentally, I was thinking about you the other day and thought I must call,' she says.

'Oh, really, I'm intrigued,' I say, as I like to do my best to be a good sport.

'Well, apparently there is—and I'm not sure if you're aware of this or have given it any serious thought—a rather shocking decline in male fertility at the age of thirty-five. Of course, what made me think of this is your birthday. It's not too far away. Tom, you're almost thirty-five! How did that happen?'

'Good question. The answer to which is, I am not entirely sure. The important part is, I'm okay with it, with being thirty-five,' I say.

To be honest, I must admit I was aware of this news. I'm not sure how. Maybe I clicked on clickbait article with a headline like '*Thirty Reasons You Know You Are Getting Old*'. When my mother tells me she's been reading about my declining chances of producing offspring, she isn't too concerned. She continues to assure me that she has faith

I will 'eventually' sort myself out. I think she would just be happier if I was moving at a similar speed to my sister and her impending wedding.

My mother was ecstatic when she first heard about the wedding and ever since that day, fifteen months ago, she has been working to help my sister plan the biggest wedding the town has seen in years. When I say helping, what I really mean is directing, as at times it has appeared she is more invested in the wedding than my sister.

My sister's attitude to the wedding is somewhat laid back. I would go as far to say, it is apathetic. Sometimes, I get the impression that she gave in to, rather than embraced, the idea of marriage.

When I first heard the wedding news, I was a surprised. A few months previously, Sarah and I had talked about how it was going with Jack, and she was not overflowing with enthusiasm when she told me: 'Well, he's hardly the love of my life.'

This was an eye-opening answer. Wasn't the love of your life the only person you should consider marrying? After thinking about it, I realised I'd heard many stories of people who got married, and at some later point admitted that they did it because they thought they should rather than because they had found their soulmate.

'Then why are you with him?' I asked Sarah.

Sarah laughed: 'I like him, and we have fun together. It's only that he doesn't lift my heart, and the earth doesn't move. Despite what women might have told you, Tom, it's what we want. If only a little,' Sarah said.

'Careful, Sarah, you're making yourself out to be a dyed-in-the-wool romantic,' I said.

'Oh please, I have high expectations, that's all. I have the first-class degree and I have the MBA and a job that I enjoy just enough. I deserve the partner to match. There's nothing romantic or old-fashioned about that.'

'So, if that's all true, why aren't you out there looking for the perfect person then? Rather than Jack, who "doesn't make the earth doesn't move"?'

'That's a good question, and I've thought about it a lot. My basic conclusion is that another man is not the answer,' Sarah said.

I wasn't sure how serious she was being when she said this. Sarah dated a girl at university, and after they split up, she said it was always about the person rather than the gender and hasn't dated another girl since.

With talk of declining male sperm count out of the way, my mother cuts to the chase about why she's calling.

'Oh, there is one other thing; there is something going on with your sister. Have you noticed anything?' she asks.

I'm intrigued when I hear my mother say this, as I am always the last person to find out. Despite being twins we do not see each other that much, and we are not as close as we used to be. One of the nicest things about opening the café and doing it with Sarah is that we have spent time together. Although she doesn't confide in me.

'You know I am always the last to find out. You know what she's like,' I say.

'Yes, of course, but she's been more so.'

'What do you mean, more so?'

'Well, hard to pin down. Maybe you could speak to her? See if you can find out what's happening.'

'You know she won't tell me anything,' I say.

My mother ponders this for a second. 'For my peace of mind, would you call her anyway? I think you'll catch her if you try now.'

I look at my watch. I will be late now, and I imagine Adam sitting in the pub wondering where I am. He'll probably think I am having some post-dating meltdown and hiding in my flat to avoid discussing how my dates are going.

'Of course, I'll give her a quick call.'

'Perfect, and I have to say I'm very happy to see how you two have reconnected of late with the café, and now she is helping you with your love life, which is it is wonderful,' she says. 'Anything to report yet?'

'Nothing yet, but I will keep you posted.'

'Please do, you know I'd love to hear.'

I say goodnight to my mother and keep my promise by immediately attempting to call my sister. I fully expect it to go straight to voicemail—Sarah never answers her phone. But Sarah picks up on the second ring, which takes me by surprise, and she jumps straight in.

'What's up, Tom? Has something happened at the café?' Sarah says, pausing. 'Or are you calling me about your dates?'

'Both seem to be going well. Besides, you speak to Julie almost as much as I do,' I say.

'You know I like to check in on our venture. I love the café. I don't want to work in one, but you know I love it anyway. And I hear your first two dates have gone quite well. I'm impressed,' Sarah says.

'What, you mean, given that when you came to the flat you said I was terrible at dating, and not very good with women generally?'

'Look, you should do what you always do, and ignore me. Women still seem to go out with you. So, what do I know?' With these words Sarah sounds almost concili-atory.

'I'll take that,' I say. 'Besides, it isn't about my dates; that's not the reason for my call.'

'I'm so glad to hear that, although that said, your next date is a friend of mine so try your best and all that.'

The way Sarah puts this sounds exactly like one of those sports teachers before a rugby game. He knows full well his team of thirteen-year-old boys are hopeless and hopelessly ill-prepared and are about to take a pounding on the field.

'I will endeavour to be amusing and charming,' I say.

'That is a good plan. Just try not to talk about *Star Trek* or anything, she hates that.'

'I don't even like *Star Trek*.'

'Really? I'm sure you used to.'

I let this go rather than go into a detailed explanation about *Star Trek* and *Star Wars* that Sarah has no interest in.

'Moving on; Mum called, and she's concerned.'

'That's interesting. I hadn't expected that,' Sarah says. With that, I know something is going on, and it sounds like something big. My sister tells my mother everything. What is she hiding?

'It sounds like you know she thinks something's up?'

'Do I, now? That's very intuitive of you, Tom.'

'What have you been up to, Sis?'

'I… well… nothing…' And she pauses.

Sarah is rarely flustered, and it is like she has been caught off guard. She is usually cool and measured. For a second there, it sounded like she was going to open up and tell me something, and then thought better of it.

'Nothing going on. It's work, you know how it is. Oh, that's right, you don't. You float around at the café now, don't you?' And there she goes, snapping back to her old self.

I take minor offense at this. I am at the café first thing every day and I close with Julie at five.

'I'm at the café all week,' I say.

For a few beats there is silence on the line, and I'm not sure what is happening as I wait for Sarah to speak. Something is definitely up with her.

'Sorry, I know you are. Julie says you rarely take time off. She's full of praise for you. You need to take a break. God knows, we all need a holiday after the last year or so. Maybe visit Marcus; isn't he always asking you to visit?'

I haven't thought of Marcus in ages, and there was a time when he *was* always asking. It has been almost eighteen months since he and Victoria left London, and a long time since we spoke. I need to give him a call, as I miss hanging out with him. London isn't the same when your friends leave. It is as if the city becomes bigger and emptier. I know this is another sign that I need to move on with my own life, just as my friends have already done.

'I'll give him a call,' I say.

'That's a good start. As for Mum, there isn't anything to tell.'

'Really? It sounds like there is.'

There is silence on the line again. This time, I know Sarah is weighing up whether she should tell me anything about what is going on, as it clear that something is happening.

'Okay, I promise I will tell you in good time. It's complicated, and now isn't the time to get into it. Please don't press me and don't say anything to Mum.'

'Of course not,' I say. But I am thinking that whenever people say 'it's complicated' it almost always suggests that their relationship is about to implode. Except that can't happen to Sarah, as she is with Jack, and they are getting married. Maybe I should check on this.

'I take it your wedding plans are all thundering ahead?'

'Mmm, last I heard.'

It is an answer that doesn't suggest Sarah is chomping at the bit to get down the aisle. Rather the opposite. I don't think it can be pre-wedding jitters, as she isn't the kind of person who gets those.

'Okay,' I say, as I am not sure how else to respond.

'Look, why don't we meet up, go for dinner? I'll message you. You'd better run along now. You're late for your drinks,' Sarah says.

How does she know I am meeting Adam? No doubt they have a WhatsApp group, and she is updating him even as we speak.

We say our goodbyes and hang up. I sit there on the couch for a moment looking at my phone. I am thinking about change, and it is as if I can feel the currents brewing. Maybe it is that awareness you get every now again about our place in the world, and our connection to it, as the blue marble we call home hurtles through the deep darkness of the universe. Something altered during our phone call and, unless I'm wrong, more significant change is on the way. I don't know what it is, only that, like a gathering storm, it is out there and blowing its way towards us, and when it hits life will be different for us all.

-

When I leave the house, it is a warm light summer's evening outside. The street is quiet. An old woman with long white hair is walking a small white dog. I recognise her from the park, and on the confines of the pavement, we smile as we approach each other. I cross the road to the pub.

The Auld Triangle is a great big old pub that is suitably warm and worn and tucked away on a side street that guarantees there are never more than ten people inside at any one time, other than when Arsenal are playing at home. Outside, there is a sign that reads: '*We have beer as cold as your heart*'. Now, two dates in, I would say my heart is a warmer than it has been for a while.

Inside, there are a few people huddled at the bar, and other than that, most of the tables are empty. Adam is sitting in the corner, in one of the nooks, away from the raised platform area where the big screen hangs from the ceiling, and golf is being shown. There is a pint of beer waiting for me as I take my seat.

'Sarah said you were going to be late,' Adam says.

'Well then, you know as much as I do. I had an unexpected flurry of phone activity. It's been a weird evening,' I say. 'Something is going on with Sarah.'

At first Adam does not say anything. I look inquiringly at him, and he offers a blank expression and no information.

'It is a strange time,' says Adam. 'And I have no idea what she is up to. Besides, we're here to talk about you. How do you feel after two dates?'

As I consider my response to his question, I realise that I am feeling optimistic, even though neither of the dates I have been on so far are leading anywhere. In different ways I enjoyed both of my dates, and I am still thinking about that kiss with Jules. It has been a long time since I kissed anyone, and I realise I have missed it. I miss that spark between two people, that human connection that brings people together. The truth is, if she rang me tomorrow and said 'let's meet', I would, but I don't think that is on her agenda.

The important bit about my second date is that I learnt something fundamental about myself, which I had forgotten in all the pandemic strangeness. I miss being with someone, kissing someone, and that maybe somewhere in my future there will be children. I never expected that and understanding this has surprised and got me thinking. Adam was again right. I am starting to understand that these dates are not about the destination, they are about the road I am travelling. They are about a journey, and I don't know where that might end up.

'I never thought I would be grateful to be dating again, but I am. Even though my first date was almost a disaster, I liked Alice, and the second one with Jules was unexpectedly revealing,' I say.

'You're welcome,' Adam says. He sits back in his chair with a broad satisfied smile on his face, as if his work here is done. 'I spoke to Alice. She said that you are the kind of guy that she would date, if she wasn't going out with someone.'

I will take that—only I am not sure I believe it. I have heard it once before from a girl I liked at university. She said almost the same thing, telling me that I was cute and that she would consider going out with me if she wasn't already with someone. It is like going for a job and being told that while you were not successful, they will 'consider you for future posts and keep your CV on file', to be saved in some folder and never looked at again.

'I hear your date with Juliette went well,' Adam says.

Was he smirking? Does everyone know everything about my dates? It is as though reports of my dates are being filed in real time to the WhatsApp group.

'I liked her, and yes, I can see you have heard, we did kiss, but that is as far as it went,' I say.

'Good for you. It absolutely doesn't matter if the date goes anywhere, if you're progressing.'

'I think I might be, which is a surprise. I'm not sure I saw it happening.'

'Good. I'd focus on your next date,' Adam says, and checks his phone, and smiles. 'You'll like her, I'm sure.'

'She is a friend of Sarah's so I'm worried. Are you going to tell me anything about her in advance this time?'

Adam looks at me and takes a deep breath. I can see his reluctance. Having set the rules, Adam doesn't like to change things. 'She is a lawyer, and her name is Miranda.'

I am wary about lawyers, I'm not sure why. Will we have anything to talk about? I am also worried that she probably got better A-Levels than me. Why I am worried about A-Levels almost seventeen years after taking them, I do not know. Adam must see my expression.

'Try not to read too much into that. People put too much stock in what people do for a living,' Adam says. 'It's a form of unconscious bias. We rule out people who we think are not like ourselves. In this case, you would rule out Miranda as she doesn't work in the media.'

I know Adam is right on this point. Should what we do define who we end up with? I have been guilty of this behaviour in the past, thinking I was helping myself by only going for people who did something like me, only was probably in reality engaged in a self-limiting act. I mean, look at me; I thought I would be a journalist until the end of my career. I considered myself a dyed-in-the-wool hack always looking for the next story until I reached a point where I realised I could no longer do it, and now I am happier than I have been in a long time, doing something completely different. Life changes in the moment.

'Well to be fair, neither do I,' I say.

'That is true—have you updated your CV to food services?' Adam thinks this is hilarious and laughs.

I am sure that my friends think running a café is not a proper career, and it is true that there is no room for pay rises or promotion. I don't care. I don't want a career. I even deleted my account on LinkedIn mostly on the basis that as a website it is almost entirely pointless, and no, I don't want to read your blog.

'Adam, I don't even have a CV anymore, I don't need it, and that is part of the point,' I say.

'A very good one too. I was joking, but seriously, though, I think it took real courage to change like that and to do something else. I think that's why more people don't do it. It's a success to celebrate. Let's drink to that.'

We raise our glasses and touch them together and take a drink. The two of us are quiet and reflective for a moment. I feel a sense of pride and achievement. I am glad to be out tonight; I have missed nights like these when we would sit in the pub, have a few drinks and our conversations were honest and unguarded.

'I could see you with Miranda,' says Adam.

'Really? Are you sure? I never saw myself with a Miranda. I remain open, though.'

'Glad to hear it.' Adam pats me on the shoulder. 'That's all you need to do. Oh, I should say that your date with Miranda will be quite short. She only had a small dating window.' Leaning forward, he adds, 'She's incredibly busy, which is not a big concern, but there is that.'

I process the words 'small dating window', and I wonder if she actually used those words, and I don't know why, but I think she did. I try to remain sanguine and tell myself that lawyers—like bankers—do seem to work hard. It reminds me of a funny tweet I saw where someone had made a play on the famous Mark Twain quote about how if you find a job you like, you never work a day in your life, only this one read 'If you find a job you like, work is all you will ever do'.

I am still thinking about this, about the differences between living to work and working to live, when Adam drops a small bomb on me.

'So, with that in mind, I have arranged a second date on the same day. I thought it might help you maintain your dating momentum. I realise it is upping the pace, but I think it will do you good,' he says.

He looks at me, gauging my reaction to the idea of two dates in one evening. I search my feelings for a moment as the idea sinks in. I have never been on two dates in a day, but if it increases the chance of meeting someone, then why not? One thing I never knew I needed in my life was dating momentum and yet here I am, moving into the dating fast lane with multiple dates on the same day.

'Okay, I'm game, and are you going to give me any details about date number four?' I ask.

Adam sits back, folds his hands in his lap, and offers a big smile. He looks tremendously pleased with himself.

'That's the other thing; date four is a mystery date. I thought it would be good to mix it up, a wild card so to speak. I can't tell you a name, and there won't be an email either, so no details. You'll have a little time between the two, and I'll text you a location.'

'How am I supposed to find this mystery date?'

'Oh, don't worry, she'll recognise you,' he says with a smile.

I can't help but feel Adam is enjoying this. What I don't understand is why the mystery. It makes me think that Adam is up to something, although I can't work out what. I wonder if she is someone I know, and my mind immediately jumps to Beth, and I feel a rush of blood to my head. I realise that I hope it is Beth, as I miss her, and I want to see her. I want to tell her that I think about her, that she often floats unbidden into my thoughts. More importantly, I want to say that I worry that if anything happened between us, I would screw it up, and that would be the end. That's what I want to say—only I am not sure that I can do it.

'That seems like an unfair advantage,' I say.

'Really, it isn't. There's nothing to worry about, and I promise you will enjoy this date. You really will, and I would love to tell you more, but I don't want to give anything away. Part of this dating experience is about finding the right kind of person, which is why you're meeting a range of people. Please, don't ask me to tell you anymore because I'm not going to,' Adam says.

Chapter Fourteen

'There She Goes'

I spend the night tossing and turning and thinking about my mystery date, or more to the point, thinking about Beth. It reignites my memories about that night after Marcus and Victoria's leaving London party.

At work the next day, I don't say anything to Julie in the café other than that I have two dates. One with a lawyer and the other being a mystery. Julie loved the idea of a mystery date and hit me with her speculation about the kind of person the enigma could be throughout the day. Without knowing it, her thoughts mirrored mine with one of her first suggestions.

'Imagine if it is someone from your past.'

'Why do you think it might be that?'

'Mystery girls are always from the past,' Julie said, pausing. 'I might watch too much Netflix.'

We both laughed at this, but TV plotlines or not, Julie had a point. It had to be the answer. Where else did mysteries come from? They were always unfinished business from your past. Her suggestion only confirmed what I had already been thinking: that my mystery date tonight was with Beth.

Before that, my first date tonight is with Miranda, and it is taking place in one of my favourite London locations. We're meeting at the 5th View café at Waterstones bookshop in Piccadilly. Even though this place is in the heart of London, I like the fact that it never gets too packed—primarily, I think, because you have to make it past Russian literature or military history on the fourth floor to get there. Not a big draw for passing tourists.

From there, it is a short walk across the river for my second date at the British Film Institute bar, which is another favourite bar, tucked away on London's Southbank. With its cosy couches and views across the water, it is a great dating destination. So, whoever my mystery second date is with tonight, they have chosen well. It must be I tell myself, Beth.

Waterstones Piccadilly is the best big bookshop in London, and a visit is worth it for the view across London's skyline alone. You rarely see the city this way and get to take in the Victorian rooftops, abbeys and statues, and glimpses of London's history mixed in with rising modernist glass towers.

This is the profile Adam has sent me, written by Sarah, along with the note telling me she only has thirty minutes. She sounds great, and it's a shame we only have a short time to chat when there is a lot to talk about.

Dating Profile:

Name: Miranda Franken

Age: 36 Height: 5'7 Build: Slim

Hair: Auburn Eyes: Green

Occupation: lawyer

General: Miranda is gorgeous and one of the cleverest people I know. One of her best qualities is her generosity of spirit. She's

> incredibly open and upfront and is a great listener. When you have a conversation with her, it feels like there is a connection taking place. That said, she will keep you on your toes, so make sure you bring your most brilliant self.
>
> Miranda is also hilarious and has a spiritual side that you wouldn't ordinarily suspect from a high-flying lawyer. She's very much into mysticism and New Age thinking. We met at a meditation and yoga retreat in Glastonbury.
>
> She is a keen runner, has run several marathons, and is also a former triathlon competitor. Make sure you mention your love of fitness and running.
>
> If Miranda ended up being the one, you'd be lucky. I'm super hopeful about this date. Keep me posted.

Like many people, I started to run more during the pandemic and graduated from being an occasional runner to someone who can drag themselves out on a regular basis. What I am not is enthusiastic about the activity, and I wish I were. I don't understand people who get joy from running mile after mile, although I'd like to be able to do that. If I ever wrote a book about the subject, I would call it *The Reluctant Runner*, which would feature the epigram: "Running is for the body, walking is for the soul."

As I make my way out of Piccadilly Tube station, it is almost six. I have five minutes before the date, and while I am just about on time, I am later than I'd like. I prefer to be there first, to get seated and comfortable. I feel less nervous about what is about to ensue. It means that when whoever it is I am meeting arrives, I can see them walk into the room and avoid the embarrassment of casting my eyes around trying to locate my date.

I make my way through the busy bookshop, full of women browsing and tourist couples with colourful rucksacks bumping into things. I climb the wide staircase and make my way to the fifth floor. At first, I am taking two stairs at a time and leaping ahead, as this is how I tackle stairs. However, I slow my pace, as I realise that I will be perspiring by the time I make it to the top. Not an attractive first impression.

There are a few empty seats on the top floor in the outer bar area, which has the air of an old theatre bar, dark and outfitted with soft, deep-red comfy benches and high-backed armchairs. I walk towards the main bar which, in stark contrast, is flooded with light, thanks to the floor-to-ceiling windows that look out over the roofs of Victoria and Westminster. It is a sunny day, and I can see clear across the city as I enter, and the top of the London Eye is just visible over the river.

Turning into the bar, which is humming with chirpy cocktail conversation, I scan the room, hoping to be first here. I am not. In the far corner of the room, tucked away with her back to the wall, is a slim woman sitting on her own. High cheekbones, and a sweep of auburn hair, that nestles on her shoulders. She is dressed in a sleeveless black top and black trousers. It must be Miranda, and she is striking to look at.

When my eyes reach her, she is already looking my way. She has seen me first. I feel exposed, as if she is wearing x-ray specs and gazes through me. Whatever it is she sees,

I am not sure she is enthralled. There is no smile, and if I had to describe her expression as our eyes meet across the room, it would be one of disappointment or even gloom.

I raise my hand, executing a half-wave, and do my best to smile as I walk towards her. Arriving at the table, I am awkward, and when I stop, I am not sure what to say by way of immediate introduction, so ask her name—almost, I realise, in the hope that the low-spirited expression that greets me does not belong to my date, Miranda, and instead to some similar looking random stranger, even though I know this not to be the case.

'Miranda?'

She looks up at me, giving me a further appraisal, and does not break a smile or exude any warmth of expression.

'Uh-huh,' is all she says.

'Tom; really nice to meet you,' I say, to which she nods.

Wedged next to the wall, the table Miranda has chosen is only big enough for two slim people. My chair is tucked in at a right angle to the wall, making squeezing in tricky.

Tangling my feet with the metal chair legs, my effort at taking a seat is a performance. Miranda still hasn't said anything, so I do what I always do in these situations and try to fill the conversational space with waffle.

'Sorry, I was a bit late,' I say. 'Usual nightmare on the tube. There was a massive crush at King's Cross. We sat there for ages.'

Miranda nods at this and offers no comment on my travel tribulations. The silence stretches, and it is excruciating. All other conversation in the bar fades away, and it is one of those moments when it feels like everyone around is tuned in. This, even though I know that no one is paying any attention to us.

'Shall we get a drink?' I ask.

I am hoping my suggestion will break the ice and help us navigate the freezing seas our date is battling, and spark some much-needed conversation. At the very least, we can discuss our drink choices.

However, this is not the way it turns out.

'Do you mind if we don't?' Miranda says.

For a second, for a beat or two, I think Miranda might have misheard. But she looks at me stony-faced, and the message I am receiving loud and clear is that there is nothing wrong with my hearing. This date started frostily and has now frozen over. Adam did say Miranda only had a small dating window, and the window is now, it seems, closed. I am amazed at this rapid rejection. It hits me that I am on the shortest date I've ever been on. This must be a dating record.

'Okay,' I manage.

'You're not my type,' Miranda says.

'Right.' At this point I should give up and leave, only I persevere. I want to hear the reason why. 'How's that?'

'You don't have an inner light, no spark,' Miranda says and shrugs. 'I know we won't get along, I'm an excellent judge, and in my experience, if there is no spark in the first thirty seconds then there will never be one.'

I am at a loss for words. *I have no inner light?* I find myself mutely nodding and trying to work out what to do with this information.

'I thought I looked pretty much like my picture,' I say by way of reply.

'Oh, you do, it's a good picture. The thing is, you can't tell from pictures or Zoom calls. You don't have the right kind of energy that I'm looking for.'

'Got it… So, you can tell this just by looking?'

'I can,' Miranda says.

At this point, my fight has gone. If I had a white flag, I would raise it. I am officially on the world's shortest date. Was that even two minutes? It might have been less. I think you get longer if you go speed-dating. This is like ultra-dating: one look, no hello, then a goodbye.

'Well, I think I might get a drink.' I say this, half thinking that as the date is over, we might sit and chat for half an hour in a platonic way. Miranda has other ideas, and she looks at her watch, and no doubt thinking of her dating window.

'Well, enjoy your drink. I am a little short on time—I did tell Adam—so if you don't mind, I'm going to go,' she says.

Before I even have the chance to reply, Miranda, without another word, is on her feet. She squeezes delicately between the two tables and gives me a blank nod. The kind you might give to a passing acquaintance in the street. This is the extent of her goodbye.

Miranda walks out of the bar. She does not glance over her shoulder, and then she is gone. My date is over.

I'm speechless, and I sit there stunned by what has happened. I feel like a complete loser, and even more so as I found Miranda attractive, and given we had a few things in common we could at least have had a conversation. What did Sarah say in the notes she gave Adam? That Miranda was '*open, and… a great listener*' and that '*when you have a conversation with her, it feels like there is a connection taking place*'. There was tonight no sign of any connection being made.

My second date is not until 7.15p.m., and I time to kill before I need to start walking in the direction of Jubilee Bridge to the Southbank.

A waiter comes by, and I order myself a beer. Drinking on my own in bars isn't something I do, but tonight I need a beer. This is why I hate dating. Profiles can be so deceptive. They sound promising, but the reality can be light years away. No amount of algorithmic profile-matching could ever have predicted tonight's outcome. On the plus side, there is no way my second date can be as bad as this. *The only way is up*, I tell myself.

My beer arrives, and I down it quickly while reading Twitter on my phone. I then have what I am sure is a dumb idea, only I can't help myself. I hadn't planned to note any of these dating experiences on social media, but since I've been on the shortest date ever, I feel like saying something.

This is never a good mindset to approach social media. It is, however, too late for that. An idea has formed in my head. This date, I convince myself, must be worth reporting to the world. I a quick tweet:

> I have just been on the shortest date ever. Less than two minutes. Her name was Miranda, and she said I did not possess an inner light. She left before we ordered drinks and did not say goodbye. #ShortestDateEver

I read the words over, and then hit send, not bothering to see if anything happens as I fully expect nothing will. Putting my phone in my pocket, I finish my beer and leave the bar, before heading down into the interior of the bookshop and the fiction section on the first floor. If nothing else, buying a book always cheers me up when I'm feeling down.

A few people are sitting in the scattered armchairs, and a dozen or so more are shelf-surfing. With no author destination in mind, I start drifting from display table to display table and stop at American Contemporary. Then I look up—and do a double-take.

There's Beth.

She's across the room, standing by a table of contemporary women's fiction, holding a book. I forgot she works nearby. It is the first time I have seen her in a long time. She is dressed in a black tea dress; her blonde hair is much longer than I remember. It is like post-lockdown hair that she has rolled with. It is down to her shoulders, and it suits her, she looks great.

I remember how Beth and I talked about books when we first met, and how *Wuthering Heights* was a novel that we both loved. We re-read it together, discussing it as we went. After that book, we continued to choose other books taking it in turns to pick, and without even thinking about it, we formed Beth and Tom's private book club. I miss that as well.

I find myself looking at Beth, smiling. Then experience a terrible sinking feeling as I realise Beth is not my mystery date. I am lost for a moment in thought, and my mind is swimming. If not Beth, then who? I have no idea.

I consider two options. 1) To stay and say what needs to be said; or 2) to leave. Despite obsessing and thinking through what I could say to Beth, the first thought that pops uninvited into my head is to do the latter; to turn around and leave before she sees me. That way I can avoid any difficult conversation. Running is not the answer, but I cannot bring myself to say what I need to. Besides, after so much time has passed, I'm not sure Beth would even want to hear it.

I steel myself, take a breath, and walk towards Beth. She doesn't look up, and I stand by the table, almost alongside her, before she notices me. She is holding a copy paperback copy of *The Year of Magical Thinking*, which strikes me as a perfect title for the days in which we have been living because we need, perhaps, some magic in our lives. I could definitely do with some now.

'Any good?' I ask.

Beth looks up, half smiling before she sees who is speaking.

'Oh, look who it is,' she says.

Thrown off-balance by her hostility, I force a smile and try to recover. At the very least, I want to tell her that it is good to see her, as it is. I feel good, even after what happened in the bar with Miranda. Seeing Beth after all this time, despite how we left things and how I let it drift, has lifted my mood no end. I am unsure where to start, so I go with the facts.

'I dropped round recently,' I say.

I am not sure why I say this. I think maybe only to find out if she was in that day and watching me via the Ring camera in her doorbell.

'I must have been out,' Beth says. 'What was it you wanted?'

That is the question, isn't it? I start slowly and with some kind of truth.

'I miss you,' I say.

Beth gauges me, and I know what I've said has fallen short of what I need to say. But now that I am here, I have no words—my ability to express myself, be bold, and make that leap of faith has gone. I am back to worrying about what would happen now if she rejected me. If Beth has changed her mind and no longer feels the same. I swerve and, sensing that I have nothing else of importance to add, an annoyed expression flicks across Beth's face.

'Well, I'm sorry about that,' says Beth. 'What are you doing here, anyway? It's a bit unlike you these days to actually go anywhere, isn't it?'

This remark stings, and I suppose it should. It reminds me how I have hidden away since the pandemic started and until now not left my local area.

How small my world has become, is the thought that strikes me.

'I was on a date,' I say.

'And where's your date?' Beth asks.

'She left pretty much as soon as I arrived,' I say.

'Well, maybe she didn't like what she heard,' Beth says.

A sharp, wincing pain strikes me. I feel as if my heart has been skewered. I know she is talking about us, and I know she has every right to respond in this way.

'I don't think I was her type.'

'Well, dating is difficult, isn't it?'

'I have another date,' I say, glancing at my watch. 'In a little while. It's a mystery date, and I thought it might be with you.'

Beth stares back at me and looks mystified. 'What on earth would make you think that?'

I start to speak, say something, only it is more of a mumble, and I trail off, standing there opposite Beth. I cannot say anything else, and we are silent, left with the sound of pages being turned, books being placed on piles, a hush of voices, in the quiet of Modern Fiction. When she finally speaks, she does so with an oblique response.

'I have to go,' she says.

I am desperate to claw something back, and I blurt out my following line without any thought. 'Maybe we could get a coffee some time?'

'Will it be on the house?' Beth asks.

I'm puzzled for a second or two before I comprehend what she means, and when I answer, I feel like a complete idiot.

'I was thinking of somewhere else,' I say.

Beth nods at this information. 'I'm sure our paths will cross at some point.'

Before I can say anything else, a middle-aged tourist with a salt-and-pepper beard, and round-rimmed glasses stops at our display table. He picks up a book and starts to read the back cover. I am far more annoyed by him, at his interloping, than I have any right to be. He looks up and smiles at the two of us, and I glare at him. He theatrically recoils, says 'excuse me,' rather tartly in a German accent and leaves. After scaring away a tourist, I find I do have to say something.

'Look, I wanted to say—' is as far as I get before Beth butts in.

'Yes, Tom, what *is* it you want to say?'

This is my chance, and I am about to blow it. I cannot say what I need. It is too hard. I cannot bring myself to talk about my feelings, and the problem is, when you remove those from the equation, when you boil it down and once the vapour has cleared, you aren't left with much. You don't have enough words left to say anything meaningful. So instead, I make a mess of it, and this seems to come as no surprise to Beth.

'I thought we could hang out sometime,' I say.

Beth looks at me blankly, wondering, perhaps if I uttered that sentence, which fell so short of what was needed.

'Is that really what you thought after all this time? Goodbye, Tom.'

With that, Beth turns on her heels and leaves. I swear, tonight, all I have done is watch women walk away from me.

Watching Beth go, I realise I miss her more every moment, and I can see no way of getting back to her.

Chapter Fifteen

'Two Doors Down'

In a partial daze, I linger for a short while in the fiction department after Beth leaves. I feel as if the air has been let out of my body; I am physically deflated and replaying our conversation. Why did I tell her that I thought she might be my mystery date? It was so lame and weak that I am embarrassed.

I check my watch. I have thirty minutes until my actual mystery date, and I am considering leaving the bookshop and heading home. At least there, I can collapse on the couch with a beer and watch *Gilmore Girls* and feel sorry for myself. I am edging towards this plan of standing up my mystery date when I mentally slap myself. I've done enough staying at home, and it would mean standing someone up. That is a horrible thing to do to someone, which I know I would hate to happen to me. So why would I do it to someone else?

I walk out of Waterstones and loiter on the street as people stream by. Beth is long gone, and I stand for a little longer before I move off. I turn into Jermyn Street and walk past the men's tailors and shops selling expensive men's shirts and skirt the edges of Trafalgar Square where tourists are sitting on Nelson's lions, taking pictures in the dazzling evening sunlight.

I climb the steps to Jubilee Bridge and start to make my way across the river. The sunshine has brought the crowds out and the bridge is thronging with people, many of whom are heading the same way, to the bars and restaurants of the Southbank. With its slender steel beams and cables rising along its length, the bridge, running alongside the railway line, looks like part of a great ship that has been moored in the middle of the river.

It is only a short walk to the BFI bar along the bustling riverfront, and I remain at a loss, still feeling discombobulated after my surprise encounter with Beth. A date, a surprise encounter and now a mystery date are almost more than I can bear for one evening. However, as I close on the bar, I find myself perking up. Whatever happens next cannot possibly match the first part of my evening for its sheer awfulness.

Through the main entrance, I make my way to the bar area and start to look around. I have no idea who I am looking for having now firmly established that my mystery date is not Beth. I order a beer at the bar and find myself a seat on a plush orange sofa. It is so good to be back here. I used to love this bar with its jumble of comfy couches and soft lamplights, giving it a relaxed nineteen seventies vibe and making it an ideal bar for a date.

I sip my beer and check my phone, continuing to glance around the bar. I see no one who looks like my date, but then I have no idea what it is I am looking for. I open Twitter again and wish I had not done so. My *#ShortestDateEver* tweet has already received a dozen likes, and a few comments and people are retweeting it. I am not sure how I feel about this. I had thought that it would attract nothing more than tumbleweed like most of my tweets. One of the comments simply says, '*This is not a nice*

Tweet', and another says, '*I feel sorry for Miranda*'. I consider deleting the tweet for a moment and decide not to because this is about as much attention as it is likely to get. People move on so quickly on social media, and I cannot imagine anyone remembering my *#ShortestDateEver* tweet come morning.

I flick to Instagram and am scrolling my feed when I look up and see a woman standing at the bar, looking my way, and smiling. And just like that, I time travel and tumble back to university. Audrey was one of the coolest girls I ever met and for some reason, she liked me enough to go out with me, for a short time, at least. Despite this, when I think about her, the word that springs most to mind is 'unobtainable'. Even when I was with her, she felt that way, as if she was slipping away almost as soon as we started to date. Back then, with her Louise Brooks haircut, a hint of an American accent from her mother, and her revolutionary left-wing politics, she did things her way. Causes and struggles, placards and slogans, Audrey was a member of one of those tiny left-wing groups forever leafleting, and for a while, I was a fellow traveller. More moderate than Audrey, though left-wing enough not to offend her political sensibilities. She made it clear that she drew the line at dating Tories, or almost as bad, Lib Dems.

The sleek, sharp bob cut is gone, and her brown hair is tied back in a ponytail, although not much else has changed. Audrey gives a shake of her head as if she cannot quite believe it is me. I know how she feels, and I only hope this is the mystery solved.

I am not sure if it is only me, but isn't there often one person in new couples who likes the other more? So, they are never even, not quite equal. They like you enough to date you, but it always feels like they're holding back. That was what it was like being with Audrey.

We only went out for a few months in our second year at university before she dumped me. I did not take it well. She said I was 'petit bourgeois', and had no real commitment to the revolution, which was, of course, true. I thought turning up to the odd meeting, handing out leaflets and going with her on a couple of demonstrations was more than enough. It wasn't. This, despite me also standing outside Sainsbury's with her and a few others shouting 'Get your copy of *Socialist Power*' at disinterested shoppers.

I wonder if she has changed and if her politics still guide her romances? I am guessing that they no longer do by the fact she is walking towards me.

Audrey is dressed casually in jeans and a stripy blue top with a cream jacket. She looks smart and, I don't know, grown-up? Is that what the change is? University is a long time gone, and this isn't the girl I dated all that time ago. This is the grown-up woman.

She stops in front of the couch, and I find myself standing, noticing as I do that her eyes are as green as I remember them.

'It's so good to see you, Tom,' she says.

'You too, long time. Can I just check that you are here to meet me? I am supposed to be on a mystery date.'

'I am your mystery date.'

I am confused and delighted. I don't understand any of it. How can Audrey be here?

'That is such a relief. Let me get you a drink. What can I get you?'

I get Audrey a glass of red wine from the bar and sit down next to her on the couch, where she begins to answer my questions, and tell me how this date came about.

'I bumped into Adam randomly maybe a month ago, and he mentioned you and what he was planning. I said I'd love to see you again, and I always regretted how I treated you at the end. I took myself way too seriously, was intense about everything, and frankly, I was an asshole to you,' Audrey says.

When she says this, it makes me think about the ways that people change, and how, as we grow up, and our beliefs in certain causes and our values evolve. Audrey was one of those who had a naturally rebellious heart and could galvanise people—she loved megaphones and a slogan and knew how to use them well.

'We were all pretty serious at times, I seem to remember,' I say.

'At times, but I was so full of politics that I found it hard to see anything else.'

'And now?'

'It all seemed so important, and I am sure some of it was. I'm not sure what we achieved. Don't get me wrong, I enjoyed every minute, and I don't have any regrets, but what I do have are a couple of people I idly wonder about. That's why I'm here, as you've always been one of them. You were always nice to me, even after,' she says.

'Really? I always thought I was too eager to please.'

When I say this, the words float out of my mouth without much thought, and they prove to be self-revealing and characterise my time with Audrey. Like a puppy, I would have done almost anything, and I don't think anyone wants that. That's how relationships end up being one-sided, isn't it?

Audrey assures me that this was not the case, and it is a reminder that how we see ourselves is often not how others see us at all.

'Don't be so hard on yourself,' she says.

We park the past there and make our way to the present like two explorers with torches, sharing stories, to light the way ahead. We exchange mini-biographies and career highlights in the decade or so since university. After working as a campaigner for various charities, I am not surprised to learn that Audrey has found herself working for the World Food Programme in London.

'After I left Bristol and did an MA in Manchester, I knew what I wanted to do. That's when I fell out of politics. You'll love this bit. I got thrown out of Socialist Power for being ideological soft,' Audrey says.

'They kicked you out? You sold so many papers.'

'I know! And I called you petit bourgeois,' Audrey laughs.

'True story,' I say.

'I'm sorry. To be honest it was a relief. I realised I'd done my time, and I wanted to do something where I could help people, which is what matters most to me.'

Audrey was always fighting and was always going to do good, one way or another, and now she is making a real difference rather than playing politics. Although I am aware that this hindsight-driven view is laughable in its predictability and would find no favour with our more youthful selves.

'I'm more than impressed,' I say. 'In comparison, all I can say is that I make good coffee.'

'It sounds like what you've done is build something, and books and coffee rate very highly on my list of things that are good about the world and worth living for,' Audrey says.

To me, this sounds like a generous compliment and one I am happy to take. Besides, I do genuinely feel the same about books and coffee.

After a couple of drinks, it is like the years since we last saw each other have fallen away. We could be sitting now, as we did then, in some bar in Bristol, talking the night away. Unlike then, I do now like to get some food instead of just drink. I am reticent to suggest this in case Audrey has other plans, and my suggestion brings our evening to a rapid halt.

'Do you want to get some food?'

'You read my mind,' Audrey says.

'The food is pretty good here.'

'I have something else in mind.'

Little more than thirty minutes later, we are back at my flat, arriving only a few minutes before the pizza. I am in the kitchen opening a bottle of red wine, while Audrey is putting on some music.

'You've been making mixtapes?' she calls.

I walk from the kitchen into the lounge, hand Audrey her wine, and explain my lockdown hobby.

'I'm impressed and somehow saddened that I never got a mixtape,' she says.

'Well, you have arrived at just the right time. I have both the ancient equipment and mad mixtape skills. I can't promise anything, but you might find yourself in possession of a tape at some point very soon. Of course, I'm guessing that you will need to find something to play it on,' I say.

'As much as I hate to say it, that's what Amazon is for, right?'

Audrey rifles through the tapes before finding one she likes, and she holds it up to me. It would be that tape, wouldn't it; the mixtape that I made for Beth, with its list of carefully written song titles. I think Audrey is going to comment on it, but she doesn't.

'This one okay?'

'Works for me,' I say.

Audrey turns on the stereo and drops the tape in. There is that satisfying clunk and hiss of cassette tape as the music kicks in with the Bright Eyes song 'First Day of My Life', and he is singing about how things are different now.

We sit on the floor, leaning back against the couch, drinking wine, and eating our pizza, and it reminds me of one night, at uni, sitting on the floor of a crowded bar when there were no seats. It is the kind of thing that neither of us would consider now. We would be more worried about getting our clothes dirty or being told to move.

I am not sure how many drinks in we are when it happens, and when it does, it feels like a natural progression of the evening—as if we were always heading in this direction. There is a moment when we are talking, when I turn to her, waiting for her to reply, only Audrey doesn't say anything. Instead, she looks back at me, and it is a look that says, *if you are going to kiss me, then now is the moment.* I tilt my head and move it towards hers, and I am relieved to know that I have not made a mistake. Our lips touch, and we kiss, and we kiss unhurriedly and as if we have all the time in the world. It is a kiss that is new and fresh, yet familiar at the same time.

It is as though we exist in two places, the past and present, and those memories are carrying us forward. Our slow kisses gather pace and we move closer and hold each other, our hands starting to explore.

I lift my lips from Audrey's and come up for air. I suppose, given that it has been so long, and this night has come out of nowhere, I want to check that this is okay. Audrey must be reading my mind as she asks me the same question.

'So, what next?' she asks.

I stand and offer out my hand. Audrey stands too, and we hold each other and kiss again and sway to the music as Damien Rice sings 'I Don't Want To Change You'. We dance out the song, and the next one begins to play as, still holding hands, we turn and walk to the bedroom. We undress each other and fall onto the bed. Our lips touch, and I start to move my lips over her body.

In the morning, when I wake, the first thing I notice is that Audrey isn't there. I check my watch. It is early, not even six thirty. For a moment, I think I dreamt the whole thing. Did I somehow manage to conjure Audrey out of the past and reimagine her in the present? It seems almost as likely as Audrey and I sleeping together. It is then that I hear movement coming from the lounge, and I smile in relief. The good news is that I did not lose my mind in lockdown, and I guess that Audrey has been to the loo or is making coffee. My mind then begins to race off, sprinting through the rest of the day, and wondering if we can have breakfast together and meet up again later. Whatever happens, I know I want to see Audrey again.

She walks into the room, and it is at this point that reality hits. The first word that pops into my mind is 'unobtainable'. It is what I thought yesterday when I remembered when we first went out, and I am thinking of that word again, because Audrey is fully dressed. Not only is she dressed, but she also has her jacket on and is ready to leave. I sit up in bed, and I am about to get out when Audrey holds up her hand.

'I am really sorry about this, and you will hate me,' she says.

'Okay, I'm a little confused...' I say.

'I wasn't entirely honest with you—or Adam when I met him. I should have said that I will not be in London for much longer,' Audrey says.

'How much longer, exactly?' I ask.

'I got a job with the food programme in New York. I'm transferring and flying at the weekend. It's closer to my mom, who I miss,' Audrey says, sounding more American by the second.

'It's Friday,' I say, and don't ask me why, but I feel the need to state the obvious.

'I know, and I did say you are going to hate me, but I wanted to see you, and—'

'Don't say it.'

Surprised, she asks: 'What?'

'I think you are about to tell me that you owed me last night,' I say.

Audrey laughs hard at this. 'God, no. I would never do that. I don't owe you anything. A chance came my way to see someone I liked a lot once, and I wanted to take it. Life doesn't always do that; you need to grab it while you can.'

I feel a shift, something stirs when Audrey says this, and I am not sure what it is. She's right though, you need to do that.

'That's a huge relief. I enjoyed last night,' I say.

'Me too.' Audrey says. 'I loved seeing you, and I want to be honest now; I have no idea when or if I will be back.'

I nod at this. I do feel hurt, only I don't feel that bad. I always liked Audrey, and spending time with her has been one of the best things that has happened to me in a long time. That does cushion the blow that she is about to walk out of my flat and back out of my life like a guest appearance from the cast of the Ghosts of Girlfriends Past.

I get out of bed, and I don't care what happens next only I want to kiss her again. I stand in front of her, pause, waiting for permission almost, and Audrey smiles, and leans forward. I put my arms around her, and we kiss.

And then it is time to go. I pull on some jeans and walk Audrey out of the flat. We stand on my doorstep, and she leans forward to give me a goodbye kiss.

'I'd still really love that mixtape, if that isn't too much,' Audrey says.

'I do love making mixtapes, so I am afraid I will probably make it for you,' I say.

'Thank you, and if you're ever in New York, then find me.'

I have a fleeting thought about that, and I wonder if I will ever be in New York, if I will ever leave London, and then the thought is gone, and I am waving goodbye to Audrey, as she turns onto the street. I watch her walk in the direction of the tube station. I stand there a while longer until I can no longer see her, and then I close the door.

Chapter Sixteen

'Cornerstone'

After saying goodbye to Audrey, I shower and get ready for work. It is only when I am out of the shower that I check my phone and notice that I have numerous WhatsApp messages, including from my sister and Adam, as well as too many Twitter notifications to count.

In a panic I check Twitter, and to my dismay I find that my *#ShortestDateEver* tweet has gone viral and not in a good way. There are thousands of likes and retweets. The hashtag is trending, as is the name, Miranda. There are hundreds and hundreds of comments as well, most of which do not have nice things to say about me. I'm struggling to work out what has happened. I could not repeat the success of this tweet if I tried. Most days it is hard enough to get a single 'like'.

I reread what I posted, and I am bewildered. It was the most innocuous of tweets. I didn't say anything mean or derogatory. It was a description of our date, which like my tweet, was barely 280 characters in length.

It is only as I scroll down the comments that I find a tweet from Miranda. This is what she has written:

> You are an absolute arsehole. I feel violated by what you've done to me. I was

> honest and nice to you, and this is how you repay me? You've humiliated me with your tweet. Never contact me again. Men like you shouldn't be dating anyone. #WorstDateEver

Somehow from my harmless tweet, Miranda has taken a great offence. She has let rip on Twitter and done so with a tweet so packed with invective that it has exploded my timeline. Her words have attracted roving rent-a-trolls and legions of angry online users who seem to spend most of their time hanging around and waiting for a pile-on to take place. Then there are the people who revel in misfortune, and delight in schadenfreude, and feel the need to chime in with comments such as 'Lol', 'ha ha ha', or 'no one is going to date you now, mate', and 'what a pariah'. I am most offended by that last comment, as only a couple of weeks ago, my friends were calling me a hermit, and now I'm a pariah. How does that even happen? I am having a Kafkaesque moment.

I am struggling to see how can the #ShortestDateEver can be the #WorstDateEver? There wasn't enough date material there to make anyone conclude this. If we'd had a drink and chatted for a while longer, then I could understand. That never happened; all I had time for was to say hello, and by then, Miranda was already leaving. It was a case of hello and goodbye.

Last night is proving to have been a whirlwind of women in my life from Miranda to Beth and Audrey.

I am baffled. All I can conclude from #ShortestDateEver is that I do not understand social media or understand women.

I think 'nice' is being generous. 'Blunt' sounds like a better description of our brief encounter. Even I would stay for at least one drink. Hell, I'd stay for two without too much arm-twisting if the conversation was flowing. I enjoy swapping stories, to hear how others are faring in the dating trenches.

I am also wondering how Miranda could feel 'violated'? Miranda might not be the most common of names, but there have to be quite a few of them out there. There is no way that anyone could have attributed my tweet to this particular Miranda, the lawyer. Even the best of investigators would have trouble connecting her to my inoffensive tweet. That said, I suppose it is a moot point. After our date, she must have checked my Twitter account to see if I'd written anything and then responded with both barrels, no mercy and no social media prisoners taken.

I stop reading the replies after a while. There are too many, and they are making me angry, and I need to get to work.

As I leave the flat, I check Twitter one last time, and the tweets are still rolling in. I shut the door behind me and begin my walk when my phone rings. It is Adam. It isn't even seven thirty. He must have seen my tweet and will want to know what happened with my double-date night.

'You've gone viral,' Adam says.

He does not sound disappointed, and I am sure that he is delighted by what has happened to me. This is the perfect material for his book. If I had only gone on one date, it would have generated little material. I have gone on four dates now, and three was all it took to go viral.

'I don't understand it,' I say. 'My date with Miranda was really a chance for her to see me in the flesh and hit the reject button. I barely said a word.'

'Sarah did say she could be picky.'

'Funnily enough, no one mentioned that.'

'Look, it's a process; people like what they like. Not every date will work out. Now tell me about your mystery date,' Adam says, and I can feel how pleased he is with himself; it is as if his achievement with Audrey is wafting down the line.

'I will give you that you really pulled an ace out of the pack. You know I always had a thing for Audrey, so you have my gratitude. It was good to see her; it was the best evening I've had in so long. Unfortunately for you, and your book, one thing she omitted to tell you is she's moving back to New York, like, in a couple of days.'

'You're kidding, I thought she might be the one.'

I nod at this. I thought the same thing at one point. However, Audrey remains what she always was, unobtainable, and on our date, we were those two proverbial ships passing in the night.

'Same. She's still Audrey, and it was kind of wonderful to see her again. So, thank you,' I say.

Despite being zero for four, rejected out of hand by my third date, suffering a next-level bad encounter with Beth, and being the subject of a social media viral pile-on, I am hopeful about what happens next. I know a lot of that is down to Audrey. It makes me want to get on a plane to New York and not come back, although I know as soon as I arrived any magic the two of us had recaptured from the past would swiftly die. Our night together is over, it came with a time stamp and the clock has run down, and I'm okay with that.

'You're welcome, and I'm glad to hear you're still sounding positive,' Adam says.

'Yeah, it was a rollercoaster of an evening because you know who else I saw?'

There is a pause on the other end of the line, which is weird, and I can't quite work out why.

'Who did you see?'

'I saw Beth—although she wasn't that over the moon to see me.'

'Well, hopefully your date with Audrey made up for that,' Adam says.

I'm surprised he doesn't want to talk about it more and interrogate me on the encounter. I mean come on. It has been almost 18-months since Beth and I last saw each other, and yet nothing.

'It did. Look, I'd better go,' I say. 'I'm almost at work. There is coffee to make.'

I hang up on Adam and enter the café. The lights are on, and Julie is busying herself behind the counter. Before I get a chance to greet her in French, she jumps right in and cuts straight to English.

'I am sure you do have an inner light,' she says.

I laugh. I am sure I do, too; I am sure that we all do. It is sometimes just a case of finding it. 'Thank you. If only you could help me convince Twitter.'

Julie giggles. 'It's why I so rarely go on the internet.'

I look at her with an inquiring smile as I try to square the circle that Julie's words so obviously suggest. 'And yet you still saw it on Twitter?'

'*Mais bien sûr*. Everyone looks at Twitter.'

She appears to be correct. After all, even Miranda, who is more concerned with inner lights than algorithms, is on Twitter.

As the morning wears on, the café fills up. A variety of mums arrive, ranging from those who look like they made it with some degree of difficulty, dragging reluctant toddlers in tow, to those with sleeping babies who look to be enjoying motherhood's occasional quiet moments. A couple of dads pop in with small children, too. I recognise one, and I give him a slight nod and say hello as he walks in with his young son. It is the guy who I saw playing guitar in the bar, as I made my way to Allison's that night. I always wonder what his story is.

Julie and I often speculate about customers, wondering how their lives came to be as they are. The café is like a fishbowl, where all life is displayed, and some lives appear more interesting than others.

Some of the work-from-home regulars arrive and sit down with their laptops, their eyes darting around for the tables closest to power points. Then I see Beryl enter. A slight woman in her late fifties, Beryl has short grey hair, and is always stylishly dressed, and is one of our best customers. She's also someone that I do know more than a little about—she writes crime fiction about a middle-aged female detective and is a *Sunday Times* bestseller. Her main character is a bossy British police officer, a Cockney cross between Jane Tennison and Miss Marple, who rose through the ranks in London's East End and has spent thirty years battling male prejudice.

Beryl started turning up at the café as soon as it opened, introducing herself and her work that, yes, you can also purchase right here. She is on book five and likes to write here in the café. She even mentioned it in an interview. '*I love the books, the people, and the bustle of the Shakespeare Café. I wrote the end of this book sitting there. I urge you to do the same.*'

Beryl likes to chat, and even someone like me, who does their best to avoid conversation, has not escaped. I have given myself over to it and accepted that when running a café, there are some people who you must embrace.

Beryl has the oldest laptop of anyone who comes to the café. It is a substantial old machine that makes a right racket. Its keyboard clatters like an aged train coming down the tracks. It is the closest thing in the computing age to a typewriter. I wondered why she put up with it, and once asked if she had ever considered upgrading.

'This is my lucky laptop,' Beryl said. 'I am going to type on it until it goes up in smoke.'

Today, Beryl gives me a wave and takes her usual window seat in front of one of the bookcases. Julie is about to walk over and take her order when I tell her I'll go.

'Are you sure? You know she likes to chat in the mornings,' Julie says.

'Beryl's my favourite customer,' I declare.

Julie gives an amused chuckle. 'I never knew you had a favourite customer.'

'Just the one.'

I straighten my blue waist apron that I have taken to wearing in the café, and walk over. Julie bought the aprons for everyone and had them embroidered with 'Shakespeare Café'. I was reluctant to wear it at first, never seeing myself as an apron-wearer. However, I now like to wear it and consider it part of my essential work uniform, part of my working shield. During the day, I never take it off. So much so that I have left the café still wearing it, and only noticed when someone pointed this out to me in the street.

'Morning, Beryl,' I say. 'How's the writing going?'

The writer sucks in air and shakes her head. 'I am at a tricky stage. Martha,' who is Beryl's detective, 'has always been on her own, and in this book, I wanted to give her a man. Not for sex, but someone to be with, in a platonic way. A special person with whom she has a deep connection. My editor isn't keen on the idea. She wants me to stick to the crime. Nice tweet by the way,' Beryl adds with a chuckle.

I offer my hands out: is there anyone who does not know? Beryl is on social media and does lots of promotional work for her books, although I didn't think she paid much attention to it beyond that. It does, as she has told me, become a significant distraction.

'Oh, you saw that,' I say whilst completing a semi-theatrical step backwards with a hand on my hip.

'I think everyone did. I try to keep up with the zeitgeist. I've got TikTok in my latest book. My publicist has suggested I do one of those TikTok pointing videos. I must say, I'm quite keen,' Beryl says. 'My real interest, though, is how criminals use it. They love social media. It's the wild west of endless scams.'

'So, what do you think?'

Leaning forward, she looks up at me as if sharing a secret: 'There are some angry people out there. It's illuminating reading the comments. Can I offer you some advice?'

There was me thinking it was the barista's job to offer sage advice to customers they come to know through careful observation. I am nervous about saying yes, for some reason—perhaps because I'm afraid of what Beryl might say. It is as if the advice of strangers will be more penetrating because they see you in a different context to those who know you well.

Seeing that I am hesitant, Beryl smiles reassuringly and touches my hand. It is a soft, protective pat and one to usher away any troubles. It is as if she has been waiting to offer me this advice for a long time.

'I like to tell people to follow their heart, that's all. Often, it is the heart that leads them in the right direction. If they're listening,' she says. 'What does yours say, Tom?'

My face heats when Beryl says this. I think it is the mention of the heart. I feel exposed and transparent. It is as if this customer has seen straight through me, like I am made of glass, and my failings and faults are illuminated. Each small crack and all the tiny chips that I have picked up along the way.

'I'm not sure I know how to do that,' I say. I'm surprised by that. It doesn't sound at all like me. Or maybe it is a revealing moment of honesty plucked from the shield behind which I hide.

'Oh, I'm sure you do, you just have to tune in, and then you will hear just what you need,' Beryl says.

Is it that simple? I wonder. Is that all you need to do? Is all I need to do on my upcoming dates a matter of adjusting the frequency to be on the right wavelength?

I smile at Beryl and begin the process of batting off such thoughts, shimmying away from the awkward feelings that they conjure up from inside. As I said, I am not sure that is me. Besides, I need to get Beryl her coffee. She has a book to write.

'I'll get your coffee. The usual?' I ask.

'The usual.'

Chapter Seventeen

'Talk Tonight'

I'm on my way to Islington to have dinner with my sister Sarah, and I must admit to being apprehensive. Something is going on, and I have no idea what it could be. When she suggested dinner, I was almost sure it was a figure of speech and not something she planned to follow through with. Sarah not only followed through, but did so swiftly, which is a new development. She messaged me a time and place and booked a table. True to form, she did quip in her message, 'don't worry, I'm paying'.

Works for me, besides, I am sure I will pay in other ways. Sarah will no doubt enjoyed my #WorstDateEver debacle along with everyone else. I have a slight breather of a few days before my next date, which isn't a date as such but, in Adam's words, 'a dating experience'. It's a speed dating event that Adam has organised as part of the research for his book. We're all Adam's guinea pigs, now.

Sarah and I have spent quite a bit of time talking over the last year although much of that was via video calls. It is rare for us to have dinner like this.

I take the tube to Highbury & Islington and walk half-way down Upper Street until I come to the French restaurant, which sits beneath an ornate-looking copper-brown building that looks as if it might have once been a department store many decades ago.

When I arrive, my sister is already there, and I can see her sitting at a window table. There is a bottle of white wine on ice by her table, and she has a glass in front of her. She doesn't notice me from the street, watching her as I walk past. Inside, a waiter in a shirt and waistcoat asks if he can help me, and I point towards Sarah. He nods at me, smiles, and moves off. The busy tables are full of young couples all leaning close and talking in muted tones, and middle-aged diners chatting about the day.

'You look like you've been here for a while,' I tell her as I sit down.

Sarah smiles and looks cheerful. She pours wine and waits for me to take a drink. The wine is a delight on my lips when I taste it—chilled, clean, and crisp.

'Good choice, this is delicious,' I say.

'Good, isn't it? Jack hates wine. Hates it.'

As an opening gambit, this was not how I imagined the evening beginning. I am always surprised that Sarah complains about her long-term fiancé to me, and so often. It is the one thing about which she is indiscreet. If Jack were here too, she would still do it, and I am sure he would laugh it off like wiping rain from his face. I had wanted to dive straight in and find out what is up with Sarah, but I am getting the feeling that I should tread carefully.

'That's a healthy attitude. I'm sure you can find something else you like drinking together to ensure future matrimonial harmony,' I say.

'Oh, I rather had another solution in mind.'

'So much for young love.'

'Talking of young love—I mean Miranda—I feel I should apologise. I did tell Adam she could be frosty.'

'Adam said picky.'

'Well, that too. Look, to be honest, I did not hold out much hope for the two of you, but she is very attractive, and I thought you might be able to swing it. I did put that on my first draft of her dating profile for you, but Adam changed it to "super hopeful".'

Sarah gives a shrug, and I shake my head. I wonder what Adam is playing at?

'I will take that as a vote of confidence, but there was no way on earth I was ever going to be able to swing that. She wanted to leave almost as soon as I arrived, and you know what happened next.'

'OMG. I couldn't believe it. I don't even know how people go viral, and then you come along, and I still don't know,' Sarah says.

'I know, right? How is it possible? I have no clue.'

From there I fill her in on my date with Audrey, and skip any mention of Beth as it is a subject I don't much want to talk about.

'Well, I'm pleased for you, and you sound upbeat, which is also good to see, after… well, you know what I mean.'

I do know what she means: the last year or so, where I got comfortable being alone. To best honest, I wasn't ready, and I had to wait until now to do this and start dating again.

'I have another date next week. Or more to the point, I'm going to Adam's speed-dating event.'

'It increases your odds, no?' Sarah says, taking a sip of her wine.

'That is the theory. If the worst comes to the worst, and I still don't meet anyone, maybe you could sit me next to someone at your wedding.'

My sister rolls her eyes and takes a large gulp of her drink and places her glass down with purpose. She presses the palms of her hands flat on the table as if bracing herself.

'Okay, about that. Take a deep breath. I'm going to tell you what I brought you here for,' Sarah says.

My mind spins like a roulette wheel, the ball bouncing from hole to hole, as I try to work out what it could be. Is she about to abandon her career in the city and open a yoga and meditation studio? Does she want to open another café? Is she going to run off with Jack and confound my mother's wedding ambitions? Maybe jump on a plane and head for Las Vegas and be married by an Elvis Presley impersonator? She likes a little bit of the king, some 'Love Me Tender' or 'Suspicious Minds', on the car stereo. Or maybe they will drive for the Scottish border and opt for Gretna Green. That is not a bad option at all. The wedding has grown in scale, and Sarah, when it comes down to it, likes things done simply.

'You're not going to be sitting next to anyone at the wedding,' she says.

I knew it! Question is, will it be Nevada or Scotland? 'You're going to Vegas, aren't you? I think that's a really good idea. You will disappoint Mum no end, but there's a lot to be said for spontaneity.'

Sarah shakes her head, looking at me quizzically. 'I'm not going to Vegas.'

'Really? Gretna then? I almost think that is more romantic.'

'I agree,' she says, pausing, taking another drink. 'But I'm not going to Scotland either.'

'Now I'm really confused. You're deleting me from your wedding list?'

'Don't be silly.' She reaches forward and takes my hands. 'If I ever have a wedding, you will be there… just not at this one as there's not going to be any wedding.'

At first, I'm not entirely sure that I heard what she said, but I know that I did. She is planning to kill my mother after all, as that is what cancelling her wedding will do.

'You have been with Jack for… I don't know, forever.'

'I know, and now it's over. You don't have to worry about Mum, she knows. I told her earlier, but other than her and Jack, only one other person knows,' Sarah says.

As soon as she says this it all makes sense. While they always looked like a good couple, almost like one of those couples you see in stock photos, there were moments when they just did not get on. And Sarah did say that Jack was 'hardly the love of my life'. In retrospect, it is obvious that this is the kind of thing people say when they are not in love at all.

Despite Sarah telling me this with a serious face, I find that I need to double-check, to confirm that tonight is not part of some complicated and stupid joke, which is the kind of thing I could imagine Jack being behind and my sister going along with—albeit with a good deal of reluctance.

I have so many questions, I don't know where to begin. I start at the beginning with the obvious one first.

'Why?'

'I wasn't in love with him, and I haven't been for a long time, and it hit me like a brick in the first lockdown, and that was it. I knew we were over. I didn't want to marry him. I also understood that if the pandemic hadn't struck, I might have married him and lived a life that I didn't want.'

This makes me think of what Beryl said, about listening to your heart. This is what Sarah had done, and her heart had told her not to marry Jack, and she had acted upon it.

I am thinking about how many lives got so turned around in the last year or so. What would have happened to us all if this massive change and consequent new normal hadn't come along? Would we have remained stuck on the tracks of our lives, like express trains, thundering down the line until some point far in the future when we finally hit the buffers? Would I still be working away at a keyboard in an office I had come to hate? Would Allison still be together with Paul, complaining and struggling with childcare and work, and would Sarah and Jack be getting married? What about Beth? Would we be friends again or remain as estranged as we are? The last person I think about is Larissa. I cannot stop thinking about her.

It is as though we have been living a life of 'ifs', and that somewhere out there, running along parallel tracks, are our former lives, continuing as before; unmarked by change. Only something happened, and we branched off. Our lives diverged from our established paths as the world shifted and shook, before allowing us to move forward anew.

'But you said yes to Jack?' I say.

'I know, and I didn't want to get married then either. He took me by surprise when he dropped down onto one knee and that makes it trickier to say no. It's hard to decide on the spot and even tougher if you have nagging doubts.'

'But you still said yes?'

'I know, and I said yes because I thought that would ultimately be a precursor to breaking up. But I wasn't quite ready for the whole "marry me or leave me" discussion, which is what it would have become. It was a stupid thing to do,' Sarah says.

'Hang on, let me get this straight. You said yes when Jack asked you to marry him because you thought getting married would lead to breaking up? That makes no sense, you know that, right?'

'Surely, you've heard about marriage being the road to divorce?'

Of course, I've heard of the road. In the same way that I've heard of the Highway to Hell. I always thought it was a joke made by couples who were nervous about taking the plunge, as opposed to unwilling.

'I thought it was more a turn of phrase than a plan of action,' I say.

Sarah smiles at this. 'You will be pleased to know that Mum has not taken it too badly. She says she's happy to take over organising the cancellation. There's quite a lot to do.'

'She does love to organise,' I say, nodding.

'There was one other thing I wanted to tell you.'

I take a drink of my wine and then a second and give my head a shake. No, I am all out of options. I have no idea what is coming next.

'I am all out of guesses,' I say.

'Really? I thought you might have an inkling about this one. The second thing is something I have known for a long time. I was in love with someone else. When lockdown happened, it came to a head. I would never have done anything about it otherwise. The opportunity was there, and we both decided to act.'

It makes perfect sense when she says this. This is why she is so smiley. There is a new man on the scene. Of course, I understand now. My sister is following the classic two rules of breaking up. The first rule says there is always someone else involved. If there weren't someone else, it would be simple, and that's the second rule. It's never simple.

'I'd like to tell you that I had some idea,' but I didn't,' I say. 'So, who is it? Do I know him?'

Sarah surprises me again, smiling and nodding. 'You do, and there's no complication. They're single, and they're gorgeous, and we're best friends.'

When she says this last part, she looks at me evenly, and with a smile. I know right away who she is talking about, and I suppose I have always known. She nods, gauging my reaction, seeing the recognition on my face. I have it all wrong with my useless assumptions.

'It's Allison, isn't it?'

'I wasn't sure you would guess so fast.'

I nod in agreement. I am I think surprised at myself, only I have always thought those two were so well suited. Allison and Sarah have been best friends for as long as I can remember. From school until now, Allison was always around. They have travelled similar paths, having had relationships with other women at some point in their love lives, before long-term relationships with men followed and then foundered. It is as though Sarah and Allison shipwrecked on the same rocks, washed up on the same shore, and then found each other again, and came to the obvious realisation.

'I'm happy for you, I really am. You two are so good together, you always have been. I could not imagine a better partner for you,' I say.

'Thank you, I appreciate you saying that very much,' Sarah says.

'I imagine it is just very comfortable to be together.'

'It is, but it is so much more than that. It's love in all its colours, and I couldn't be happier. I'm all in with Allison, and I don't think I have ever been that way with anyone before.'

I find I am sucked in by Sarah's smile, by her obvious happiness. It is good to see.

'I am so glad to hear that, and to know my sister is with someone who is one of the best people anyone could be with.'

'I feel the same. Allison wanted to tell you. So don't blame her, she always wants to share things with you, ever since we were kids. I, on the other hand, like to keep things back, but you know that.'

'I do, and really, I am okay with that. I like it when at least some things don't change. I need that reassurance.'

'I know you do,' says Sarah, and she gives my hand a squeeze. 'You know what it is? It's like being found.'

I hold my hand up at Sarah; *stop*, I am saying. I am feeling inordinately emotional, overcome almost; my eyes are feeling moist. I don't know what's come over me. Sarah's words are moving me, and that last part hit me. It is what we all want, isn't it? What we are all missing? To be found. After I have recovered enough, I wonder how they finally connected.

'How did it happen?'

'In lockdown we talked all the time. We've always shared our lives and been honest with each other, and I didn't want to lose that, and I didn't think that I could keep that realisation back, so I told her. I said, "This is how I feel", and she started laughing,' Sarah says. 'She said she had always felt the same and that maybe this was our moment.'

Her words make me think about our shifting world again, how this shake-up has created new connections for some, sending their lives spinning in new directions.

'So, what about you? I worry, you know? I might not technically be any older than you, but I feel like the older sibling,' Sarah adds.

'I know you do, and that is also okay. Don't worry about me, though, I have six more dating experiences waiting for me.'

Chapter Eighteen

'Between The Bars'

Sarah and I continued drinking in the restaurant and at the bar down the road. We were pretty drunk when we left, and it was a good, happy kind of drunk. The kind we had not been together for a long time.

When I got home, I messaged Allison. Just a few words, nothing more. I just wanted to check in as I knew she would have spoken to Sarah.

> Congratulations, delighted for you.

Allison texted straight back.

> I heard you had a few drinks! Let's get an early coffee in the park before work. See you at eight.

In the morning, I am up and ready by a little after seven. Allison texts me that she will see me soon—only I am far too distracted by what has happened overnight.

I have a message from a *Daily Mail Online* reporter. It is from someone I vaguely know, Clare Jones, who I follow on Twitter from my days as a reporter.

Would you be interested in a short interview about your viral date? We love the story.

I cannot imagine anything worse. All I want from the *#ShortestDateEver* is for it to stop. The last thing I want to do is talk about it. I send a quick firm no, being as polite as I can.

Wow, that is a great offer only I'm not sure there is anything to say. It was a really short date. Lol. Thanks anyway.

I send this message hoping that will be the end of it only it is not. I get an immediate response.

Sorry to hear that. The thing is we've run a piece on the Mail Online, and we have an interview with your date, Miranda, and thought you would like the chance to respond.

Classic tabloid journalistic trap. You have got to be kidding me. I do a quick Google search and I find the article. It is a take-down story. Not only have I been screwed on Twitter, but now I have been trashed online. They have taken my profile picture from Twitter and featured it prominently, along with a stunning picture of Miranda, which she no doubt supplied.

Former Journalist Dubbed 'Worst Date Ever' by Twitter

A former crime reporter, Tom Martin, has been labelled the worst date ever by Twitter users after he insulted his date in a tweet.

The tweet went viral after women across Twitter took offence and rallied in support of the woman he met, Miranda Franken, who has spoken exclusively to the Mail Online about the experience, which she described as 'traumatising'.

'Dating is hard enough without men like this feeling the need to publicly humiliate women online after they have been rejected. I tried really hard to like Tom, but found him a closed and negative person,' Franken said.

Martin's date with Ms Franken is one of a series of dates arranged for him by his friends. Ms Franken described how she had been matched as one of ten dates that Martin is going on in the coming days.

'I feel sorry for the other women he will meet, and I'd like to warn them to steer clear. There are nice men out there, but unfortunately my experience with Tom Martin has shown me he is not one of them. For me he is the worst guy on the internet,' Franken said.

The story continues to drone on and on after that, in the classic vein of a *Mail Online* story in a bid to fill as much space as possible. The website has included a selection of other tweets, none of which paint me in a good light.

I continue to stare at the story, knowing there isn't anything I can do about it. For a moment I debate sending an angry message back to Clare protesting at her story, and asking her whatever happened to sticking up for fellow journalists? Only I know that in the age of online news and the need to generate clicks, none of that counts; anything goes, and no prisoners are taken.

I flick back to Twitter as another direct message appears.

> If you change your mind, let me know, we can add your side of the story at any time. BTW I love the idea of your ten dates. Sure, that would make a story too. Best Clare :).

> Thanks Clare, I will definitely think about it, and will be in touch if I do.

I don't add that this will only happen once hell has frozen over, and am left once again whining to myself, how this could happen? The thing is, if I am honest, I brought it on myself. The rule should be, unless you have anything nice to say, then avoid Twitter, as you will end up in some tweet storm blowing a gale of angry internet at you. I should never have tweeted anything in the first place. Maybe I should delete all my social media accounts now? I reject this idea as an overreaction. All I can do now is dig in, and hope that it blows over soon. I really hope no future date reads this, as being called 'the worst guy on the internet' is not a good look.

The buzzer to the flat goes, and I put my phone away. I am hoping Allison has arrived, and we can have a coffee and I can forget about going viral for a while.

I open the door to find Allison standing there looking summery in a blue dress and white cardigan.

'Morning,' Allison says. 'You never told me you planned to become an online pariah.'

I roll my eyes at this and offer my hands out as I close the door to the flat behind me.

'Funny. What I can tell you is that it is incredibly easy to become hated by the internet. All you need to do is open your mouth and wait for someone to take offence, as almost inevitably they will,' I say.

Allison laughs at this. 'You of all people should know this.'

'You'd think so, although having once been a journalist is no protection.'

I fill Allison in on my messages from the *Mail Online*, as we set off down the street towards the park. As we walk, Allison asks me for details of my other dates.

We cross the road, navigate the bustle of Finsbury Park station, pass the bowling alley and the Twelve Pins pub on the corner, and then stroll into the park, and along the tree-lined drive to the boating lake, which is where I know Allison wants to be. She loves the water, and every time we've ambled around the park, we always go by the route that takes us around the lake.

As we approach the bench where I often sit, I look across, and I don't see Larissa sitting there. I don't see anyone at all.

'It isn't the greatest park in the world. It isn't quite big enough to lose yourself, but it does have a boating lake and ducks,' Allison says.

'It's the best part.'

'It is, and I like that we both love that. We haven't done this walk for a long time now.'

I nod in agreement. Pre-lockdown, pre-the-new-normal, when our lives all started to spin in uncharted directions and to settle into alternate orbits, when Dylan was first born, I would come on occasion with Allison, and sometimes Paul, for a walk. At that baby stage, Dylan slept and ate, and we would do long, slow, coffee-drinking circuits along the road that loops around the park. We would sometimes head down Parkland Walk, the nature trail that follows what was once a railway line, with its abandoned platforms and railway arches.

We come to a halt by the metal railings around the lake, and watch a short old Mediterranean-looking man, Greek or Italian maybe, taking out bird feed from his crumpled and well-used bag and feeding the ducks on the lake. The man smiles and offers some a handful of seeds to Allison, who gratefully takes them. With a gentle nod, he turns, and walks off with his hands folded behind his back, following the fence around the edge of the water.

'I wanted to tell you about me and Sarah ages ago,' Allison starts. 'And then we waited. I'm not sure why. I think maybe it was because, after sneaking around for months and then not sneaking around so much, we wanted to be sure that it was the real thing and that we weren't having a moment brought on by the weirdness of lockdown and life being turned upside down.'

'I'm really pleased for both of you, and I never knew you were so good at sneaking around. With you two it's the real thing, you can tell,' I say.

Allison laughs, a small gentle laugh, and nods in agreement. 'It's the real thing.'

'I'm happy to hear that. If you two get married, you know you will be my sister-in-law?'

'I do. How do you feel about that?'

'You've always been part of the family so making it official feels perfectly natural,' I say. 'Besides, you two have always been as thick as thieves.'

'We are much thicker than we used to be. The funny thing is that none of it was planned. If things hadn't broken down with Paul, I might have continued to live my life. Had another child, hit two-point-four children without any kind of pause. Isn't that what happens? It blows my mind thinking about it. How we could have all these different lives.'

Allison's words echo my thoughts of those parallel lives that race alongside each other, separated by light and energy but shadowing us all the same.

'More than anything, it is the best news. Sarah couldn't be with anyone better,' I say. 'It seems like you have the life you deserve.'

'Thank you for being so good about this. It makes me love you more,' Allison says, and she opens her arms, inviting me in. 'Come here,' she says, and we hug by the side of the lake, and she holds me for quite a long time.

Afterwards, we stand together, looking out across the water, as sunbeams catch the ripples and sparkle in the sunshine. I ask if the pair of them have any plans or are thinking about the future. I realise I dropped marriage into the conversation rather casually, although I realise it is early days.

'What happens next?'

'I don't think anything "happens" next. We're going to be partners and see where we get to. We don't have a road map.' Allison turns to lean on the thick black railings, and as she does, she hands me some of her seeds that the man gave her. 'Come on,' she says. 'Feed the ducks for me. There is something I wanted to talk to you about.'

'If it starts with b and ends in h, then really, I think we both know what you're going to say.'

'Are you sure?' says Allison. 'I'm not sure that you do.'

'Didn't we have this conversation recently? Where you told me that she's going to meet someone, and then that will be it for Beth and me?'

'That's what I told you, and I'm telling you again now. This is your last chance to do something about it.'

'Well, now you've told me. I can't say I haven't been warned.'

'I know, and the thing is, I wish you would take it more seriously.'

I throw my hands out and offer a smile. Right now, I am the most serious I have been for a long time about dating. I have been on four dates, and next week will attend the speed-dating experience Adam has organised, which he is running at a bar in Piccadilly.

'I am serious. I'm so serious I've gone viral. I maybe as well be on a Wanted poster—or possibly Not Wanted is more accurate. If at the end of this I am still single, you can tell me this all over again,' I say.

Allison shakes her head at this and looks quite sad for a moment. 'I think you might find it's too late by then. Just so you know. I think Beth is reaching her cut-off point, which might mean even though she is super bright, she might do something stupid.'

I have no idea what a cut-off point is or why it might cause Beth to do something regrettable. Allison is looking at me with a superior expression, so I ask the obvious question, which is what she has been waiting for me to do.

'Okay, I'll bite. What is the cut-off point?'

'I'm so glad you asked, and really? I can't believe you don't know what it is. I know you've led a more sheltered life of late, but this is something you need to know about. It is part of the same demographic shift you're going through, that led Adam to drag the rest of us along on his dating intervention,' Allison says.

'Go on.'

'Do you remember my friend Anna, the lecturer?'

For a moment, I have a flashback to a date I went on with Anna. We only went out once about six years ago, and then I never called her again, which I then regretted. This annoyed Allison, who had persuaded Anna to go out with me in the first place, and Anna, who later told people at a party that I was an idiot—which in retrospect is a fair assessment. It's okay to have a few regrets, only make sure you don't dwell on them too much.

'Of course, I do, and in my defence, that was ages ago,' I say.

'Saying something was "ages ago" and using the words "in my defence" isn't an actual defence, you know that, right? Just for future reference in case you are ever arrested,' Allison says. She is grinning and enjoying my discomfort at this trip down memory lane far too much.

'Funny,' I say.

'I thought so. Anyway, this isn't about you. Anna started going out with this guy called David. She went out with him for about two years. He was terrible for her. He was a musician who she finally dumped because he was lousy and inattentive (forgot dates, birthdays, like, everything) and generally no good (he cheated). Not to mention the fact that he owed Anna thousands of pounds almost entirely as the result of a cocaine habit,' Allison says.

'Wow. She deserves better than that. I liked Anna.'

'Did you? Not enough to go out with her again,' Allison says, pausing for a beat or two. 'I'm joking. Mostly, anyway. About five months ago, she got back together with him, and now she's pregnant.'

'And again: wow. David does not sound like outstanding father material.'

'Father material? Are you claiming expertise?' Allison is laughing hard at this.

'No, although I had this idea that fathers would generally teach their kids to play cricket and football and build brilliant model Lego constructions rather than educate them on class A drugs.'

'Is that your game plan, Tom?'

'I don't have a game plan, but at least I am dating. Anyway, why is Anna with David and what has this got to do with Beth and the cut-off point?'

'I'll get to that. Anna used to say that he could play the piano rather beautifully. He played to her when they first went out, wrote her a song. She used to think it was sexy. Then he sold the piano and spent the money on drugs.'

'He sounds like the opposite of a catch. More anti-catch.'

'Do you mean the antithesis?'

'I mean that. What I don't understand is, why so rash on Anna's part? She always struck me as a rather sensible girl, which is why you two get on so well together.'

'Oh, you're charming. Sensible? I have a BMW Mini Cooper Sport. It's very nippy. What do you have?' Allison asks indignantly.

It is true. She does have a relatively cool-looking sporty red Mini.

'Fair point. Look, I meant sensible in a good way.'

'I'm sure Anna will be as thrilled as I am to hear you say that.'

'I'm going to reappraise her. She might lose her sensible girl rating. She might in fact be a really rather rash girl. So, what happened?'

'Anna reached her cut-off point. That's what happened. She decided ages ago that her cut-off point was thirty-five. She said she didn't care if she had found the right man, she wanted to be pregnant by then,' Allison says.

'So, David got a call back because Anna was running out of time in the great game of musical partners?'

'Now you get it, and that's what I am saying to you. David got the call back. You can't always cast the right guy. I should know—and I told her that as well. It was too late. Her mind was made up.'

'I almost feel for the David. He probably thinks Anna wants him for his music and his future fathering skills. So much for true romance then.'

'Welcome to true biology.'

'Maybe it will be the wake-up call he needs,' I say.

Allison shakes her head. 'I don't think so. David will be gone in a year. I am not sure he will last as long as Paul. She'll meet someone else. It's depressing. When we were young, I always thought that we—and by that, I mean you and our friends—were somehow going to be different to our parents, only we are similar in so many ways. Too many ways,' Allison says.

I nod in agreement, only pausing to reflect if perhaps these are the thoughts of every generation. Do we all think that we will be different, breaking the mould that our parents set? I am sure I thought the same. That somehow, we would not repeat the mistakes our elders made. When we have fashioned our own mistakes, and they are modelled on those of our parents before us. It's like some vast, self-repeating merry-go-round where everyone continues in much the same way, but with small progressive improvements.

'I know what you mean,' I say.

'If you do, then maybe you'll hear what I am saying,' Allison says.

'Are we still talking about Beth?'

Allison throws her arms out in a dramatic fashion like a conductor lifting an orchestra to crescendo. 'Of course, we are! We always are. I only hope you now understand how critical things are.'

With that, we start to walk around the lake again, the water rippling in the sunshine like a silken sheet. We do one last circuit before work and talk about other things.

Chapter Nineteen

'You're the Best Thing'

The following week, I attend Adam's speed-dating night, which is being held in the upstairs of a bar on the Haymarket near Piccadilly Circus—an area that I am being drawn back to time and again.

After navigating Piccadilly station's warren of exits, I make my way past groups of tourists drawn to the statue of Anteros, posing for selfies and, like me, maybe pondering questions of love. I move onto the busy Haymarket as people stream by, to and from the tube, and I see the glass-fronted bar ahead, which is my destination tonight.

The bar is jammed on the ground floor, so I head straight for the stairs, where I am greeted by a bouncer standing by a red rope at the foot of the staircase. He has broad shoulders and a shaved head, and on his exposed forearm a tattoo of Pegasus is partially visible, which makes me think of Greeks and their gifts. The bouncer inspects my invitation, checks it against an iPad list, and gives me a perfunctory nod. He lifts the red rope, and I step forward to the glass stairs. As I walk, I feel almost like I used to in my former life, as if I am back in the swing and out on one of those nights that could go anywhere.

There are a lot of people in the upstairs bar, some standing in small groups and others alone. The lights are dimmed, and it looks as though there is an even split between men and women. People are awkwardly chatting, a few propping up the bar and standing ready in corners of the room.

Adam has recruited a select number of people via social media who he says he has evenly matched after having everyone fill in a questionnaire and then filtering the results. This way, he says it is 'almost guaranteed' that some of the people who are attending tonight's event will meet a suitable match. These sound like famous last words. Does Adam mean as well matched as I was for Miranda? Someone I hope not to see again, and who has slayed me on social media.

When Adam and I spoke about the event on the phone, I asked him what he thought my chances were tonight of meeting someone I might get along with.

'I think they are the same as they have been since the start of this process,' Adam enthused. 'By that, I mean very good. Just try not to go any more viral. A self-imposed social media blackout might be in order.'

I am not sure I would agree with "very good" given the mixed results so far. I have had some good dates and enjoyed meeting Alice and Jules although neither date went anywhere. Audrey's entrance into my life, on the other hand, was an outlier. Less a date and more a one-night-only revival of our relationship; fun, drunken, ending in sex, and not to be repeated.

I have enjoyed it though, dating again, and I am grateful, so baby steps, right?

I find Adam talking to a woman in a smart blue skirt suit, holding a clipboard. She has long wavy blonde hair, which hangs loose around her shoulders. Adam gives me a wave, beckons me over, and introduces me to Claudia from the event company.

'I've been hearing everything about you, plus I saw Twitter. I never met anyone who went viral before,' Claudia says, by way of introduction.

I laugh nervously at this. 'Neither have I.'

Claudia doesn't answer directly. Instead, she smiles and says: 'I'm sure you will meet your match this evening. You are the last to arrive. Here.' She peels a sticker from her clipboard. 'This is your name tag, and the number of your first date.'

I try to smile as Claudia hands this to me, and in fact, helps me stick it on my T-shirt. Name tags: I was not expecting that.

'Thank you,' I say.

Perhaps noting my less than enthusiastic response to the name tag, Claudia explains.

'It's a time-saver and an icebreaker, and the good news is, Tom, there is no worry that your name has been spelled wrong. We have a Gordon here, and they printed his name as Godot,' Claudia says.

'Playing the waiting game, is he?' I ask.

Claudia stares blankly at me when I say this, as she asks herself why I would make such a terrible joke. It is a good question. Adam smirks, and Claudia offers a curt: 'Yes,' and excuses herself. She says she has to get her gong.

'Did she say "gong"?' I ask.

'You'll understand what she means in a minute,' Adam says. 'More importantly, are you ready?'

'Any last-minute advice?'

'Funny you should ask. The thing to remember is that you get three minutes with each person. So, think of them as micro dates. Don't waste time. You need to use it wisely.

Three minutes will flash by. Ask the questions that you want the answers to. I put all this in your dating pack to help guide you through the evening,' Adam says.

This would be an excellent moment to admit that I didn't read the 'dating pack'. I mean, seriously, whoever reads the instructions? Isn't it much better to muddle through and later Google a solution, thus still achieving a sense of satisfaction? I don't know. That could be me. Besides, how difficult can it be? Wait, what am saying? This is dating, anything can happen.

'I'm sure it will be fine,' I say.

Adam looks at me suspiciously. 'You didn't read it, did you?'

'I did not.'

Adam throws his head back in dismay. 'The way to think about it is, how can I make things go right? That is my final bit of advice for you.'

'Is this all going in the book?'

'Everything is going in the book. I need to set up some time with you to do some interviews. I want to capture everything that has happened if that's okay and then write it up,' Adam says.

I nod. I was wondering when he was planning his detailed dating debrief sessions.

Looking around the room, I see equally attractive men and women here tonight. Adam's recruitment policy has worked well if looks alone are anything to go by. I see one woman with a short blonde bob I am drawn to; she is cute, and I can't help looking over.

'Anyone you noticed?' Adam says.

'Maybe one or two, but difficult to see, what with it being so dim in here.'

'I did try to brighten it when I looked over the venue. Honestly, it is worse with the lights up. It makes it look like a large interrogation room, which I am not sure is the dating experience that people are looking for.'

'Point taken.'

'Anyway, here we go,' says Adam.

At this point, it becomes apparent that I did not mishear Claudia. She appears at the edge of the room with a large copper gong and whacks it with a mallet. Everyone stops talking.

This is Adam's cue, he steps forward and, in a booming, authoritative voice, he addresses the room. He goes through his spiel, which is close enough to what he has already told me. We're reminded that we only have three minutes, and should use them wisely, after which we must move along to our next date. Tonight, he says, it will be the men who do the moving from table to table.

'Let's get going, and remember to enjoy yourselves,' he yodels.

The women make for the ring of tables and chairs positioned around the edge of the room, and the men hang back, watching the women go. The men check their numbers and shuffle off to find the corresponding table. With the dim lighting, this makes for a confusing start. Men bump into each other and peer down at table numbers before finding the right one. It is like a metaphor for dating.

I find table seven where I am to start my dating journey tonight. I take my seat and find I am sitting opposite a pretty woman with striking long red hair that falls in loose ringlets to her shoulders. However, Claire—this is the name on her tag—does not look pleased to see me.

She sighs, and a sour look spreads across her face. She seems to deflate in front of my very eyes.

I have flashbacks to my date with Miranda, who would have been an ideal participant in tonight's activities. She was a fan of the fast date.

'Hi,' I say, and then run out of words, derailed by Claire's dour-looking and less-than-pleased-to-meet-me expression. I find myself responding in kind and feel myself physically shrink, sitting across from Claire.

'I recognise you. You're that guy whose date went viral. I read that story, and thought, who would do that to someone?'

I do think about explaining that I did not do anything to Miranda, other than turn up and offer to buy her a drink. Given Claire's reaction, I don't say this, as I feel it might be a pointless exercise.

'I do think that it was blown out of all proportion,' I say.

'You would say that though, wouldn't you?'

This is a damning criticism from someone who doesn't know me and has met me for less than twenty seconds. That's the problem with social media, or one of the problems. People think they know you, and they draw conclusions and pick their sides. Claire, it is safe to assume, has picked Miranda's side.

'I suppose I would,' I say, at a loss.

'To be honest, even without what you did, you're not my type.'

'Ditto.'

Claire appears offended by this and looks at me, aghast. 'Ditto? Who even says that?'

I offer my hands out. I am beginning to think that speed-dating is the worst kind of dating invented. It is worse than two-minute dating, and that is saying something. I am also reappraising what Adam said about three minutes being a short time. It is already feeling long.

Claire looks at her watch and looks back at me. I get the impression that she wants to sit in silence. As I am contemplating this, Claudia bangs her gong.

'Okay, everyone,' Claudia calls. 'Let's date!'

It is only at that point that I realise we haven't even officially started yet.

Okay, so one of the things that could make speed-dating worse is someone calling out 'let's date!'. I do my best to put a smile on and make the best of the situation. I am not sure if it is possible to rescue this date, but maybe we can make it bearable. Even if we are ill-suited, I'm not her type, and Claire has formed an opinion based on my viral moment, I can act interested and ask questions.

'Well, why don't you tell me what your type is, then?' I ask.

'Ryan Gosling.'

Oh really, I'm thinking. *Of course, he is.* I mean, why wouldn't he be? What with him being fit, good-looking, the star of numerous movies and being the best Ryan on the internet.

I was hoping she would give me a little more, and so I pressed her. 'What is it you like about Ryan Gosling?'

Claire rolls her eyes at me and makes an 'uh' as if this question is beneath her and requires no elaboration. I was hoping for at least something like 'because *Blue Valentine* is one of the most captivating and real films about a couple struggling to rekindle their relationship, or that *Blade Runner 2049* was a brilliant update, with a perfect twist, to a classic Ridley Scott movie'. As these are all strong contributing reasons as to why Ryan Gosling is the best Ryan on the internet. The other Ryans do not come close. In lieu of actual dating, I would happily spend the remaining two and a half minutes of our date discussing these films.

'It's kind of obvious,' Claire says finally.

Okay, and at this point, I make a snap decision not to say anything else. He does, after all, top the fantasy list for a lot of women, which is fair enough. But, while fantasy is fine, reality is better—although that seems ironic in my case, given my current questionable mental state.

Although I have decided to sit in silence, I find myself saying something else. Before I can stop it, my mouth has engaged without using my brain and, well, to be honest, the results are poor.

'That's pretty optimistic of you,' I say.

'Twat.'

I nod at this. I think about explaining by saying 'what I meant is that Ryan lives in Hollywood, and you live in London, and— oh, what's the point?' I clamp my mouth shut and sit there in the contemplative bubble of silence that envelopes the two of us. Claire is staring glassy-eyed into the middle distance as the sound of conversation and laughter echoes around the room.

I sit there, willing Claudia to bang her bloody gong. Finally, she is on the scene, and she hits it hard. Claudia and her gong are, I think, living their best life. She is either a huge fan of *University Challenge* or Marc Bolan, and this whole gong thing is her tribute. Either way, I am okay with that. As far as I am concerned, Claudia can let rip with the gong for as long as she likes.

I stand without a word, half thinking I should leave in silence. However, I cannot bring myself to do this.

'Nice to meet you. Good luck with the rest of the evening,' I say.

Claire stares silently back at me with an intense look of loathing. I think she is summoning her inner psychokinetic powers to fling me through the air. I depart without another word being spoken.

I move to the next table hoping that I am not going to speak all evening about how I went viral. Hopefully, my date with Claire is the evening's low point and that whatever comes next will be better. The only direction of travel from here is up. I am sure Adam would be impressed by my sanguine approach.

My next date is Lydia, and she smiles, and I smile, and we introduce ourselves. She has short dark hair, pale skin, and big brown eyes. She looks beautiful. I am already feeling much more cheerful. I would happily date Lydia if that was a possibility. However, this is not to be. After the smiles and introductions, Lydia jumps straight in. It is clear that she, unlike me, has read Adam's dating pack and clearly explains her aims and objectives and what she hopes to get out of this speed-dating experience.

'I'm a doctor and a vegetarian. I will be honest and tell you that I'm only really interested in dating other people who work in medicine and who are vegetarians,' Lydia says.

I nod at this, indicating that I understand where she is coming from.

'Okay,' I say, thrown off balance by this start.

'Do you work in medicine?'

I shake my head. 'No, I run a café bookshop.'

Lydia looks disappointed but manages a smile. 'I do like the sound of that. Are you a vegetarian? I would settle for a vegetarian.'

I do like a woman who is prepared to compromise, as at least through this route, there is a hope that we can find some common ground. I have had long spells of being first a vegetarian, then a pescatarian and finally, a flexitarian. That said, I am a long way from the lentil-eating student where my brush with politics and vegetarianism started and then ended.

'Not really. I do eat meat, although I should say my meat-eating is mostly at a burger level. It is the one thing I have found hard to give up,' I say.

'I'm not sure we're that suited. I hate burgers, which is a shame, as I think you look nice. Tell me about your café. I love books and coffee, and will make a beeline to visit it,' she says.

What a sweet thing to say. It makes me smile. Lydia comes across as so genuine, and despite not being suited, I like her. We whizz through our three-minute date, exchanging short biographies with each other. This takes us to the end of our date, as Claudia bangs her gong, and even though it did not result in a planned future meeting, it has gone well. I thank Lydia, tell her that it was nice to meet her, and hope she finds who she is looking for.

Lydia offers a bright smile. 'You too. I enjoyed chatting with you.'

I am up and on to my next date. She is a slim woman with wavy long blonde hair and is wearing cool black glasses. She looks like an attractive librarian.

Her badge says Ariel, and when she says hello, she has a very soft voice. Ariel reminds me of Beth in her looks, and with the name there is a Sylvia Plath connection. I bought Beth Sylvia Plath's *Ariel*, for her birthday a few years after we met, after she left her treasured copy on a train. I gave it to her as the two of us sat in one of

London's best old pubs, The Lamb in Bloomsbury, which I had chosen as it was a place that Plath had spent time when dating Ted Hughes. On opening the book, Beth said, 'That is the most thoughtful thing,' and before I knew it, she leaned forward and kissed me on the cheek. I looked at her, caught for a moment in the gaze of her blue eyes, which are the colour of moonstone and clear winter skies, and didn't know what to say. After a few moments, I mumbled, 'you're welcome' or something similar. It was a moment, looking back, that I should have acted upon, and I never did. I am such an idiot. It is such moments that have led me to where I am now. I wonder where Beth is and if she is dating anyone.

My mind snaps back, putting thoughts about Beth to one side, as Ariel asks me a question.

'Tell me, are you enjoying this?' Ariel asks as soon as I take my seat.

'It's been hit and miss,' I say. 'My first date rejected me within seconds, which was okay but…,' I pause at this point, and feel I should come clean. 'I went viral on Twitter, after a bad short date, and it was in the *Mail Online* and—'

Ariel holds up her hand and stops me. 'I didn't see it on Twitter, and I never read the *Mail*, so you are safe.'

'I am finding dating can be very prescriptive about what people want.'

Ariel laughs at this. 'That does sum up dating. Although the very thought of going viral gives me palpations, I won't judge you. I thought I would try this, but almost as soon as I signed up, I knew it was a mistake.'

'How so?' I ask.

'I made a belated new year's resolution that the next person I date I must be desperately in love with. Otherwise, what is the point?'

When Ariel says this, I smile at her, charmed by her words. She is also right; otherwise, aren't we going through the motions and ignoring our actual emotions? I understand where she's coming from. People are fed up with wasting their time on people who aren't right for them, compromising too much and going out with people just because that is what is expected of them. I think of the last woman, Lydia, who said she would settle for a vegetarian, and of Anna. Why should they have to settle for anyone?

'It has to be worth trying,' I say.

I mean, doesn't it? If you have tried everything else, maybe it is time to shoot for the moon and accept nothing less—low earth orbit isn't good enough.

'If I'm not desperately in love with them, I'll at least have to like them quite a bit. Besides, I don't think I have ever been desperately in love, and frankly, I find that depressing. What about you? Have you ever felt that way? I'd like to know. It seems important, and I'd like to know that at least someone has,' Ariel says.

I think about it, and there is no one in my past I could point to and say I was desperately in love with. There have been a couple I liked a lot. Larissa is in that category, as crazy as she made me.

'I don't think so, at least not yet.'

Ariel nods. 'You don't sound like you have given up. That's a good sign. Why don't you tell me about yourself?'

I share my story with Ariel, and she shares hers with me. It turns out she is not a librarian, rather she is a museum curator working at the Imperial War Museum.

History is her passion, she says, and like that, three minutes zips by and the gong sounds. All there is time for is to say goodbye.

'Nice meeting you. Good luck,' I say.

'You too, and good luck,' Ariel says.

I am up and off. As I approach my next date, I can already see it is the attractive slim blonde woman I noticed earlier. I smile, and the first thing I notice is that she has a small button nose and high sharp cheekbones. Her blonde hair cups her jawline as she looks down. When she looks up, I find I am caught for a moment by her eyes, which are a pale grey that looks like the colour of English skies on September days. Her name badge says Amy, and after we have said our hellos, she asks me what I do. I give her my brief bio, and Amy tells me hers: she's a fiction editor for a publisher and spends most of her time reading.

'How's it been so far?'

'I was volunteered for this, and I didn't have high hopes,' Amy says.

'Same. My first date lasted about three seconds, which is weird as recently I went on what I thought was my shortest date ever, which then blew up on Twitter...,' I pause for a second, giving Amy an opening, and as she smiles, I continue: 'She took one look at me before hitting her reject button,' I say.

Amy leans forward, like a conspirator, and in a soft voice, says: 'Well, I haven't hit my reject button. Tell me something about yourself.'

This is a good dating question, asking for some reveal that I suppose we do not tell other people.

'I usually tell people that my favourite novel is something very worthy and obvious like *The Great Gatsby* or

Jane Eyre, but I love *The Secret History*. I've read it three times. I have no idea why,' I say.

'I love that book as well. I love all of Donna Tartt's books,' Amy says.

When she says this, it makes me happy. It is one of those moments when you know that within a few words of conversation, you have met someone who might be a kindred spirit.

'Your turn,' I say. 'Tell me something that you don't normally tell people?'

Amy gives this some thought, and the seconds tick by. Three minutes is sometimes too long, and at other times not long enough. I wonder if the two of us could sit here for the rest of the evening, set up a diversion sign, and allow other dates to bypass us.

'Okay, so I tell people that I love yoga, although that isn't true. I don't, but I go all the same. I find it a grind, maybe because it always feels like I am lumpenly going through the movements. I am not one of those feathery light women who flow through yoga and land like a cat. My bones are like lead, and I land like a Labrador. On the plus side, it does stop me from piling on wine pounds. I also say I prefer documentaries, but if you pushed me—and not hard—I would rather watch a rom-com,' Amy says.

'Same, I would rate *When Harry Met Sally* as one of my favourite films,' I say.

'Agreed, I will always have what she's having, and on that note, do you believe men and women can never be friends?' As she says this, she takes a sip of her drink, and keeps her eyes on me. It is, of course, a leading question. I have met people who, when asked this question, are adamant that they cannot. However, I don't believe that for a second.

'Not for a second. They can be friends,' I say.

'Interesting,' Amy replies.

'What's your take?'

Amy gives a slight shrug. 'The jury is still out.'

'I suppose most of the time, men and women don't go looking for friends, do they? Friends seem to happen, where this,' and I offer my hands out to the room, 'only happens with difficulty.'

'I hate dating, and probably wouldn't have come along tonight if my arm hadn't been twisted. I would be at home watching Netflix and be as happy.'

When Amy says that I get that funny feeling. It is as though we are in perfect synch. Until recently, that was me as well. I would be at home streaming some TV series midway through season three and not worrying too much about the fact that I hadn't been out and hadn't seen anyone other than work. And yet, here I am, socially back in the world and engaged in this dating project, which has reconnected me with Adam and the rest of my friends.

'Dating is hard,' I say. 'Although I did come willingly.'

Amy sits back in her seat, crosses her arms, and taps her forefinger to her cheek as if she is giving an issue some thought.

'The crazy gong lady is about to do her thing, in about, I don't know, twenty seconds or so,' she says.

'I met her, and I can confirm she is attached to that gong. I am guessing it is not a prop and rather an object she uses in her everyday life. You're right, though. Our time is short. This has been the best three-minute date I've ever had,' I say.

'I like your speculation, and I agree. It has been entertaining. If you want, we can chat in the bar afterwards.'

'I'd like that—'

Right on cue, Claudia bangs her gong. I have a dozen questions I would like to ask, and there is no time left to ask them. I can see other people are already on the move, and a tall blond-haired guy is approaching our table. He offers a grin, and I take this as one of dating solidarity and my prompt to depart. I don't want to go, and I don't want anyone else to talk to Amy. I'm worried that she might like them more.

'Enjoy the rest of the evening,' I say.

'See you later,' Amy says.

'Looking forward to it.'

-

I move on to my next date, which is with a brunette woman called Louise, and it makes me think I have not met anyone called Louise for a long time. There was a period when all I had to do at a party was turn around and I would bump into a Louise, or a Sara. They probably said the same thing about men called Tom.

My date with this Louise starts well. We smile and chitchat about how our previous dates have gone so far.

'It's better than I thought,' Louise says. 'I thought it might be worse than online dating, which is godawful. The bonus is there is no way for guys to send you dick pics. Why do they do that?'

I shrug, having never done this. I have no idea. To be honest, I am not a huge fan of my own penis, and the idea of photographing it and sending it to other people is bizarre. But hey, what do I know?

'I promise you I've never done that.'

'Really? You look like the kind of guy who might,' she says, and before I get a chance to ask her what she means by this, she moves on. 'Let me ask you another question: have you watched *Star Wars* or various Marvel movies multiple times?'

I shift my shoulders awkwardly in response to this question. I feel exposed sitting there. It turns out that speed-dating is as hit and miss as real dating. You can go from one fantastic date, where you feel an instant connection, to this. From hero to zero, in the space of a few minutes.

'I am not going to lie to you. I have,' I say.

'I thought so. You also look like the kind of guy who does that too,' Louise says.

My impression so far is that my date is very heavy on judgement and over-uses the phrase 'you look like the kind of guy'. It is like I have been placed in a bucket with lots of other men who also seem the type, whether we are genuinely similar or not. Sensing that we will not be meeting again after our three minutes is up, my only mission is to keep this date on an even keel.

'How can you tell?' I ask.

'I have experience. My ex-boyfriend, he was like you. I put up with him for ages, and he forced me to watch endless superhero movies, which are terrible and basically incomprehensible, and then he left me. In retrospect, I am grateful for it. He was overweight and never exercised. I've run two marathons since he left,' Louise says.

I am detecting a note of bitterness in her voice, which is my signal to tread warily. I have about one minute thirty seconds to go, and I am confident I can make it to the end without incident. I am impressed by Louise's marathon achievement. It is something I cannot imagine doing.

'That is amazing, what you have done,' I say.

'Thank you. I'm proud of myself.'

'In my defence,' I start, and then I find myself pausing, again. I must stop using this phrase. 'Superhero movies are not my thing. For transparency, it is mostly *Star Wars*.'

Louise shakes her head. She is not buying this. 'It's all the same. I want to meet someone who doesn't have a cult-like obsession with ray guns and spaceships and is a permanent resident of Earth. Instead, using their time to think about how we can save the planet. It's like Bezos and Branson wasting their boy buckets of cash to fly around the moon.'

'I think technically, they are flying around the Earth.'

I utter this comment in an absent-minded way, and I don't even know why I say it. I again forgot to engage my brain before talking. I realise too late how it might be perceived. The thing is, I agree with her about the rocket ship dreams of the planet's most prominent billionaires. It is a waste of money that they could be doing something more useful with on the planet we live on. This is what I should have said. However, I think it is too late either way.

Louise groans at this and rolls her eyes. 'Did you just correct me? Try to cancel my thoughts?'

'Technically—only I meant to say I agree with you.'

'Word of advice for your next date; don't bury the lede.'

'Got it. Thank you.'

'I will say this, you are not horrible-looking, and you probably do something interesting with your life,' Louise pauses, and holds up a hand, a stop sign. 'That's not a cue to tell me what it is, because I'm not interested. I work in PR, and I won't bore you about that either. All I am saying is that if you get out there more, you might find you like it better than staying inside with your ray guns.'

I want to tell her that I don't have any ray guns, only I don't think this will help my case. Louise and I might never get along, but while she is dismissive and cutting, she is also intelligent and attractive. In other words, despite her best efforts to repel me, I cannot help but like her. People don't usually come out with advice like this, which she served effortlessly up as if she were knocking balls over the net on the tennis court.

'That's good advice,' I say. 'I appreciate it.'

She smiles at this, pleased, and it is like we are back where we started our three-minute date, with smiles and a hello.

Claudia bangs her gong, and I stand, giving Louise a departing nod, which she returns. I move on to my next date.

The next few dates pass without incident. Most of the time, on my subsequent dates, I am thinking about how I am closer to chatting to Amy again. Meeting her has made coming along tonight worthwhile.

Once the final date concludes, Claudia bangs her gong for the last time. I sigh in relief. Adam steps forward and brings the formal part of the evening to a close.

'I hope everyone has enjoyed taking part tonight. You all have surveys, which have been emailed to you. It would be appreciated if you could take the time to fill them in. Other than that, please enjoy a drink on us at the bar, and if there is anyone you want to continue a conversation with, then there is no time like the present.'

I walk across the room and congratulate Adam on the evening. He's done an excellent job of pulling this together. I liked his concluding mini speech. I am feeling in tune with the whole 'no time like the present' vibe.

'Nice speech, that all went pretty well,' I say.

'I can't wait to read your feedback, and tell me, did you meet anyone?' Adam asks.

'There was one woman.'

'Oh really, where is she?'

I look around the room, and spot Amy standing on her own by the bar, almost hiding in the corner. I'm surprised there isn't someone else talking to her, and even thinking this makes me want to rush to her.

'The blonde woman by the bar,' I say. 'Her name is Amy, and this rarely happens to me, and it is not the kind of sentence I ever imagined myself saying, but I think we had a connection.'

Adam smiles, pleased at this. 'See? It works. The good news is, I do not know her, and so I cannot provide you with a mini-biography. I would walk over there now if I were you.'

'Wish me luck.'

Adam claps me on the shoulder, and I walk towards Amy and join her at the bar.

'Buy you a drink?' I ask.

'Oh, hello again, and yes, I'll have a vodka tonic,' Amy says.

I order her drink and get myself a beer. We clink our glasses and share brief stories about the rest of our dates, which can be filed under the category of so-so.

'So, where were we?' Amy asks.

'The jury was out on whether men and women can be friends, and I think I was going to ask you who twisted your arm to get you to come along tonight?'

'Ah, I thought you might ask that. There is a bit of a story. It was my ex, which is bizarre, right? Your ex wanting you to date again? Don't you think?'

I consider this. It sounds like another loaded question. It could be strange, although it might just be a case of a couple ending on good terms and wanting good things for one another. That said, I am convinced that sounds more like fantasy than reality.

'Maybe he wanted you to have some fun and to meet someone,' I say.

'Mmm,' Amy starts, pausing to take a sip of her drink, gazing up at me. 'You might be right. Why did you presume it was he?'

I am thrown by this question and caught red-handed by my own unconscious bias.

'Good question,' I say. 'Honest answer is force of habit. I will have to work on that.'

Amy smiles. 'It's okay, I did set you up for that, to be fair. I should have maybe said this right at the start, only I liked you right away, which doesn't usually happen to me. It would have complicated things and wasted our three minutes of time.'

'It doesn't happen to me either,' I say.

Amy nods. 'I'm glad. The thing is, I haven't dated a guy in years.'

I nod back, continuing to smile. It strikes me that Amy is another person thinking about her life and choices, which is why she is here tonight.

'So, all of your most recent relationships have been with women?'

'They have. I was open to men, and have dated them, only I've almost always preferred women.'

'I see, so how long has it been?'

'Let's just say a while.'

'So why now?'

'I don't know. I thought I would take a look and see how I felt, and here we are,' Amy says.

'Well, I, for one, am glad you decided to come along tonight. You were my best date.'

'Thank you, and likewise. I appreciate you saying that. It's been much better than I thought it would be.'

'Glad to hear it. I will say this, and I never normally would say something, having just met someone, but I like you, and we seem to have a lot in common. I think we should go out, you know, on a proper date.'

That is as bold as I have ever been. I am much better at hiding how I feel, deflecting it with self-deprecation, than saying it out loud. I never leap like that into the unknown. Tonight, though, I think I must. I feel good for having said it, but am nervous in anticipation of her reply.

'That's sweet of you to say, and I think you're right. I've loved talking to you more than anyone I have met in a long time. The thing is, what I realised tonight is that I don't want to be with anyone, in terms of a relationship. I want to be on my own.'

I feel as if I have been side-swiped when Amy says this. Taken by utter surprise. I never saw it coming. I am lost and confused as well. Unless I am mistaken, Amy and I agree that we have a certain chemistry, and isn't that the whole point of this?

'You lost me,' I say. 'You want to be on your own?'

'The thing I realised, when the world stopped, and we all hit the pause button, is that I prefer not being with people. We spend so much time trying to make other people happy, to make it work with other people, and not enough time trying to make it work with ourselves.'

Amy pauses for a beat and takes a drink, trying, I think, to work out how her words are landing. Quite hard, is what I would say, although I understand them and recognise what she is talking about.

'I worked in an office, spending most of my time reading manuscripts. I could have done that anywhere, and when I got the chance, I found I liked the alone time, and the calm. I'm an introvert who was forced to be an extrovert, and I was never happy in my skin, and now I am. Lockdown allowed me to find myself, and I don't want to lose that,' she says.

'I completely understand,' I say.

'Tonight, only confirmed to me after years of unhappy relationships that while there are nice people out there, and yes, I do mean people like you, I don't want to be with them. I want to be with me. Does that sound weird?'

'I'm not sure it does.'

'I don't want to feel forced to be in a relationship—after more than a year of being more or less on my own, Zoom calls aside, I found I was happier. Yes, I agreed to go out tonight, but mostly so I could prove I had done it and wasn't shutting myself off,' Amy says.

'I'm not sure what to say. I like you, although I understand how you feel. I think I felt some of what you talked about too. Although having been jolted into dating again, I enjoy it, and like being with other people, and deep down I know I want to be with someone,' I say.

Amy smiles beatifically and gives a small sad shrug. 'We are on different roads but, that said, I would like to see you again. I mean that sincerely. I could imagine sitting in a pub with you chatting and feeling no pressure, and I like that.'

'You mean as friends?' I prompt.

She nods. 'I do mean as friends, I can't offer any more. If that isn't so bad?'

I shake my head. No, it isn't bad at all. On any other occasion, at any other time in my life, it might be a good idea. However, tonight it isn't.

'I hate to say this, but I am going to say no, as lovely an offer as it is.'

'So, what you're saying is that men and women can't be friends?'

'It seems that way. I never thought I would say that, but I suppose that is my answer. I don't think it used to be, only it is now.'

I am surprised by my words. I am not sure what is happening. As I stand there, I find that my thoughts are circling back to Ariel and thus to Beth. To the poetry, the books, the drinks, and all the conversations we shared. I think of all the moments that we spent together, and how they were slowly building, week after week and year after year. Beth and I were friends for a long time, and then we weren't. I blew it. I could not own up to my feelings, I got scared and I lost her. I don't want to start that process again. I realise I am not looking for more friends. I have been friend-zoned by women, done that, grown up, and now want to be with someone. The same is also true, I suppose, of Beth. As I think about how we are not friends anymore and are unlikely ever to be so again, a wave of melancholy sweeps over me like a thick fog, which obscures the road ahead.

'That's a shame,' Amy says.

'I think so too,' I say.

'So, I suppose we are saying goodbye?'

'I think we are, and I don't want to.'

She nods mechanically. 'I know you don't.'

'It was so lovely to meet you, and I mean that. I feel like we squeezed so much into few minutes.'

'I feel the same, but I don't want to prolong this,' she says. 'As much as I would like to chat to you for the rest of the evening. I'm going to go. I do wish you luck, and hope you find what you're looking for.'

'You too,' I say.

Amy steps forward and gives me a small hug, and without another word, she turns and walks away. I watch her go as she steps onto the glass staircase and descends as if into another world. She does not look back. She disappears from view a step at a time, and then she is gone.

Chapter Twenty

'Every Beat of the Heart'

The next day I am at the café telling Julie in the mid-morning lull about my speed-dating evening, and how it ended with Amy.

Julie has a sad smile on her face when I finish telling her this, and says it reminds her of one of Jasper's favourite films, *An Affair to Remember*. While I am not sure it is on that level, my meeting with Amy does feel precious. You do not always meet people who make such an immediate and lasting impression. Only a few of these people come along in a lifetime, and I have the feeling I have already met my quota, at least for now.

'That you parted like that makes me blue,' Julie says.

'It is what she wanted, or at least she wanted to be friends, but that never works,' I say.

'And not what *you* wanted. That means she was nearly but not quite the woman for you. It is a good thing.'

I am puzzled by this. How can it be a good thing? 'It is?'

'Of course. As I can tell, you are closer now to knowing what you want. Otherwise, you would have become her friend and been quite unhappy, I think.'

She is right. I am almost sure that is what would have happened. It's hard and ultimately ruinous to try and be friends with people you want to date. When one of you wants more than the other, it seems to be a recipe, as Julie says, for unhappiness. It never ends well. I did put myself on the line and was honest about what I felt, which feels like another sign of growth.

'I think you're right, and I really don't want to be unhappy,' I say.

Julie smiles as if again I have reached the correct solution.

'You are happier now than I have seen you in a long time. These dates have been good for you,' she says. 'I think you are making progress, no?'

I nod in agreement, despite my half surprise at this. It is only in looking back at the dates that I can see how far I have come, and the progress made. From being a person who was no longer going out, who wasn't meeting people, I am out there again. This prompts me to check Twitter.

Julie notices what I am doing, and laughs. 'Only a few tweets I saw today. You will miss them when they have gone,' she says.

I smile at this and shake my head. I did not enjoy my fifteen minutes of viral social media fame, and I am glad that it is over. 'I don't think so. As much fun as it is being kicked about online, I can live without it.'

At that moment the door to the café bangs open, and a large buggy is manoeuvred inside by a tall woman who has another child strapped to her chest. It is the mums' coffee morning, and I rush over to help with the door, as another two buggies arrive.

A little after five I leave the cafe, and walk to the park. I have been neglecting Larissa. Stepping outside, I find I am blinking in the sunshine. It is dazzling, and the warmth and fresh air feel good on my face after hours inside masked in steam and indoor lighting. I head across the busy road, through the gates and up the wide avenue where the tall trees are casting long afternoon shadows today, then turn and head up the hill towards the lake. There I can see Larissa sitting on the bench, facing the water, dressed as she always is in black trousers and a white T-shirt.

'Where have you been? It's been ages,' Larissa says by way of greeting.

'It feels like all I've been doing is dating,' I say.

'I want to hear all of the news.'

I run Larissa through the highlights of my recent dating life, from Audrey to my viral social media disaster, to speed-dating and Amy, and the other women.

'Tom, I thought by now you would have found success with at least one woman,' Larissa says.

'You would have thought so.'

'It's a litany of near misses and close shaves. It does also seem you have exhausted girls whose names begin with the letter A. Maybe it is time to move on down the alphabet.'

'I'm not sure taking an alphabetical approach to dating is all that scientific,' I say.

Larissa laughs loudly at this. 'There is no science to the heart. Surely, you have learnt that much by now?'

I nod emphatically. I have, and my thoughts turn back to Emily Dickinson and her wise words on the nature of the heart.

'I have but it is like after so many dates, I feel I am running out of time,' I say.

'I think you're right, but not in the way that you mean. What is the worst story you ever told me about yourself?'

As soon as she says this, I know what she is talking about, although I don't immediately see the connection.

'The tequila story.'

'That's right, and I want you to think about that story now, and what you learnt.'

I sigh, and still do not see why. I feel like I am at a session with my non-existent therapist, which is weird in so many ways given where I am now and who I am with.

But anyway, this is the story: Beth invited me to a party. It was being held by an old friend of hers from university, Poppy, who was having a Mexican-themed birthday, and there was a free bar. Waiters were circulating the party wearing ammunition belts with shot glasses across their chests.

Drinking tequila, Beth said, did seem the obvious choice, and I nodded enthusiastically at this idea, and neither of us gave much thought to what would happen next. A night of tequila shots, it turns out, is a terrible idea, at least for me.

I reached a point—and it wasn't even very late in the evening—where I could barely stand. Beth was gloriously unaffected, while I ended up holding onto her arm for the rest of the evening, which seemed to infuriate Poppy, who remonstrated with me.

'She's not a doll,' Poppy said.

'Pop, it is fine,' Beth replied.

Poppy did not like this answer either and scowled at me. Despite being terrifically drunk by this stage, and only having a loose grasp of what was going on, I can still see Poppy's face. Her expression then rapidly changed as I vomited not only over my own shoes but those of Beth and Poppy as well.

I have never heard someone scream so loud. Poppy lost her shit in record time. She was apoplectic, steaming with rage. This was not helped by Beth deciding to laugh. She claimed later this was not a nervous response but rather the fact that she found it hilarious, even with sick splashed on her boots.

'Get him out of here! I never want to see him again,' Poppy shrieked.

Beth helped me out of the bar, and we got in a taxi, and made it back to my flat. My memory of the chain of events that followed is vague. I worked out in the morning that Beth had not only helped me into bed, but she had also cleaned up my face, and slept next to me.

It was the sweetest thing. I couldn't believe she had done that for me. I wasn't sure I would do that for someone else, and I told her this.

'I'm sure you would. Besides, I was worried you'd be sick again in the night and drown in your own vomit. Then I'd never be able to tell that story again at your expense,' Beth said.

'Fair point,' I said.

When I finish relating the tequila incident to Larissa, she looks at me with a satisfied look on her face, as if to say that her work is done.

'Who else would do that for you?' she asks.

I think for a minute, and my mind surfs through a list of names in my head. I don't come up with a single person and obviously, the state of our current relationship means that Beth wouldn't do that for me now, either.

'No one,' I say.

'I rest my case, and yes, in case you were wondering, that's what I mean by it being time to move on down the alphabet,' Larissa says.

'Okay, you've made your point. I still have two dates to go.'

'And what do you think you're going to find?'

I shake my head. I have no idea of what I will find. I only know that whether it is because I am a completer finisher or something similar, I am going to make it to the end of these ten dates.

The following evening, I am sitting upstairs in one of my favourite Soho pubs, the Dog & Duck, a thankfully almost untouched Victorian pub decorated with gorgeous tiles on the walls and large mirrors. It has a small upstairs bar, named after George Orwell, who drank here in the 1940s, and it is a perfect, tucked-away spot for another date. I chose it when Adam requested a central London venue in which to meet today's date, Carolyn, whom I have only vague memories of from when we met at Marcus and Victoria's wedding.

Even being on familiar ground, and enjoying the feeling of being back again, I am feeling apprehensive. Not so much about the date itself, but more how this one came about. It is Victoria's suggestion, and I remember her mentioning this at her 'leaving London' drinks. The pair are good friends. Adam called Victoria as part of his bid to find as many varied dates as possible. If I screw this up, Victoria will come down on me like a ton of bricks falling all the way from Yorkshire. I only know this as Marcus sent me a text message telling me not to balls it up.

This was one of many messages that have been coming my way from Marcus and Victoria, with the latter leading the charge.

Victoria has been messaging me all day about the date, telling me she's convinced she's found the ideal woman for me. She went on to say that Carolyn was good at 'fixing people', and that she 'loves a project'. This makes me sound like one of those run-down houses you see on property TV shows that people buy to renovate. The kind of place they refer to as a 'fixer upper', which requires a lot of TLC. As it is Victoria, and protests are not allowed, I wasn't even slightly offended.

There is no sign of Carolyn in the upstairs bar. I get myself a beer, take a seat and wait. Given it is an early evening at the start of the week, there are only a few people up here. I am sitting at a small table in the corner. There are a three guys propping up the diminutive bar, and another couple, in their twenties, with their heads leaned in close, looking furtive, as they talk.

After a while, I check my watch and see that Carolyn is now a good ten minutes late. I wonder if I am about to be stood up. It is at this point that a message flashes on the screen of my phone. It is from Victoria, and before I read it, all I can think is that she is checking in. This is not the case.

> You might need this. It is Carolyn's mobile number.

Before I get a chance to type a reply another message flashes up from Victoria.

> I'm sorry. I didn't think this would happen.
> And when are you coming to visit us?

Confused about the first part of the message, I reply to the second part in same way I have been replying to messages from Marcus asking me this same question ever since they left London almost eighteen -months ago.

Soon.

This is all I type, and Victoria swiftly replies with a ROFL emoji, which does seem fair enough. I have as yet made no plans to visit them or to visit anyone else that involves leaving London. Travelling across the city on nights like this after so long at home feels like more than enough for the moment.

I put my phone down and no sooner is it on the table again than it starts to ring. There is an incoming video call. I am starting to suspect from Victoria's message that something is rotten in Denmark, and at this point I am reaching the conclusion that Carolyn is not coming. I accept the incoming call and see Carolyn's face on the screen.

'Hello,' she says.

It has been a long time since we met, and she also looks different from her picture, which must have been an old one. She had much shorter hair than it looks tonight on my phone. It is now like a cute, grown-out pixie cut, blonde with dark roots, that looks almost gold on screen.

Her voice is sheepish, and I get the impression she is about to apologise for her non-attendance at our date.

'Hi,' I say.

There is an awkward pause as I wait for Carolyn to speak while she looks at me, twiddling with her hair.

'I'm sorry about this, I'm not coming tonight. But I didn't want to completely stand you up so I thought I would call,' she says.

God, dating is weird and hard, and I don't know what. It has been a long time since I was stood up, and it has never happened like this. It is almost like being back in the early days of lockdown when everything for a while was only a Zoom call away.

'Okay,' I say, doing my best to be cheerful.

'I thought I was ready to go out again and do this, and I really want to... I got dressed, did my make-up and then I found I couldn't leave the flat, which is weird as I leave it to go to work, but there you have it.'

I understand immediately that fear of getting back out there and being in the world again. Isn't that what happened to me? And wouldn't I still be at home, binge-watching TV if Adam and my friends had not got together and staged this dating intervention?

'I get it. That's completely fine,' I say. 'At least after you hang up you can turn on the TV. Thanks for letting me know, I do appreciate that.'

Carolyn smiles, and it is all warmth.

'Thank you for being understanding. I had an idea though, and you can tell me if it's stupid. Really, that is okay, but I thought we could hang out. I have some wine, and I am sure you have a beer there. Maybe we could just talk like this. What do you say?'

My first instinct is to say no. I thought we were over virtual dating, meetings, and get-togethers, only now I am not so sure. Maybe we are not over them at all, and maybe that is no bad thing. I think, *why not?* I mean, she is there, and I am here, and I am happy to be out. Besides, she is also a TV reporter, and we have journalism in common, which always makes life easier.

'I mean, why not?'

'I'm so glad you said that,' Carolyn says.

The two of us start to talk, and I ask her about her job in TV, and she tells me that during the pandemic it became a real grind although she isn't entirely sure what else she wants to do. She says she feels burnt out, and I get that. She is having the same thoughts that so many, including me, had during the pandemic that led to the great resignation, as people quit their jobs around the world.

'I like the sound of what you did, quitting your job, but I have no idea what I would do,' Carolyn says.

As our conversation progresses, the couple sitting along from me are starting to pay attention. Or more to the point, the guy does. He is huffing, and growing irate, and then he decides to let rip.

'Do you mind turning your phone off? We're trying to have a quiet conversation here. It's a pub, fella, not a Google Hangout,' he says.

I stare at him, disbelieving. I take a breath as I am furious on two levels, and I can feel the rage building. I absolutely loathe people who call me 'fella'. No one has any excuse to use the word.

'One moment,' I tell her, and I put my phone on mute. I don't want her to hear the next bit.

I turn and glare at the bearded interloper. His girlfriend is looking uncomfortable, and she is leaning forwarding telling 'Josh' to 'leave it', which I get the impression he does not want to do.

'If I want to sit in a pub and talk to someone on a video call I will—because it is 2021, and the world has changed. No one, if they can help it, has to do anything the same way anymore. People don't have to go to the office, they don't have to get on a train or a bus. They don't have to do the same shitty jobs. They don't have to socialise the same way either. Stay in or go out or do both. Whatever works. That includes this. If I want to sit in a pub, have a beer and talk to someone on a video call, I'm going to do it. It isn't noisy. We're not shouting, and everyone can hear themselves talking. So, who cares?'

I look at Josh and he looks set to explode. His lips are drawn so tight his cheeks are red and puffed out like a hamster. I think he might be about to throw himself across the room.

Only just then, one of the three men at the bar, with thick blond hair, who is dressed in jeans, shirt, and jacket, and who looks like an account man who work in advertising, starts to clap.

'Fuck, yeah,' he says. 'Love it.'

The other two men he is with laugh, and he turns to them. He offers his hands out.

'Guys, that is a manifesto I can sign up to,' he says.

I find myself smiling. I look at Josh who now looks deflated, as if someone has popped his anger bubble. He looks at me disdainfully, but seems in no mood to pursue his case.

I pick up my phone, and take it off mute, as everyone in the bar resumes their places.

'Sorry, Carolyn,' I say. 'Where were we?'

-

The most important thing that happens regarding my virtual date with Carolyn is that Victoria is happy. I get a message telling me that she is pleased with how I stuck with it, and spent an hour or so chatting with Carolyn in the pub. Even if, by the time we said goodbye, it was clear that she was not quite ready to join the physical world of dating again.

Adam was even more pleased. He was almost overcome with joy when we did a telephone debrief the next day no doubt seeing it as excellent book material. I have no problem with this as, if I learnt nothing else from my evening with Carolyn—and everyone else who briefly joined our conversation—it was that it is okay to do things differently now. We do not have to do everything as we did it before, it is okay to say no, and okay to say you would rather take another approach instead.

At the end of our telephone conversation, Adam asks me a question.

'You've come a long way since we started this, and you've reached date ten. I didn't think you would. I am proud and impressed. So, are you ready for your final date?'

I am as surprised as Adam that I made it this far. I wasn't sure I would either, and yet here I am. It has not gone entirely to plan, but it does feel as if progress has been made.

'I think I am,' I say.

'I think you are too,' he says. 'I hope it goes well, and given how well you've handled your previous dates—viral moment aside—I'm sure it will.'

'Hey, at least I only went viral once,' I say.

Adam laughs. 'That is the spirit, and I know you must be sick of hearing this by now, but this last date is a good one. Have fun.'

Chapter Twenty-One

'Are You Ready to be Heartbroken?'

A couple of days later, those words are still ringing in my ears, as I wake up on what is the morning after the night before. It has all gone terribly wrong. This was never meant to happen. I say this as I wake, fully dressed, on Rachel's couch, rubbing the sleep from my eyes and feeling like I never slept. I have no immediate recollection of how I got here. All I do remember is that the evening started well.

I look around, and it is only then that I notice Rachel, who was my date last night, and her flatmate, sitting at the table in the adjoining kitchen. I am confident that I did not meet the flatmate last night, although I cannot be one hundred per cent positive about this.

'Oh, look, he's awake,' the flatmate says.

'Morning, sleepyhead, would you like a coffee?' Rachel asks.

'How did I end up here?' I ask. 'And yes, I would love a coffee.'

'Oh, the usual way,' Rachel says.

'The usual way?'

'You got drunk and passed out,' Rachel says, looking up from her phone and offering me a smile.

Right. It has been so long since I found myself ending up somewhere like this that it is all a bit of a shock. I try to reclaim some of the events of the previous evening. I know how it started. I met my final date, Rachel, a painter whom Adam knows, in a pub in Hoxton.

Rachel has long dark hair, big brown eyes and is slim like a long-distance runner. She is someone who you would describe as attractive, and no one would disagree. It also turned out that I recognised her, if only vaguely. She has been to the café a few times, which is where I knew her face from.

For our date, after meeting at the pub, we went to an exhibition of a friend of Rachel's at the White Cube gallery in Hoxton Square. As unbearably trendy as it can be, I like Shoreditch, although the ratio of men modelling excessive amounts of facial hair is high. The artist's thing seemed to be symmetrical Modernist grid designs, with some early career screen printing work also on show that nodded to Andy Warhol. At least, this is what Rachel told me.

There were drinks at the gallery and drinks in a bar later, and then there were drinks at Rachel's flat, which added up to quite a lot of drinks, and that is about where my memory cuts out.

'How are you feeling?' Rachel asks.

My head is fuzzy and there is a pounding rhythm coming from the back of my skull. It has been a while, but I think it is safe to say I am hungover.

'Not great. Did we meet last night?' I ask the flatmate. 'My memory is somewhat hazy.'

'No, we didn't. I'm Charlotte.' The flatmate, who is blonde and breezy, says smiling brightly at me.

'Good to know,' I say. 'I had not intended to get anywhere near this drunk. I never do that—at least, not anymore.'

'Well,' says Rachel, turning on her chair towards me. 'It's good to do the things that we used to do, every now and again. Just don't make a habit out of it, though.'

'That's a good rule,' I say.

'Let me get you that coffee,' Rachel says. 'How do you take it?'

'Black,' I say.

As Rachel busies herself with the coffee machine, Charlotte comes over and collects the duvet cover that had been thrown over my sleeping form.

'Here, let me take that,' she says.

'I should probably just go.'

'No need to rush off. Have your coffee, recover. Doctor's orders,' Charlotte says.

When I look at Charlotte in confusion, she smiles kindly at me. 'It's okay. I'm a doctor. I work in A&E at the Whittington.'

I smile, relieved. I am also in awe of the work she does in the NHS, and it makes me think for a moment about what we owe her and everyone else who works for our health service.

Rachel brings me a coffee and plonks down next to me while Charlotte sits in the armchair opposite. I try at this point to think if anything happened between us last night. I am ninety-nine point nine per cent sure that nothing did, but I feel the need to check.

'Just for clarity, did anything…' and I offer my hands out in lieu of completing my sentence, relying instead on the tried and tested universal sign language for the question, did we have sex.

'The answer to that question is no. We didn't have sex,' says Rachel, who then laughs loudly.

I am relieved and disappointed to hear this. On the one hand, it is good to know that the universal sign language still works and that I did not do anything too stupid (other than drink too much), and on the other, Rachel is attractive, and I blew my chances. On balance, I think the events worked out for the best.

'You were far too drunk,' she says. 'And to be honest, so was I. I think we had a good time, though.'

I smile at this and decide to take this date as a win even if I might not be able to recount all the details of it.

'I think it's really cool what you've been doing,' Charlotte says.

'You do?' I ask just so I am sure what she is talking about.

'Yeah, the dates. Adam told us about them,' Charlotte says.

Adam, it turns out, is sharing this story with everyone. I am fine with that; I did, after all, agree to go on the dates in the first place.

'Oh, I didn't realise,' I say.

'Oh yes,' Charlotte starts. 'We all met up, didn't we, Rach?'

Rachel nods at this and takes a sip of her coffee.

'All of you?' I ask.

'Yeah, for drinks and food with Adam and his girlfriend,' Charlotte says.

That's funny. I didn't even know he was dating anyone. He kept that very quiet, which is even stranger given that he has been sending me on these dates without filling me in on what is happening with his own love life. I would go so far as to say that he kept it secret.

'That's curious,' I say. 'I didn't even know he was seeing anyone.'

Rachel gives me a funny look, and then looks to Charlotte. Something is going on here, and I am not sure what.

'Odd,' says Rachel. 'I thought you two were friends.'

'So, did I.'

'And do you know what's strange?' says Charlotte. I shake my head, no I do not. 'Adam's girlfriend said she knew you,' the doctor continues.

Now I am intrigued. Adam's secret girlfriend knows me? I have no idea who it could be.

'Really? What was her name?'

'She was lovely,' says Rachel.

'Wasn't she?' adds Charlotte. 'Scottish girl, called Beth.'

I am no longer intrigued. I am ready to explode.

Adam is dating Beth? That cannot be true. Even though I know I have no right to feel this way, I have been stabbed in the heart. Adam and I have spoken about Beth numerous times over the years as I went through phases of wanting to go out with her, and never doing anything about it. He knew that, and thus it follows that Adam must adhere to the unspoken rule that you cannot date women your close friends have previously declared their love for. I have done that with Adam. He knows how I feel about her. We have sat up late discussing Beth, with him urging me to do something about my feelings, which of course I never did.

'What's wrong?' Rachel asks.

'Adam knew I liked her. She was my friend, and we had one of those on-off flirtations that never went anywhere, and then I messed it up,' I say, and my voice cracks as I speak.

'Ah,' says Charlotte. 'Well, this is awkward.'

'What happened?' Rachel asks.

'Well, it turns out that Beth felt the same way, and right before the first lockdown she came out and said how she felt. She laid it out for me, and I bottled it like an absolute bottler.'

'Definitely the worst kind of bottler,' Rachel quips.

'Rach,' Charlotte says. 'And as for you, Tom, I'm so sorry to hear that, but surely you must know by now you are an idiot.'

'That thought has crossed my mind,' I say.

'So why didn't you tell her how you felt? Break it down for me,' Rachel says.

I pause at this point and think about Beth. I picture her in my mind. Those calm blue eyes, her easy smile, and how one way or another she has been on my mind for a long time. Over the years, those feelings rose and subsided, as if with the tides of our lives. There has been ebb and flow right up until that moment when Beth declared her feelings.

'Because I was scared. I knew if we got together that would be it. We'd have to work at it and make it work. I worried about if she didn't like me or... I don't know what. But mostly that,' I say.

'That's the chance you take,' Charlotte says.

I know she is right. People have been saying this to me for a long time. I have been putting it off for too long and allowing fear to rule my emotions rather than my heart. Beth was right. Allison was right. Beryl was right. Ariel was right. Charlotte and Rachel were right. Everyone was right, and the only person who was wrong was me. I am the odd one out, and the last to know. I think that is maybe something that comes with age. I am sure I used to be good, if that is the right word, at wearing my heart on my sleeve. Not so much anymore.

I know what I need to do. Maybe it is too late, I don't know. What I do know is that I have to go, and I have to go right now.

'I should go,' I say.

'Doesn't right now feel like this is your time?' Charlotte says.

When she says this, I know what she means, and I nod. It is as if the stars are now aligned, and the hour for me to act has finally come about.

Chapter Twenty-Two

'I Miss You'

I leave Charlotte and Rachel's flat and step out into the Sunday sunshine of Stoke Newington. I walk at speed through the park, skirting the large lake and catching a bus to Finsbury Park on the far side.

It is still not much after eight when arrive home. I consider running straight to Beth's house, but then I look at myself. I am dishevelled, and probably don't smell too good either. I open the door, sprint for the shower, and as I am washing one thought hits me. If it is true about Adam and Beth, then Allison and everyone else must have known. This makes a joke of the whole intervention. It makes a lie of the whole thing. Everyone was offering me dating advice while lying about what they were doing. I was dating and they were sneaking around. First Sarah and Allison, and now Adam. All three of them lying. I don't mind about my sister, there was a lot going on with her, but Adam is another level. That is a betrayal.

I hop out of the shower, dress, and call Allison. I want to hear from her before I charge over to Beth's house. It takes a good thirty seconds for her to answer, and when she does, I don't waste any time.

'You knew, didn't you?'

This provokes a hollow laugh that tells me all I need to know.

'Allison?'

'What? What?' she says, her voice flustered, and then I hear her whisper under her breath ('*he knows*'). She must be in bed with Sarah.

'I heard that,' I say.

'Look, I'm sorry. It was Adam's idea, and that's all I have. We went along with it as you needed that intervention. It got you out in the world. It got you dating. In retrospect, we all misled you, and for that I'm sorry,' Allison says.

'I'm going round there,' I say.

'I really wouldn't do that.'

'Too late.'

'I think that ship has finally sailed. I told you and I told you to do something about it.'

'I'm still going round there.'

'Is there any way I can talk you out of this?'

'No, there really isn't.'

'Wait for us, we're coming round.'

'You'd better be fast,' I say, and I hang up.

Leaving the flat, I walk with purpose. I don't care if the ship has sailed. How serious can it be? If I do nothing else, I will see Beth and say it. I have to tell her how I feel, and even if nothing ever happens between us, at least I will have said it. So that later, there will be no regrets, and I will be able to tell myself that I did everything possible.

It takes less than ten minutes to walk through the quiet Sunday streets to Beth's house. It is only just nine o'clock, and there are few people around.

Allison's Mini Cooper is pulling up as I arrive, and she is stepping out of the car as my sister climbs out of the other door. This is, I realise, the first time I have seen them together like this, as a couple, and it makes me smile.

They are both wearing leggings and hoodies and looking like they jumped straight out of bed and into Allison's car and broke the speed limit to get here. The only person who isn't here is Adam, and the thought of him and his lies makes me seethe with anger.

Before I can do anything else, Allison steps between me and the path to Beth's house.

'On the scale of ideas ranging from one to ten, this idea is zero-rated. I'm here to tell you not to do this,' she says.

'I appreciate that, but I'm going to do it anyway. Besides, it was only a few weeks ago you were still telling me to do it.'

'I know—and you refused.'

'And I regret that now. I'm going to say what I should have said years ago,' I say. 'You don't have to stay. I am happy to suffer ritual humiliation on my own.'

Allison and Sarah look at each other, and some unspoken agreement is made between them.

'We're staying. I don't want you to get hurt,' Allison says.

'Listen to her,' says Sarah.

'Look, I appreciate all you have done—I do—but I'm going to press her doorbell. I imagine she'll be annoyed, but I have to do this. You should be happy, you were right. It took me a long time to realise it.'

'You're an idiot,' Sarah says, which is a very Sarah thing to say. 'Why couldn't you have listened to everyone years ago? If you had, we wouldn't be in this mess.'

'Well, as my sister, I think you have already answered that question. I'm an idiot.'

Without waiting any longer, I sidestep Allison and walk down Beth's path, and I press the bell. I hear that familiar Ring tone that sounds like a train blowing its whining whistle as it rattles down the railway track.

I turn to look back at the two of them, my chorus, who stand on the pavement, my doom foretold. I'm waiting, and if their expressions are anything to go by, for the worst to happen.

We are all listening to Beth's house, listening for any signs of life to indicate that someone is home. I am confident she is in; it's Sunday, and early, so Beth has to be here. I push the button again, and the Ring sounds inside the house.

This second ring sparks a response, and I hear activity—footsteps coming down the stairs, and the door opening.

For a couple of seconds, the distance between the flash and the bang, I think I am ready for what is about to happen next. However, I'm not. It isn't Beth who opens the door. It is Adam. He is dressed in a pair of boxer shorts and a T-shirt, and he looks as surprised to see me standing there as I am to see him. The flesh of my face creases, my features folding into a perfect picture of disbelief. Despite now knowing that Adam and Beth are together, I cannot believe what I'm seeing. I want to ask him what he is doing at Beth's on a Sunday morning, only I already know the answer.

I am speechless. I do not know what to say, presented as I am with Adam staring back at me.

He folds his arms and appears for once to be lost for words. I can hear more footsteps coming down the stairs and Beth appears in pyjama bottoms and a T-shirt. She comes to stand alongside Adam.

I look at the two of them, and I ask myself the question, how did this happen? It is a stupid question. *I let this happen.* I had every chance. I am so angry that all of this has been going on, in secret, behind my back and I am frothing with explosive indignation.

'You weren't supposed to find out this way,' Beth says.

This way? Is there another way, as I can't think of one?

'What way was I supposed to find out?' I ask.

'Why are you here? What do you want?' asks Beth. 'You should go.'

I don't know why but I am hurt by this, wounded by her words. Beth doesn't want me here, and now that I am here, I don't want to go.

'I have something to say,' I manage.

'Okay, say what you're here to say and leave,' she says.

'I really wouldn't,' Allison says.

I turn my head, half looking back at her. I know there is perhaps little point in saying this now and that I should turn around and go home. It's awkward and embarrassing, and no one wants an audience in situations like this. Only I have an audience, and while the ship might have sailed, come hell or high water, I am not turning back. I am here. I am going to say it, otherwise I might never say it. It will end up being a weight I carry around with me for a long time to come. It will be my largest ever regret, and it will weigh me down like a heart made of lead.

'When you told me how you felt, and I didn't say anything… The truth is, I was scared. Too scared to admit how I felt. I should have said something and told you that I feel the same way, and I always have. I wish I'd been brave enough to do that, but I wasn't, and here I am. I'm saying it now. I know I'm late, only if I don't say it now,

I never will. So, here I am, saying this. I miss you, and I want to be with you, and that's it.'

As soon as the words leave my body, I feel lighter, like my soul is made of warm air and it is rising through my body like a wave.

I wait for Beth to say something, to respond, for someone to say something, but as the seconds tick by, no one does. I am left thinking that this cannot be the way it ends, can it? Surely not like this, there must be something more. Then the reason why no one is speaking, why Allison and Sarah are looking at their shoes, and Adam is silent, becomes blindingly apparent.

'Tom, we're getting married,' Beth says.

On a scale of zero to ten, with ten being *this could not have gone any better*, we are at less than zero and falling fast. I wish I could get control of my mouth, only that doesn't seem possible, and I find myself repeating the last thing Beth said, like some sort of delayed echo.

'Married? You mean, as in…'

I hear my sister groan from somewhere behind me, muttering 'oh god' as the glare of excruciating embarrassment withers us all like the desert sun. Right now, I want to shrivel up and die. My sister's words do seem to perfectly express this car crash of a moment, which has come complete with an audience. Hitchcock said to 'always make the audience suffer as much as possible', and I think I have more than sufficiently achieved this.

'I mean, as in a church,' Beth says, spelling it out for me so that there can be no mistake.

I want to ask when and how all this came to be, although I'm worried that I will never get out of here if I ask any more idiotic questions. However, I cannot help myself. My verbal incontinence will not quit.

'When?' I croak.

'In two weeks' time,' Beth says.

I repeat the bare facts to myself, and they strike my flesh like bullets.

Beth is getting married. To Adam. In a church. In two weeks. Those are the details. There is no escaping them.

Right there and then, I realise it is over. I feel physically ill. My stomach is empty, and I am sick with a longing that I can do nothing about. I am crushed and I am defeated.

'I'm sorry,' Adam says. 'I feel responsible for this.'

'Sorry,' I repeat, my voice, flat and dead, weighed down by an overwhelming sense of loss and finality.

I want to tell Adam how angry I am about his betrayal. He should have told me long ago, and definitely before he set me up on any dates. Instead, he lied to me from the start. He knew I had always liked Beth. We had talked about it often, and that means as a good friend it was somewhere he could never go. That is understood. It is one of the commandments of friendship, and to break it is treachery. Of all people, why did he have to choose Beth? Why did it have to be her and no one else? I realise I never acted, and even when presented with the golden opportunity, I blew it. That doesn't matter, and it isn't the point; Adam should never have done this.

But he did.

And this is a car crash of my own making.

Like the joke about the drowning man waiting for rescue on the roof of his house, who is sent two boats and a helicopter and refuses them all as he waits for God, I had every chance, and I did not help myself. I drowned just like the man on the roof. I created the circumstances for this moment to happen. Everything I did and didn't do made this moment what it is. I should tell Adam this, and vent, to let him know how pissed off I am, only I cannot bring myself to do it.

'I really am sorry, Tom,' Adam says. 'I didn't mean for it to happen this way.'

I am incensed by this comment. What way did he expect to deliver this betrayal to me?

'Fuck you,' I say.

And on that note, Beth calls time on our impromptu gathering before it turns any more farcical, or I get the chance to do or say anything more stupid than I already have.

'I think you should go,' she says, and she looks pale, and shellshocked. Beside her, Adam looks nervous.

Still, I don't move. I stand rooted to the spot, waiting, expecting something to happen. I'm not sure what. Ritual humiliation doesn't get much better than this. It takes Sarah, her hand on my shoulder, to move me from the spot to which I have anchored myself. She is saying it is time to go. This show is over, and our run is at an end.

Without another word, I turn and walk down the path. I get in Allison's car, and we drive off with Adam and Beth standing on the doorstep watching us go.

We drive the short distance to my flat in silence. I get out of the car, walk up the path. Only when I have my key in the door, do I realise they are following behind me.

'What do you think you're doing?' I ask.

'We're coming with you,' Sarah says.

I shake my head and throw my hands out. I could not think of anything worse. They cannot expect me to talk about what has just happened. That is not going to fly. My plan is to go to bed or go to the café and work. Making coffee at least is something I can focus on.

'No, you're not. That is the last thing I want. Please go,' I say.

'I'm not sure that's a good idea. We should talk,' Allison says.

'Are you kidding me? Were you not there? It could not have gone any worse. And the worst thing? Both of you already knew and have known for ages. The last thing I want to do is talk.'

'I'm sorry, I feel awful. I did try to tell you,' Allison says.

'Not hard enough,' I say. 'So, besides that, what else is there to say?'

For a few moments, no one says anything. Mostly I think, as there isn't anything else to say. I mean, how can there be? Adam and Beth, whose names are so ridiculous in the alphabetical compatibility stakes, are getting married.

'You're not going to do anything stupid, are you?' Sarah asks.

'What she means is—' Allison starts.

'It's fine. Rest assured, I am all out of stupid,' I say.

'You know what you need?' Sarah says. 'You need to get away. When was the last time you left London?'

I shake my head. I don't recall. I stopped going anywhere when I stopped doing everything else. It has been years. I'd rather stay at home. Even before the pandemic, I wasn't good at going away. I am useless on holiday, and can't sit on a beach for more than five minutes. I'm never sure what I am supposed to be doing. However, I think the point is that I never end up enjoying holidays because I am always on my own.

It cannot, however, be healthy doing what I am doing and rarely going anywhere else. Sarah is right. I need a break, and a change of scene. After what has happened with Beth and Adam, the need to escape is trumping my desire to stay close to home. Then it hits me. I know where I need to go. I have put it off for long enough. I need to visit Marcus, as life has come full circle.

Didn't this all start on the night of Marcus and Victoria's 'leaving London' party? It was the night that Beth told me how she felt, and here I am now. Once, there were three of us. Then Marcus left and it was down to Adam and me. Now it feels like it is only me. I miss Marcus, and he has been asking me to visit since he and Victoria quit London. I also get the impression that he is a bit isolated living up there, so maybe he needs to see a friend as well.

'You're right. I'll go and see Marcus. I've left it long enough. Besides, I think right now I need bracing walks in windswept countryside,' I say.

'Don't worry about the café,' Sarah says.

I nod and smile at this comment, as I know that I don't have to. The truth about the café is that I never have anything to worry about. If I died tomorrow, other than the obvious tears and wailing, Julie would be brilliant and carry on regardless. It is Julie who makes the café run like clockwork. While I make a passable flat white and straighten the books nicely, I am not essential to its operation.

'I'm not worried about that,' I say.

'So, you're going?' Sarah says surprised.

'I am. It's time.'

Chapter Twenty-Three

'Ever Fallen in Love (With Someone You Shouldn't've)'

The next day, on Monday, having had almost a day to wallow in self-pity, I am bathing in it, as I flip back and forth between regretting what I did and wishing I had done a better job of it; that I had made more of a speech where I made clear that I was in love with Beth, and had been for a long time.

I'm not sure any of that would have made any difference, given that Adam and Beth are getting married in a matter of weeks. And that is the thing. There isn't anything I can do about it. It is a done deal. All I am left with are strong feelings for Beth, and they are not going to go away.

I know I told Sarah that I was all out of stupid, however, this appears not to be the case. I'm going to confront Adam. I'm not a fan of confrontations, and know it won't achieve anything, however, I can't help myself. What I should be doing is leaving to see Marcus rather than putting it off until later in the day.

I text Adam and tell him that I'm coming to his flat to talk about the 'situation', and he texts me straight back, saying, 'go right ahead'.

I take the bus to Crouch End and get off by the old clock tower where a busker is playing guitar and singing.

He has a gravelly voice, and a few people are gathered around him as he sings.

This is the hardest love I know,
Stuck in this life of mine,
I'm in the dark with my heart,
And I can't let my feelings shine,
Because I miss you and I miss you,
I miss you most of the time.
There's no way to let you know
We ran out of road long ago.
This is the hardest love I know,
There's no way to let it show,
This is the hardest love I know,
There's no way to let it show.

It is one of those song moments when the right lyrics magic themselves out of the radio or from the next track on your phone as the music shuffles—or in this case, present themselves to you in the street, as if this moment has been created for me, and I have been transported here to listen for a few moments to this song.

It is only after watching the busker play for a while that I recognise him. He is the guy I saw that time playing in the bar, and who occasionally comes into the café. I'm sure the music is personal to him. It doesn't matter, though, there is something about the words, about the 'hardest love' that speaks straight to me. It makes me think that the hardest love is either the one we don't talk about, the one that remains a secret until it is too late, or the love we have lost. I'm not sure which, and maybe it is both.

I have no idea what I hope to achieve by visiting Adam. The situation is a *fait accompli*. I am sure by now the wedding venue is booked, the guests invited, and the speeches ready. What is there left to say?

I turn off Park Street, take a left, and make my way up the hill to Adam's house. He occupies the ground floor flat in a Victorian house.

When I get there, I ring his buzzer, and wait for only a few seconds before he answers. He must have been ready, waiting. He stands on his doorstep, puts his fingers together like a steeple and touches them to his lips.

'This is a difficult situation, and I am sorry how it came out. I mishandled it,' he says. 'Why don't you come in and have a coffee and we can talk properly.'

I bristle at this suggestion, and am offended. The idea of going into Adam's will somehow feel like accepting this situation on his terms. It is an insult. Besides, I want to have it out with him, not have a calm discussion where I am sent away at the end of it with a pat on the back.

'You should have told me,' I say.

I cannot keep the anger out of my voice. It is rising like a foaming torrent of water flowing fast down rocky rapids.

'I should have done, you're right, and I apologise for that. We did the intervention, and it didn't seem the appropriate time. I was worried it might derail the process,' he says.

'How long has it been going on?'

Adam doesn't answer at first, and that tells me all I need to know.

'Almost a year,' he answers, finally.

I am at the same time blown away by this news, and unsurprised. It makes perfect sense. I let Beth go, and I laid the groundwork for this to happen.

'I would never have gone on any dates if you'd told me,' I say.

'I know, and I thought—we all did—that you needed to. You needed to start meeting people again. Don't you feel better for having done this?' Adam asks.

I ignore this question. None of it matters. Yes, I did feel better, and now I feel awful, and I am not going to share this with him.

'That isn't the point. You lied to me. You've been duplicitous. What you've done is a betrayal, and you know it.'

Adam takes his hands from his face and folds his arms. I can see he is not happy with that. Unconsciously I find myself mirroring him and crossing my arms also, so that the two of us are standing there, all crossed, over on the weed-ridden path.

'I don't think that's the case. I hate to boil it down to this, but the truth is, you had plenty of chances. I know you liked Beth and we spoke about it, and that was years ago. Then Beth told you she had feelings, and you turned her down,' he says.

All true, and I am, I know, damned by my own words—or rather the lack of them. It doesn't matter, I throw my hands in the air. What on earth have chances got to do with anything?

'I don't want chances. What I want is for you to not be with Beth. I want you to admit you should have told me that you asked out my oldest female friend, who you knew I had feelings for,' I say.

Adam nods at this. 'Correct. I cannot deny it. It is also true that I told you on several occasions, did I not, that I liked Beth?'

Did I not? Who says that? He sounds like some TV lawyer making his case in a hushed courtroom. Yes, Adam had mentioned it, but years ago, and only in passing. I never thought he was serious.

'You did, and what did I tell you? Let me refresh your shaky memory. I told you that under no circumstances were you ever to ask out Beth,' I say.

'You told me not to date her, and I followed that advice for a long time. I followed it to the point where Beth made her feelings to you known, and you rejected her,' Adam says.

I feel my face heat when he says this. That is not true. I did not reject Beth. That wasn't what happened. Or at least, not in my head. That wasn't what I meant. But when I think about it, I can see that I am kidding myself. I *did* reject her. There is no other way to look at it, no matter how much I try to dodge and sugar-coat it. However, I cannot bring myself to admit this to Adam. It is too humiliating. Or *more* humiliating, I should say, as I don't think anything can be as crushing as standing outside a girl's house and being spurned in front of an audience.

It makes me think of US sitcoms announcing that this show 'was filmed in front of a live studio audience'. The same is true of my humiliation. It is only a matter of time before a secret recording emerges. Adam has probably downloaded Beth's Ring video, and it will go viral on social media.

The trolls will not be able to believe their luck. *#WorstDateEver* guy has been suitably embarrassed in the most fitting of public manners. It will be my comeuppance. There will be a follow-up article on the *Mail Online*. Miranda will dust off a quote, and it will be a party. Finally, the trolls will say, I have received the social media shaming that I so richly deserve. Then I will be truly cancelled. After that, no one will date me again. I will be on some dating blacklist website that women can consult to avoid bad boys and losers. Yes, I do understand that I fall squarely in the latter category. That I am not disputing.

But all I am prepared to admit to Adam is this: 'I made a mistake.'

He offers his hands out as if to say there isn't anything he can do about that. His hands are tied. He doesn't say this, but I know he would love to.

'I'm in a relationship with Beth, and as you've heard, it is serious. I want to marry her, and I'm going to,' Adam says.

He says this as if stating the facts, which is what they are—cold, hard, unavoidable truths. He might as well add, *and there is nothing you can do about it.*

'Jesus,' I say, at a loss.

'You need to find a way to come to terms with it,' he says. 'I don't want to fall out, and I don't want to lose you as a friend.'

'You should have thought about that before you did this. I'm not going to come to terms with. It isn't going to happen.'

'I'm sorry about that. We were both hoping you would reach a point where, if you could not give us your blessing, you could at least attend the wedding as our friend,' Adam says.

He must be joking—or living in la-la land. There is no way on earth I can imagine continuing to be friends with Beth and Adam after this. We are done, as far as I am concerned. There is no going back, and there is no way forward. I would be prostrate in their company, and

I would hate myself and them. All it would do is serve to remind me of the absolute heartbreak and humiliation that I brought upon myself. It would slap me in the face every time I saw them. It would be a reminder of what I have lost. Why would I put myself through that?

'That's never going to happen, and I can't be happy for you. We're done,' I say, and I turn to leave.

I hear Adam walk behind me and call out.

'Don't do this, Tom. Think of all the years of friendship you are flushing away.'

I face him and shake my head.

'Maybe you should have thought of that too.'

Adam is still coming behind me, and he puts a hand on my shoulder. It is the only spark needed to set ablaze my anger and tip me over the edge. The next thing I do is nothing like the person I am. I never get into a physical confrontation with people. However, I can't help myself. I turn around and shove Adam hard.

He looks at me in disbelief, and then he responds in kind and pushes me back.

'You wanker,' I shout, and I push him again.

That is all it takes for the two of us to be in a shoving match, like small children in the playground bickering over a contested toy.

'Prick,' Adam responds.

'Dick.'

'Loser.'

'Shit.'

'Bastard.'

'Fuck.'

'Fucker.'

'You artless, flap-mouthed clackdish,' I say.

I have no idea where this comes from. I think I read it on Twitter.

'What?' Adam shouts, pushing back.

'You droning, half-witted hedgepig.'

'What the fuck is a hedgepig?'

It's at this point, after our pushing has reached a stage where it isn't going anywhere other than up and down the pavement, that we stop. We both know that the next step in the arms race is to fight, but that isn't going to happen. We're not fighters. The pushing only worked in tandem with the insults and having thoroughly cleaned out my book of insults, I'm now speechless. I have said all that I can say. I don't know what else to do, so I start to take a few steps backwards, with Adam staring at me and watching my retreat.

'This is over,' he says.

I am sure he is right. Where else is there for this to go? I turn on my heels and head for home.

To be honest, I'm not sure how effective that was or how much good I have done myself. I suspect the answer to those two questions is minimal in both cases. That said, I'm glad that I went, although I don't know why. Like my speech to Beth, I have if nothing else, said what is on my mind. They both know where I stand, and it is not in the wedding congregation.

I am reasonably sure that when Beth gets to hear about this, she will be furious. I'm betting that Adam sprinted to pick up his phone as soon as I had gone and called her. I imagine that seconds after I left, he was probably uttering the phrase 'you'll never guess who paid me a visit' while simultaneously updating the WhatsApp group.

Chapter Twenty-Four

'Linger'

From Crouch End, I head towards the café, although as I get off the bus at Finsbury Park station, I decide to head into Finsbury Park to see if I can find Larissa. It is earlier than I go most days, but I cannot stop myself; I am drawn to her and the park, and the darkness that lies within. I want to tell someone who sits outside of this what has happened.

I walk through the large wrought-iron gates and head up the long slope to the boating lake. There are fairground trucks and caravans parked on the playing field that adjoins the road, getting ready for the weekend.

I approach the lake and the bench, and I can see her sitting there. She must have seen me, as when I am still a good fifty metres or so away, she looks my way. I take a seat next to her, deflating rather than sitting down.

'I could sense your bad aura a mile away,' Larissa says.

'Beth and Adam are getting married,' I blurt out.

'Ah well, of course, that was bound to happen.'

'Beth and Adam?' I asked, confused by her seer-like response to this information.

'No silly, Beth, and someone; and when that did, you were always going to be on the floor,' Larissa says.

'You knew that, and I didn't. How can that be?'

'It was obvious, to me and almost everyone else, that you were in love with Beth and were never going to do anything about it. Not even when you had the chance.'

'That's what Adam said,' I say. 'I confronted him, and it descended into an embarrassing pushing match. The kind of thing you see between two people who have no idea how to fight. It capped a weekend of embarrassments. I thought I would be okay, only… I am not sure I will.'

As I left Adam and our frankly pathetic encounter behind me on the bus, I worked out what I am feeling, and now express it aloud, without prompting.

'I'm bereft,' I say. 'Lost and feeling hopeless. I thought I was heading to a better place with these dates. I was getting confident again about being out in the world. And now?' I shake my head.

Larissa doesn't say anything for a few beats. She stares into the distance, looking across at the island that sits in the middle of the lake, which I always like to think contains no small amount of mystery, even though, I am sure it has little more to offer than rats and duck poo. It is the fact that it is unknown that makes it appealing, as if it is calling out from the other side. Maybe this is why Larissa looks at it as well.

'And right now, you cannot imagine being in the world, can you, Tom?'

I nod my head in agreement at this. Her words capture how I feel. That's it, right there, in a tin.

'I don't know what to do. I'm supposed to be visiting Marcus. Only I am not sure I see the point,' I say.

'I have a suggestion,' she says. 'You could stay with me. We could be together all the time. Wouldn't you like that?'

When Larissa says this, sitting as we are in the sunshine, I slip deep into the shadows where it is cool and alluring, and her words wash over me like a soothing balm. I think I have been waiting to hear this for a long time. I would go so far as to say that I feel better. *I could be with Larissa. Wouldn't that make things much easier?*

'Really?'

'Of course,' she says. 'Isn't that what you always wanted? You and me, spending more time together?'

She is right. For ages, that was what I wanted, and I could never get it. We weren't right, only now things have changed. They are different, and so are we.

'You know it is,' I say.

'Well, then what are you waiting for?'

What am I waiting for? I repeat this question to myself and wonder what it is that I am waiting for. I have come to realise that what my longing for and loss of Beth has taught me is that I am waiting for myself and no one else.

I realise that I wasn't ready before when Beth sprang her feelings on me. I know I should have seized the day, only I didn't. Now that I am ready, I am too late. As I turn these thoughts over, I continue to be lulled by Larissa's suggestion, by her siren's call. Only in truth, I know that beneath the surface, in the place below where the water ripples, and where we often choose not to examine too closely, it is a horrible idea. I look away from the truth, however, and allow myself to sink with her words and wonder in earnest where they might lead.

Will it be easier that way? Will it sweep away my troubles, trials, and tribulations? Will it, I wonder, be that easy?

These thoughts flow through me, and I am away, as they say, with my head off in the clouds, when I hear a terrible shriek, as two geese battle it out for food. This sharp sound is all it takes to snap me back and recoil from what Larissa said.

'I'm not doing that,' I say, and wrap my arms across my chest.

She smiles at this, looking pleased, almost as if I have passed some kind of test.

'I'm glad to hear it. You only have one option really, and it isn't to spend your time with me,' she says.

'What is my one option then?'

'You need to do something about it. I know you want to, and that makes life much easier. I think that it would be criminal if you did nothing.'

'What's got into you today?'

'Oh, I don't know. I'm feeling concerned about your future. I think that's my job here, isn't it? So, what are you going to do?'

Good question. For a start, I should come clean and be honest with myself. While Beth and I were friends, I could look at her and think, *I like Beth, but*... and there's always a 'but'. Even when she was dating, I never thought the relationships would last or go the distance. I was sure about that every time.

'I always thought Beth was my back-up plan,' I say. 'And now my back-up plan is getting married.'

'I know you did, and that's the problem. Beth should have been your right-from-the-start plan. But you never fully admitted this to yourself,' Larissa says.

She has spoken absolute truth. Beth should have been my Plan A from the start, and nothing short of that. Not my plan B.

'I can't argue with that.'

'I'm glad to hear it. Now listen closely. I have a plan.'

'It's a bit late in the day for that.'

'It's only as late as you make it.'

'Your unbridled optimism and enthusiasm are, as usual, wasted on me.'

'Yes, I know, and it was ever thus.'

I raise my eyebrows and say, 'Okay, okay, so what's your plan?'

'I could tell you, but you're not going to like it.'

'Why aren't I going to like it?'

'Because it is incredibly rash and foolish.'

This is like a red rag to a bull. 'Tell me. I want to know.'

Larissa offers a delighted smile. 'I will tell you, however, there is a condition.'

'What's the condition?'

'That you go through with the plan. No ducking out, no burying your head in the sand. You must do it. Agreed?'

When Larissa says this, I know that her plan will be madcap and involve some kind of calamity for me personally. At this stage, however, I am all in. I have no more cards left to play. Right there and then, I decide that no matter what she proposes, I will embrace it. I will run with it like a player down the pitch sprinting for sporting glory or bust.

'Agreed,' I say.

'I'm so pleased. It is going to be amazing. It is the kind of story that people tell for years to come. Few things in life afford ordinary people the opportunity to be heroes. This is one of those moments. This is your chance to win her back.'

'You know, win her back might be putting it strongly as I never really had her in the first place.'

'Good point, but really, I think that's mere a technicality.'

'So, are you going to give me the details?'

'Of course. Sit a bit closer. I think you are going to like this,' Larissa says.

Somehow, I am not sure that this will be the case, and as I listen to her words, my reservations are piling up faster than cars in an almighty road crash where there are no survivors. All I know is it will be spectacular.

Chapter Twenty-Five

'Sometimes Always'

After leaving the park, I make it to the café, which is moderately busy, and no one seems at all surprised to see me.

I nod to a few customers. I see Beryl typing away, her eyes fixed on the screen, and I imagine she is in the zone. In that moment where everything flows, and I wonder what zone I will end up in if I go through with Larissa's plan.

What am I talking about? I have agreed to go through with it, and she has promised that she will come along with me to ensure that the plan runs smoothly. However, my feeling about the matter are that as soon as we put the plan in motion it will go to hell in a handbasket.

What happens after that is anybody's guess. It could be that everything happens, or it could be nothing happens. Larissa's plan is so bold; I am not sure if there is any middle ground.

I tell Julie that I'm taking a couple of days off to visit my friend Marcus and his wife, Victoria. When I tell her this, she hugs me as if I have communicated the happiest news she has heard in a long time.

'You need a holiday like a drowning man needs a rescue gilet,' Julie says.

This is a somewhat stronger reaction than I was expecting, to be honest. It strikes me then that everyone is rather pleased for me to be going away.

I take the tube to King's Cross and board a train towards the north of England. I feel utter relief when I discover that not only is there no one sitting next to me on the train, the carriage I am in is close to empty.

I put on my headphones, stare out of the window, and relax as London falls away from me for the first time in almost eighteen months.

As the train rumbles forward, I find that I am enjoying the act of travelling. I feel lighter physically and spiritually, as if I am leaving everything in the city behind; my friends, my dating disasters, Larissa, and Beth, all of it.

Although not quite Beth, as whichever way my thoughts turn, she is there, and that is okay. Beth has always been there, and I suppose she will be there for a while longer.

As I am travelling, I get an email from Marcus to tell me he will pick me up at the station. He says he must drop Victoria off at her mother's house, which is only ten miles from Leeds. This is a small relief as it means she will not be there this weekend and will not be able to grill me about my dates or what has happened with Beth. I'm sure they both know all about it, I mean why wouldn't they? Everyone else does.

In Leeds, I step off the train and swerve my way through the busy station as commuters begin their journey home. When I exit the station, I find myself standing outside a modern glass entrance. It is colder up here. You can feel it in the air; it's a few degrees cooler than London. I see Marcus almost immediately, looking at his phone.

I call his name, and he looks up, greeting me with a smile. It has been a long time, and it is good to see him.

We shake hands and walk to the station car park, where I notice one of the first changes of Marcus's life in the North. The last time I saw him and Victoria, before they moved, they had a small Audi. He has now traded this in for a black Land Rover Defender.

'Are we going off-road?' I ask.

He laughs at this. 'Cool, isn't it? I can justify it now we're living in the countryside, where there are hills and, yes, some off-road driving. Besides, Victoria said I could. She's gone all green-welly-and-Barbour wearing. She loves driving it. My only concern is that she will suggest we buy a smallholding and become farmers.'

We set off, leaving the city, bustling with development and new buildings, behind us as we drive. We hit the smaller winding roads that take us deep into the swirl of Yorkshire countryside, where the hills rise around us.

'We've had some heavy rain the last few days, so a couple of the roads are a bit flooded, and there is a small river to ford,' Marcus said.

'Ford the river? No one said there would be any fording involved.'

'Relax, we do this all the time,' he says.

'Are you enjoying it up here?' I ask.

Marcus takes a while to answer, giving it serious thought before saying anything. 'I do and I don't. I love this, the space, the countryside, and not feeling weighed down by the crippling expense of London, but I miss the people,' he says.

'That doesn't sound so bad,' I say.

Marcus laughs at this. 'You'd love it here. You don't even like going out seeing people, and there are lots of coffee shops and bookshops that are always busy.'

It's true. It does sound good, and part of what Marcus says is correct. I do prefer staying in most of the time. The thing is, I like the idea that I can go out if I want to. The power of choice brings with it freedom, and I worry that without that I would feel lonelier than I already have at times over the last eighteen months, as we have ridden out the pandemic and lockdowns.

Marcus has rung a few times asking me to visit, and I do miss him and Victoria. I just haven't been able to bring myself to go until now.

As we drive, Marcus tells me that Victoria sends her best and is sorry that she missed me.

'She was, and you'll like this, complimentary about your date with Carolyn. She thought the story of you continuing the date in the pub on the phone was romantic,' Marcus says.

'I did my best,' I say.

Marcus laughs out loud at this and tells me that Victoria said the same thing.

'Really?'

'Yeah, she turned to me, surprised, and said, "I think Tom genuinely tried! I think he might be growing." I do have some more news to share.'

'Oh,' I say nervously, wondering if they are planning another move.

'It's good news. Victoria is pregnant, and it's going to be a Christmas baby, partly why she's going to her mother's house for some rest.'

'That's amazing news, mate. I'm so happy for you,' I say.

I offer a broad smile, and I am pleased for them both, as I know they have been trying for a while.

'Thank you, it's taken us a while, but we got there. The clock's ticking,' Marcus says.

'So, I've heard, but back to you, I am made up for you,' I say.

We drive through moorland and into a small town, set deep in a valley, with hills rising above the sandstone houses and buildings, and talk of Marcus's impending fatherhood and the changes it will bring. Up a hill, we stop outside an imposing double-fronted house. Set back from the road, it is nestled in the peaks, overlooking the steeple of a nearby church and the river that divides the town.

There is no denying the stillness that a place like this brings. It carries a restorative calm that rises from the land and the lush greenery of the countryside around us.

Marcus turns the engine off and does not move to get out of the car. He turns to me.

'I should tell you; Victoria knows about Beth and Adam. She's heard the whole thing from Beth,' he says. 'So, no surprise, she did ask me to tell you that you are an idiot. She made me be sure to repeat this, so I didn't forget.'

'That does sound like Victoria.'

'Doesn't it just. Look just to make clear, we didn't find out about Beth and Adam until very recently, and if I had found out earlier, I would have told you. What Adam has done is wrong, and he should have spoken to you about it right away. The two of you should have talked about it as friends, and then none of this would have happened.'

It feels good to hear Marcus say this, and I appreciate his words. It makes me glad to be here, to be seeing him again, and I am sorry for having left it for so long. Our friendship has always meant a lot, and it is moments like this when it really counts.

'Thank you,' I say.

We sit for a moment longer, and I look out to the countryside beyond. I struggled to understand why people like Marcus and Victoria decided to leave London, but when you're here, you get it. I could see it happening to me in an instant. It's like some invisible force at work, snaking all around. Even though moving to the middle of nowhere, where I know no one and have no friends, is one of the last things on this earth that I plan to do, somehow it is inviting. Maybe it harks back to older versions of ourselves, to past lives and different times.

-

In the evening, Marcus serves up a vegetable stew he has had cooking during the day as he worked away at home, and fresh bread.

We sit and talk, catching up in a way that we have not done for what feels like an age. We have a few drinks sitting around the kitchen table, and we do not stay up late, as Marcus declares that we have an early start tomorrow. He has planned a hike for us. This must be one of the bracing walks I have heard so much about.

In the morning, after coffee and a breakfast of porridge with honey, we put on our boots, and set off. We head through the town and begin to climb up through the valley, crossing rugged open moorland that forms the Pennine Way.

Everything is different here; the air, the land. It is as if with every breath I take, I soak up the calm and quiet of the earth. It is the stillness that I find I like; it is seductive.

It feels as if you can stop spinning, and if you concentrate hard enough, you can find your centre once more.

'This must make a change to the park,' Marcus says.

'In ways you couldn't imagine. I mean, there is a lot to be said for feeding the ducks, and I genuinely never tire of walking around the park, but that's all there is,' I say.

We continue to climb until we reach our first destination, Stoodley Pike, a hill overlooking the surrounding moors, with an impressive stone monument—an obelisk that dominates the skyline.

We climb the thirty-nine steps inside the dark stone tower, and emerge to a stunning view that races on for mile after mile across sweeping moors. It feels, up here, looking out, that we are in another time entirely.

'Where can you get this in London?' Marcus asks.

'You can't,' I agree.

'Don't you fancy some of this?'

'I could see myself in a place like this,' I say. 'Only not yet. Your life is sorted, you have Victoria, and a baby on the way. I have me. I've realised that while I like being on my own, I also like having people around. At least the option of it.'

'You're right. You're not there yet. I just miss having people to go to the pub with,' he says. 'Come on. We'd better get on.'

We head down the hill and walk along rutted paths for a few miles, across the rolling open moorland before we begin to climb again. We take our time as we go, even as the wind picks up and rain starts to fall. We head up along a cobblestone path through a small, sleepy village.

We pass walkers in brightly coloured rain jackets wandering, taking photos, and we say hello, nodding to people we meet. At least Marcus does this, and after a while, I find myself doing the same.

The climb becomes steep as we leave the village and walk towards two churches overlooking the land. One of the churches is ancient and ruined, its roof crumbled and gone, and its walls stained black with time. The other, more modern, sits close by, its graveyard stretching in-front. The views of the valley are impressive, and I soak it up as we meander through the gravestones, stopping by the most famous resident.

Marcus didn't mention where we were going today. He simply said he had a good route mapped out for us. Once we have arrived, though, I remember that this is where Sylvia Plath is buried, and where Beth said she would love to visit. It had been a conversation about such a visit that had sparked her telling me how she felt, and here I am now, alone, having come full circle.

I run my hand through my hair, thinking how that seems like a long time ago. Life could have been so different. It was a pivotal moment, a fork in the road, which led all the way to here. Maybe it could have been us living in some village like this. Although hindsight is good like that, isn't it? It allows us to imagine how life would be magically different if we had made different choices and taken other roads.

I take a few pictures of Sylvia Plath's gravestone, where flowers have been recently left by fans making pilgrimages.

'Beth likes Plath, I seem to remember. She had that picture at her place,' Marcus says.

'She used to,' I say.

'I couldn't believe it when I heard she was with Adam. You messed that up.'

'That has been mentioned.'

'Come on, let's get a pint. I think we've earned it.'

We weave our way through the tumbledown graveyard, leaving the church's elegant ruin behind, and head down the hill. We walk through the cobblestone village until we arrive outside an old stone pub called the White Lion. Inside, it is not busy. Exposed wooden beams run across the ceiling, and a large fireplace sits at the centre. We order our drinks and take them outside to a wooden bench on the quiet street.

There is almost no sound of traffic, and few people are walking about this weekday afternoon. I take a few deep, clean breaths, taking it in. I wish I had come sooner. It is only when you are away that you realise how much you need to go.

'Thanks for coming, by the way. It's hard to persuade people to trek up here. Harder than I thought.'

I smile and shake my head. 'People need to see it. You're lucky. It looks like a perfect spot.'

'It's hard not to like. It's taken a while, though,' Marcus says, taking a drink, giving a shrug.

'I needed to get away, even for a day or so. Life just swept by. I didn't even notice.'

'Are we talking about Beth again?'

'Mostly.'

'I don't know what to tell you. It's a shame, and I feel for you, as I'm sure you two would have been happy, but…' Marcus trails off, leaving his last word hanging, drifting with the summer breeze.

'But?' I repeat.

'You can't expect people to hang around forever.'

'I know, and I did have a chance, and I blew it. What am I talking about? I had several chances, and I blew them one after the other. Did you get an invite to the wedding?'

I am not sure why I ask this, as I haven't asked anyone else. I am confident, however, that they are all going. Marcus does a fake cough and then quietly, under his breath, replies that he is.

'I didn't imagine Victoria missing a wedding,' I say.

'She does love a wedding, even if it is in London. If I ever even mention going to London, she feels the need to tell me she's never going back. Just checking, you're not going, are you?' he asks. 'I mean that would be awkward, probably leading to drunkenness that might be briefly entertaining, but mostly not.'

'You've given this some thought.'

'You didn't answer the question.'

I offer my hands out and I think for a second about telling him about Larissa's shocking plan, but then think better of it.

'I think you're right. It would be embarrassing if I turned up. Besides, what would be the point?'

Marcus eyes me with suspicion. 'There wouldn't be a point. She's made her choice.'

I nod at this. Beth has made her choice. My only question is, at what point do you give up?

'That is all true,' I say.

My friend looks at me as if he is trying to work something out. I can tell he suspects something. I give nothing away. Still, he presses me.

'You're going to do something, aren't you?'

I don't say anything. I take a sip of my pint and look straight back at him. Marcus nods, resigned to my silence.

'Good for you,' he says. 'Go out with a bang, right?'

I say nothing, and Marcus leaves the conversation where it falls as our talk moves on.

Chapter Twenty-Six

'Love Will Tear Us Apart'

I spend another day with Marcus before taking the train back to London, feeling altogether refreshed. I'm not sure I am ready to leave the city for good, but I have a better understanding of why people make that choice.

I walk to work feeling happier. When I arrive at the café, Julie is moving through the tables, checking everything is in order. As I walk in, she asks me to stop right there, and I eye her uncertainly.

'What is it?' I ask.

'You are smiling. You look happy.'

I am about to protest this and ask her, 'don't I always?' when I realise, I would be lying to myself by doing this. Instead, I thank her, and in French, I tell her I enjoyed being away and that I am glad to be back.

We finish getting the café ready for the day, and almost on the dot of eight, our first customer arrives. I serve the first few customers, greeting them all with a renewed sense of *joie de vivre*.

Towards the end of the day, I think about going to the park, wondering if Larissa will be there. While I mull this over, Julie asks me if I am taking my walk. Although this has been a ritual for me she has never mentioned it before.

'I was just debating it,' I say, expecting her to comment further. Instead, she smiles and heads over to a table to talk to a customer who has been sitting for too long without a drink.

After closing up, I leave the café and make my way to the park. I had been hesitant about going and had second thoughts about what Larissa had in mind. I am sure it is an awful thing to do to someone, and that maybe I shouldn't do it. That said, I know that if I don't, I will always regret it, so there's that.

Crossing the busy lanes of traffic and walking into Finsbury Park through the main entrance, I take the long way round, heading up the hill past the skate park and tennis courts, then loop by the athletics track before finally emerging around the lake.

Rounding the bend, I half thought that Larissa wouldn't be there, only there she is. She offers a smile as I approach, and I sit down next to her.

'Oh, look at you, almost a picture of health,' she says.

'I forgot it is good to get away.'

'I imagine you spent a lot of time thinking about what we discussed. You haven't had any second thoughts, have you?'

'Well, yeah, of course I have. I had lots—it is possibly the worst thing you can do to someone getting married.'

Larissa nods thoughtfully at this. 'Oh, you're right, and if someone had done it to me, I would have been seething. My expensive dress, my family, the cake, all of that would be ruined. The whole day would be tarnished.'

I look at her in horror. This is what I am talking about. How can I wreck Beth's big day when she was once a good friend? I am going to feel horrible, and she is going to hate me.

'Okay, now you've said all of that, there is no way on God's green earth that I am doing this,' I say.

Larissa wags her finger at me. *No, no, no*, she is saying.

'It is because of all I have said that we must do this. Those are the stakes, and they are high. If you feel for her as I know you do, if you want her, then you must face those risks. Don't you see?' she asks.

'No, I don't.'

'This is your grand romantic gesture, a sacrifice, and you are gambling everything. It is your very last throw of the dice. People don't do this kind of thing anymore, which is why you must. Nothing else will do. It has to be this way. You must have faith. This is your all or nothing moment.'

Now I am confused. Is she right? Or is her plan several bridges too far? I am again leaning towards her being right. This is the last moment. If I don't act now, if I don't do something daring and something less ordinary, it will be over. There is nothing else left. This is my last play, and it is a desperate one. I give a silent nod, letting what is about to come sink in.

'You're right,' I say.

'Of course, I am.'

'Okay.'

'You don't sound very convinced.'

I tell Larissa that I am with her one hundred per cent, before she corrects me and tells me that it's the other way around and that she is with me. Then she gives me my final instructions.

'Now, make sure you get your suit dry cleaned. You do have a suit, don't you?' she says.

A suit? I am not a suit guy. I have worn nothing but shorts and jeans in the last eighteen months. Even as a journalist, I rarely wore a suit. The last time I wore one would have been years ago at Marcus's wedding. As I was best man, he and I had matching Ted Baker suits. I think I remember seeing it hanging in a suit bag in the wardrobe. I do hope moths haven't eaten it.

'Somewhere,' I say.

'Make sure it is a suit, Tom. You know that jackets you bought a decade ago don't count.'

'It will be a suit,' I assure her. 'Before you go. What is our exact plan of attack? You know, so I have something to think about for the rest of the week.'

'Oh, I thought we would walk in with our heads held high,' Larissa says.

'With our heads held high. Are you sure?'

'I thought so—unless you have an alternative plan in mind?'

I think about it for a second, and then it strikes me I have a much better plan by far. 'I thought we could sneak in at the back. It seems appropriate.'

'Oh, no, we can't sneak. This is not a moment for sneaking.'

'Really? Are you sure? I am so much better at sneaking around than I am at holding my head high.'

I am still thinking this over, and staring at the island on the lake, when I hear my name being called. I think it is Larissa snapping me back. Only it is not. It is Julie, who is walking towards me.

'Tom,' she calls again. 'I wasn't sure you heard me.'

Julie walks towards me and takes a seat now that Larissa is gone. I have never seen Julie in the park before, although she does occasionally take a walk in the day.

'Sorry, I was in a world of my own. Funny seeing you here,' I say.

She gives me a small, sheepish smile that tells me it isn't funny at all.

'I have a small confession to make. I always wondered where you went. You like it here?' she asks.

I nod. 'I do. I am a fan of the ducks.'

'I think you are looking better after your trip, and I hope you do not mind me asking, are you okay?'

I am touched by this, moved by her words, which I know come from the best place. It is a good question to ask yourself now and again, and continue to ask whenever you can. Almost like an exercise where you check in on yourself, take a pulse before moving on.

So, I think about this. *Am I okay?* I might be planning something drastic, but I feel like I am more than hanging on in there considering what has happened. I also realised I have reached a turning point. One way or another, after Beth's wedding things will change.

I also believe that getting away even for a short time and thinking about what I need to do in a different space, has helped. It hasn't changed my plans, and I am taking that as a sign that I think I am okay despite everything coming to a head. What I can't do is continue to go to the park so much for Larissa. After Beth's wedding, I am going to need a new routine.

'I think so,' I say.

'I am always here for you if you need someone,' Julie says, giving me one of her slight French shrugs.

I turn to her, and we hug, which is unlike me. At least, it used to be. I might be changing again. It might be time for another new normal. Julie does not flinch or move away and is not surprised by this. It is good to hug someone, and we hold each other before pulling away.

'Thank you,' I say.

'Come on. I will walk back with you,' Julie says.

Together we leave the park, and I feel so much better for it. It feels good to talk and walk with someone else for a while.

Chapter Twenty-Seven

'Heart of Gold'

The sky is clear, a perfect ocean blue, and the July sunshine is dazzling. You could not ask for better weather for a wedding.

In Islington, we approach the church, a pretty eighteenth-century Gothic building with a steeple and green lawns to the front and side. A lone piper stands near the church beautifully playing the 'The Skye Boat Song'. We loiter on the street across the road and wait for everyone to file in.

Two white Mercedes pull up, and I know this must be the bride and her party. I can make out a figure in white and the bridesmaids dressed in dark blue.

The piper plays them in and then only the bride and her father remain. We wait for them to enter, and then walk towards the church as the bagpipes fall silent.

Despite what Larissa said, we sneak into the back, and find a pew. We nod to the piper, striking in his full plaid highland uniform, and as soon as we're through the door, we are ducking down and bending our knees in the hope that no one will see us. Apart from two small children, I don't think anyone notices us. It's a perfect stealth wedding entrance.

My first thought is: '*Wow. There are a lot of people here.*' I'm surprised I hadn't expected this many. Both sides of the family have pulled out all the stops and turned up en masse. There must be at least a hundred people.

I can see Beth, flanked by her bridesmaids, standing near the altar with Adam. Her dress is long and sleeveless. I experience a pang of longing. Even from back here, she looks stunning, and that is an understatement. She looks beautiful, and it gets me. I feel myself welling up, and my emotions are spilling over. Seeing her there, looking so perfect, breaks my heart, and I feel a terrible sense of loss. I can't say for sure that Beth and I would have made it this far as a couple, but I like to think we would have. I shouldn't have been on all those dates; I never needed to do that. I had already found what I was looking for, and I could not bring myself to accept it.

There were so many chances, but right now I am thinking of that mixtape I made Beth, and all those love songs that I put down. They would have made an awesome wedding playlist, beginning with Bright Eyes' 'First Day of My Life'. I chose that song as the first track on the cassette because I know Beth loves it. It is also a great place for two people to begin.

I can see Allison with my sister, three rows from the front. Thankfully, like the rest of the congregation, they are blissfully unaware of our creeping entrance. I spot Marcus and Victoria, who I know will be as livid as Beth.

'There's a lot more people here than I thought,' I whisper to Larissa.

'I was expecting a small huddle. This is a proper wedding,' she says.

When she says this, that it's 'a proper wedding', it hits me, like a wake-up call, and a hard slap across the face.

Reality is biting. Am I going to do this? Before this, it wasn't real, but now, with all the people and a woman dressed in white, this is serious, and grown-up. It is the real thing. I come to an immediate decision. There is no way I can go through with this.

'We cannot possibly do this. It's an idiotic idea, and we should go,' I say.

Larissa smiles as if this was anticipated. She gives a shake of her head. *No, no, no*, she is saying, *there is no turning back*.

'Don't be silly. You'll regret this forever if you don't go through with it. You must press ahead.'

My brain is spinning as it tries to assess if this is true. Will I always regret it if I don't do this? Before, I felt confident (of something at least), and now all I am experiencing is an overpowering sense of fear. My whole body is trembling.

'We have to stay on mission,' she says. 'We are here to intervene at this wedding. It is now or never.'

This makes it sound like we are on some half-baked military misadventure. No matter the consequences, the poor odds, or lack of proper intelligence and planning, we will press on regardless. It will be one of those missions where everyone, of course, will die heroically and be much talked about for some time to come.

With everyone seated, there is a reading by Allison, who walks to the pulpit and reads the words from an old wartime song that I know Beth loves called '*I'll Walk Beside You*'.

There is a hymn, and everyone stands to sing '*Lord of all Hopefulness*', and then it all starts to happen at speed, which is weird as my memory of weddings is that they take forever to get anywhere. Today, of all days, it isn't like that. Adam and Beth's wedding is a brisk affair. The vicar is already addressing the congregation and sharing those words that are so oddly familiar to us all.

'Dearly beloved, we are gathered here today to celebrate one of life's greatest moments, to give recognition to the worth and beauty of love, and to add our best wishes to the words which shall unite this couple in marriage. Should there be anyone who has just cause why this couple should not be united in marriage, they must speak now or forever hold their peace.'

At this point, I hold my breath, as does everyone else inside the church. I see a couple of heads turn. People always look. I often wonder if it is to silence any objectors, and will them not to speak.

I pray no one says anything.

'Go on,' Larissa whispers. 'Now.'

I don't get a chance to finish as Larissa suddenly thinks she is back at school and raises her hand in the air like the swot she was, ready to impress another teacher. Except no one pays any attention to her raised arm. It is now or never, and on autopilot, before I know what I am doing, I am starting to stand.

It is at that moment that I see Beth's head turn, looking back down the church. I am not sure if she sees or recognises me. I only know that she is smiling, and I am caught by her beauty. She is radiant, standing there, and I cannot go on. It would, I think, break Beth's heart, and I cannot do that to her. I would never be able to forgive myself—and right there and then my misadventure is at an end. This is where I leave.

I bow my head to cover my face, edge into the aisle, and make my way as quickly as I can to the door. I step into the sunshine and feel the warmth upon my face. The sun is shining brighter than before. It has turned into a beautiful early July day, clear and sharp rays of light making the world sparkle. I put on my sunglasses. It is a relief to be outside, and I feel like the pressure has gone.

That is not the only thing. Larissa, my 'lady in the lake', has gone as well—but she hasn't been here for a long time, and that is okay. I miss her, and I hope that wherever she is, she is all right.

I think about what I would have said if I had gone through with the plan, and cringe. I have had my chance, and ruining Beth's wedding today by telling her she was marrying the wrong person would have been an awful thing to visit upon her. Beth would never have forgiven me for it. No one would.

The piper is waiting patiently, and a photographer has now arrived. It is a brunette woman, with a short bob, dressed in jeans and a long white shirt. She looks up at me and smiles.

'Are people on their way out?' she asks.

I shake my head, and never has the warmth and light meant so much or felt so good.

'Not quite,' I say.

I walk past her and keep walking. Behind me, I hear footsteps, and my name is called.

'Tom!' Sarah is standing there. 'I saw you, and for a moment, I thought you were going to do something entertaining but monumentally stupid,' she says.

I laugh at this. 'I gave it some serious thought.'

My sister walks forward and hugs me. 'Good for you,' she whispers to me as we embrace. 'You did the right thing. Come on. There's a pub down the road.'

We walk to the Earl of Essex without saying much at all. Sarah speculates how the wedding day will end, which is something I ponder as well. I wonder if Adam has made Beth a mixtape and what song they will dance to first.

Sarah gets the drinks at the bar, and we carry them through to an almost empty walled beer garden. I take a long drink of my beer, and she sips her white wine.

'I think I managed to leave without causing a major wedding incident,' I say.

She smiles at this. 'Just about. It is so unlike you. How did you even consider such a thing?'

For a moment I think about telling Sarah that it was the idea of my dead ex-girlfriend, who I imagine I see in the park. Only, I am not sure she will see the funny side of this.

'It was the intervention that you three staged. I thought I could hold an intervention of my own.'

'I'm glad you didn't. With Beth, it's a case of *que será, será*,' Sarah says.

She is right, and I nod to this. We touch our glasses, and they chime like a bell ringing out. It must be a sign, although of what I am not sure.

'On the plus side? If you had done that, you would have gone viral again, and I am not sure you need that in your life.'

'I'll drink to that. Besides, I don't know what people do after abandoning an attempt to break up a wedding.'

'Oh, I think they do this,' Sarah says, taking a drink. 'I don't have anywhere else to be today.'

I shake my head. 'Nor do I.'

Chapter Twenty-Eight

'Here's Where The Story Ends'

I'd like to tell you something about Sunday, however, apart from knowing that it's the day after Saturday, and that it followed Beth's wedding, I can't help you. Sarah and I had a rather brilliant 'failed-wedding intervention' lunch, followed by an end-of-summer cocktail session, which did confine me to the couch for most of the next day. I drank tea and watched black and white movies.

On Monday, after calling Julie and telling her I will not be coming into the café, I keep my phone turned off. I don't want to talk to anyone or see any social media updates. The last thing I need to see are Instagram pictures of Adam and Beth enjoying their happy day.

At about one o'clock, the doorbell to the flat goes, and at first, I do not pick up the entry phone to check who is there. I worry it might be someone coming to check that I am okay after Beth got married. The bell continues to ring. Whoever is there is not going away. I am, I know, going to have to get off the couch. I ignore the entry phone, and go to straight to open the front door. The glass in the door is frosted, and I cannot quite distinguish who it is. When I open it, I see Allison standing there. Her hair is tied back, and she is dressed in a light blue strappy dress.

'Oh,' I say.

Allison smiles. 'Come here,' she says and gives me a brief hug.

'What's that for? I promise you I am fine and not in need of commiserations,' I say.

I follow her into the flat and we sit down next to each other on the couch. I want to ask Allison what happened next, only I cannot bring myself to do this. I wonder how the wedding finished, and how the party afterwards played out. Were the speeches any good? I am sure ours would have been better. Although I realise that I would have needed to have married Beth for those to have materialised.

'As you haven't been answering your phone, aren't you going to ask me?' Allison asks.

I shrug. I'm not quite clear what it is that she wants me to ask about. It almost feels like she is rubbing my failure in my face having come, as she has, to my house in person.

'I rather thought I wouldn't,' I say. 'As much as I would love to hear news about the happy couple, I thought I might skip that bit. I am now also considering packing up and moving north. Somewhere close to Marcus, so that I can avoid bumping into Mr and Mrs Adam Wright.'

'Ask me or turn on your phone.'

Okay, I think, *I'll bite*. 'How was the wedding? Was the kiss a perfect moment? What about the speeches and the first dance? Really, that is all I have.'

Allison smiles at this and shakes her head.

'The funny thing is, if you had gone through with your plan, and made your grand wedding speech that you told Sarah about, I think it would have happened—but you didn't, did you?'

Now I am confused. I'm not sure what she is getting at. What, I wonder, happened after I sneaked out?

'No, I didn't, which I think we can all agree was the right call. The last thing anyone wants after they spend a fortune on a wedding is to have someone stage an intervention. So, what happened?'

Allison points a finger at me. That, she is saying, is the question I should have been asking all along.

'Beth saw you leave—to be fair, we all saw you—and it threw her,' Allison says.

'Hang on. What do you mean "threw her"?'

'I mean just that; she wobbled. Just a little at first, an embarrassed little laugh, and then she asked for water. She was stalling, and then the wobble got bigger.'

'How big?' I ask.

'Too big to go through with it. Beth watched Sarah go, and then sat down on the step and told everyone that she couldn't do it,' Allison says.

It takes me a few seconds to process this information. It sounded very much to me like she said Beth did not get married. I can't believe it, as I never said a word—and have never been so grateful for keeping my mouth shut. Even having heard, I cannot be sure that this is what Allison said.

Why wouldn't Beth marry Adam?

'I think I need a clarification,' I say.

She smiles and gives a slow shake of her head. 'No, you don't. Beth didn't marry Adam. She walked out of the church. It was a first for the photographer. Then we went back to Beth's house with half of her family. It turned into a bit of a wake. Luckily, there was a lot of champagne available,' Allison says.

'What about Adam? Beth left him at the altar?'

'That was the last place I saw him. He called out her name as she walked off. She did turn to tell him she was sorry again, and that was it.'

My head is spinning, and my heart is racing, and it is as though it is leaving my body. Maybe I have one last chance; maybe this drowning man will make it after all.

I am not even sure what I am doing still sitting here. I jump up and grab my phone from my room.

'I've got to go.'

'I know you do,' Allison says. 'She's at home.'

I stand there for a little longer, looking at her as if I am waiting for permission until she urges me out of the door.

'What are you waiting for? Go,' she says.

I am out of the door, out of the house and running through the streets. My head is pounding; I don't let this stop me. I don't think anything can now. I push on until I turn the corner of Beth's road, and I keep running until I find myself outside her house.

I stand there looking at the door, unable at first to take those final few steps. I don't know what will happen next. What I do know is that I want to find out. I step onto Beth's tiled path and press the doorbell. I hear it chime inside the house, and wait. I hear nothing from the hallway.

And then I hear it—soft footsteps from inside.

'Beth,' I say.

There is no reply. I slide my back down the porch wall and sit on her bristled doormat. I'm not going anywhere. I pull my knees to my body.

Time passes, and I can hear Beth slide down on her side of the door, and we sit together, enveloped in our bubble of silence. More time crawls by, the minutes falling away until I am no longer sure what I am waiting for. I need to get my words out, and say what I have come to say, and at least then I will know that I have done all that I can.

'I should own up and admit that I had planned to ruin your wedding and stage an intervention, before coming to my senses and trying to quietly leave,' I say.

There is no reply, and so I do what I never have done before, and tell Beth how I feel.

'What I wanted to tell was that I know I am too late, and that I should have said this a long time ago, but I want to be with you, and as long as you know that, I'm not sure what else there is to say other than to repeat the fact that I am in love with you and have been for a long time,' I say.

I leave my words where they fall. I allow them to sink as if they were pebbles tossed into a pond. The minutes tick by, and that's okay. The important thing is, I have said all that I can.

Another five, ten, fifteen minutes drift by. When there is still no reply, I think it is my cue to leave.

'I'm going to go now and leave you in peace. I'm sorry if I had anything to do with messing up your wedding. I tried to avoid doing that.'

I get to my feet, and it is only when I am standing that Beth's voice speaks softly from the other side of the door.

'Don't go,' she says. 'You didn't mess it up. That was all me.'

This is all she says. She does not open the door. I sit back down. I am not sure what to do now. Then I have a thought, and I take out my phone.

'I made you a mixtape. There are thirty-six songs,' I say.

'You made me a mixtape with thirty-six songs?'

'I made you two tapes. I was pretty keen,' I say.

Beth laughs at this, and I hear movement, and my heart skips a beat. She opens the door and sits down again on the floor.

I turned the mixtapes into playlists on my phone. They are songs I love, and have listened to them a lot over the years. All I want to do now is share them with Beth. I hit play and turn up the volume on my phone. It isn't the same as dropping a tape into a cassette player, hearing that satisfying clunk, hitting play, and listening to the crackle. It still, however, feels good.

Neither of us moves. We sit listening as the songs play from Bright Eyes to the crooning sounds of Jeff Buckley, to Liam Gallagher, Mazzy Star to Al Green's 'Let's Stay Together'.

'No one ever gave me a mixtape before,' Beth says. 'Did I tell you that?'

'You did a long time ago, and I said I would make you a mixtape,' I say.

'Now I remember. I asked you about it, and you said you never made it.'

'I know. I was embarrassed, because the thing is, it was two cassette tapes full of love songs, and I worried what it said: that you might think I liked you as more than just a friend, which I did, only I was too scared to do anything about it. You'd said the mixtape had to have a title, so I gave it one… I called it "*Love Songs for Girls*".'

'It took you ten years,' Beth says.

'I know.'

'I waited a long time.'

'I know you did, and I'm sorry about that.'

'I'm happy you got to be the one who finally made me a tape.'

'So, am I.'

'That doesn't solve the problem, though, does it?'

When she says this, I know that she is talking about the two of us, about her and me. I have no idea what is going to happen next. Not in the following minutes, hours, days, or weeks. I have no idea where the two of us might end up. Where do we go from here? Do we have any future?

'I know it doesn't. I meant everything I said when I came to your house. The truth is—and you know it's true—I miss you. I miss talking to you, seeing you and hanging out. I miss all of that, and all of you,' I say.

'You did leave it late,' Beth says.

'I know I did, and I'm sorry about that.'

She stands, and I lift myself to my feet as well. I find I have my hands in my pockets, uncertain what is about to happen next. It feels like we have reached a conclusion.

'I think more than anything now, I want to go away.'

My face falls when she says this. I think this must be the end, and I feel a chill sweep over me. Beth looks at me and shakes her head.

'Don't be silly. I mean you and me. We're going to go to my family's home in Skye. I think we need some time, and that would be the ideal place. There's no one else there.'

I brighten, melted by her words. 'I'd like that a lot.'

'That's settled then. For a couple of weeks. Just the two of us. I want to see how we are together.'

'What do you think we will be like?'

I'm nervous when I ask this question. I'm worried that Beth might think we won't work as two people, as a couple, and that we might struggle to be in a relationship. I am not sure what I would do if that happened. Right now, I am that gambler again. I am back at the table and playing for my life. I have gone all-in. All that I have are the cards in my hands. This is, I am sure, the play of my life. It is this to win or bust. This is plan A, and there is no plan B.

'I think we'll be good together, and we will work at it. It feels like we waited a long time for this, and I'm glad we finally made it,' Beth says.

'So am I,' I say.

I feel a wave of relief. I smile, and feel as light as air and bright as sunshine, like rays of light from the heavens above have warmed my body and lifted my soul to somewhere new. Somewhere that feels right; that feels like being home. It took me a long time to work that out, and now I have arrived.

Beth looks at me and I know I have left her waiting again. This time, however, I don't need any more time. I don't need more clues or encouragement. I step forward so that I am standing very close to Beth, and reach out and take her hands in mine, as we continue to stand framed in her doorway. She looks down at them, at our hands clasped, and smiles, and then I do what I should have done a long time ago.

I lean forward, and we kiss.

A Letter from Gordon

The idea for *Blind Dates* originally came a long time ago. I always wanted to try a dating novel because it is a rich subject to read and write about, one full of humour, challenges, and a little heartbreak along the way. The thing that draws me to it is that dating stories are universal, shared experiences, as everyone is looking for someone, and that's what I tried to bring to this novel.

I also wanted to write a story that was hopefully a little different. After publishing my first book, *Songs for Your Mother*, and living through the pandemic, I had the idea of writing a story of someone who had become cut off and socially isolated and required relaunching. What he needed was an intervention by his friends to kick-start his dating life and get him back out into the world.

There was a fundamental question in my mind if anyone wanted to read anything about the pandemic. I'd had enough, for sure, but the story made sense, and I knew it would work if I approached it correctly. What this isn't is a gritty novel about the tragedy that many suffered. Nor one that deals with the rights and wrongs of the politics of what we experienced. It is a commercial fiction novel, but it squarely acknowledges that it happened and that the characters in this book lived through it, and this is the result. All the characters in this novel are changed by it in one way or another. In the same way that many of us were changed, including me.

Mental health was the most significant personal challenge, and there were elements of writing this book that was therapeutic and fun. I will be the first to admit that I needed some personal relaunching to remind myself that being cooped up at home all the time is not the healthiest way to live. And that is the story and journey of my main character, Tom. At the same time, I wanted to explore how some changes the pandemic brought were positive.

I am thinking of the people who left cities, who quit their jobs, worked differently, and changed their lives somehow.

Blind Dates is set in the same universe as *Songs for Your Mother*, and it was fun to see the characters from that book in this one—just a few small glimpses connecting the two books.

This book is also about old school mixtapes, which have witnessed a revival of late. Each chapter is a song title, and the playlist is on Spotify.

The last thing to say is that this is a book about dating and finding someone, and I enjoyed writing it immensely. It was a chance to think about a period when that was my life. It was amusing to revisit, and I hope you enjoy it.

Gordon MacMillan

https://twitter.com/gordonmacmillan
https://www.instagram.com/gordonamacmillan/
https://www.facebook.com/GordonMacMillanAuthor/
https://open.spotify.com/playlist/2wNvTFgn8W9GtGsOK2v6TT

Acknowledgments

Thanks to the various people who read this book along the way and offered feedback on it, and the team at Hera whose feedback made *Blind Dates* a better book.

Songs

'The hardest love' and 'Looking for you' by Gordon Macmillan